Beauty for Ashes

Ashes

Kathleen Neely

Beauty for Ashes
COPYRIGHT 2018 by Kathleen Neely

Contact Information: titleadmin@pelicanbookgroup.com

All scripture quotations, unless otherwise indicated, are taken from the King James translation, public domain.
Cover Art by *Nicola Martinez*

Harbourlight Books, a division of Pelican Ventures, LLC
www.pelicanbookgroup.com PO Box 1738 *Aztec, NM * 87410

Harbourlight Books sail and mast logo is a trademark of Pelican Ventures, LLC

Publishing History
First Harbourlight Edition, 2019
Paperback Edition ISBN 978-1-5223-0197-4
Electronic Edition ISBN 978-1-5223-0196-7
Published in the United States of America

Dedication

To my husband, Vaughn Neely, Thank you for
encouraging me to chase dreams.

The Spirit of the Lord God is upon me; because the Lord hath anointed me to preach good tidings unto the meek; He hath sent me to bind up the brokenhearted, to proclaim liberty to the captives, and the opening of the prison to them that are bound;

To proclaim the acceptable year of the Lord, and the day of vengeance of our God; to comfort all that mourn;

To appoint unto them that mourn in Zion, to give unto them beauty for ashes, the oil of joy for mourning, the garment of praise for the spirit of heaviness; that they might be called trees of righteousness, the planting of the Lord, that He might be glorified.

Isaiah 61:1-3

Prologue

January 1, 2006

Heaviness pressed down upon him. Nathan tried to open his eyes, but as a sliver of light penetrated his eyelids, pain exploded in his head. He hooked his arm around the pillow and pulled it to block the light. He ran a hand over the wrinkled sheets and risked opening his eyes.

He was in his own bed, fully clothed, still wearing shoes. A leaden feeling held him there, his own weight too heavy to lift. A glimpse at his alarm clock showed eleven fifteen in red lights. Sunshine forced its way through the window, and dust particles danced in the sunbeam, telling him it was morning.

Fragments of memory surfaced. Music. Pulsations rocked the truck at deafening decibels. Sam's singing. Blinding lights moving in concentric circles and changing directions. Nathan wedged his foot free of the covers and then forced his legs off the side of the bed. Once he managed a sitting position, his stomach rebelled. He remembered something else—something red in his foggy brain. A swift image ripped through his head. A spinning top. No, that wasn't right. It wasn't a toy. A car! A red car—brakes screeching as it spun and twirled before crashing into a pole.

His mouth watered and his throat filled with bitter acid. He wouldn't make it to the bathroom. He grabbed the trashcan as his stomach lost the battle.

1

Ten Years Later
July 28, 2016

Nathan Drummond's photo stared at him from the back cover of his latest release. The full-length shot captured him leaning against a tree, gnarled branches behind him, heavy with moss. It was a relaxed scene—his arms loosely folded at chest height. Coffee-brown hair and the hint of smile repeated on each novel and on the website. His publicist insisted that face recognition was as important as name recognition.

The picture captured enigmatic eyes—the steely gray hue brought an intense look, while flecks of light indicated amusement, creating a furtive paradox. A practiced look. Perfect for a mystery writer.

He turned the hardback over, enjoying the weight of it. Nathan's debut novel had only been printed in paperback. It attained mediocre success, but the second one hit the New York Times Best Seller list and stayed there for eleven weeks. His hand slid along the book jacket, feeling the rise of embossed letters.

Eight novels in the six years since he graduated from Emory had allowed him to quit his teaching job to write full time. It never got old. He couldn't suppress the grin as he snapped a picture of the cover and sent it in a text message to his mother and his sister, Leah. They had always been his top supporters, along with his dad, until his sudden death three weeks ago.

He had barely hit the send button when his phone rang. Diana's name filled the screen. They'd been dating for the past two months and had dinner plans this evening. "Hello, you must have read my mind. I was getting ready to call you."

"I have about three minutes until my next client. Just checking on tonight. Are we still meeting for dinner?"

"We are, but let's change locations. I'll make reservations at the Sun Dial."

"Whoa. Are we celebrating something?" She sounded as though she was moving around, opening and closing a file cabinet.

"The books came in today. I'm holding one in my hand."

"Wonderful. Got to go. My appointment's here."

"I'll pick you up at six." He disconnected the call and hit the button to dial his mother. She was slow to answer, fatigue evident in her voice.

"Hey, Mom. Did you see the picture I just sent?"

"I did. The cover looks great. I can't wait to read it."

"You OK? You sound tired today." In fact, she sounded tired a lot of days, now that she lived alone with her grief and a bad hip. "I'm fine, Nate. Just the same old trouble with this hip."

"So, are you ready to talk surgery? I told you I'll come to help you." His sister lived on the west coast while her husband finished his residency at UCLA Medical Center. She had flown in for their dad's funeral, but the trip was long and expensive.

"Why are you and that doctor always wanting to

rush me to the operating room? I'll know it's time when the pain from the hip is worse than the idea of surgery."

Nathan paced while he talked, a habit he'd developed long ago when he began writing. "I get that, but it makes you unsteady on your feet. There might be some merit to getting it done now. And I hear that hip replacements are an easier recovery than knee replacements."

"You worry too much. I'm planning to fly out to LA when my first grandchild is born. I've waited a long time to be a grandma."

Leah was younger than him, married, and expecting her first child. It just hadn't happened for him.

"All right, Mom. Just take care of yourself. I'll send you a book."

"You're two and a half hours away. Why don't you bring it? You might like a home-cooked meal." She liked to remind him how close he was to home.

Greenville, South Carolina, always rocked his world, taking him too close to memories he'd rather leave dormant. But he couldn't tell that to his mother. He had just spent time there for his dad's funeral and hadn't planned to return this soon. "I'll do that. But it won't be this week. I've got a few book signings set up, one here in Atlanta and then in Macon and Chattanooga."

"Why not schedule one here in Greenville? Everyone likes seeing their hometown boy."

"I'll see what I can do about that. Let's plan on a visit next week."

~*~

After riding up the scenic glass elevator to the top of the Westin, the hostess showed them to their table beside the floor-to-ceiling glass panels. Nathan pulled out a chair to seat Diana. The Sun Dial was so much more than dinner. The revolving restaurant had panoramic views of Atlanta. As the day faded, lights began illuminating the city, casting colorful halos. Diana scanned the room. "Nice. I was only here once before, and that was a luncheon. It's dazzling at night."

"Speaking of dazzling, you look lovely tonight." Diana's blond hair had been pulled back and twisted around a band caught at the nape of her neck.

"Thank you. It's been a long week, so this is a welcome respite." A crisis counselor saw many heart-wrenching situations and could never discuss them with any detail. She broad-brushed enough that Nathan knew the job took a toll on her.

The waiter brought wine for Diana and coffee for Nathan.

She pointed toward a distant cluster of buildings. "Is that the historic district? I'm losing my sense of direction."

"That happens when you're in motion." He pointed out the window, identifying landmarks. Atlanta spread before them with views of Centennial Olympic Park, Turner Field, and CNN headquarters. As the restaurant rotated, he caught glimpses of the Georgia Dome and the World of Coca-Cola.

"So, tell me about the book. Is it available in stores?"

Nathan tipped the creamer, sending a small stream of white into his coffee. "It's available online. It should reach stores within the next few days. I have a book signing here on Tuesday then in Macon on

Thursday. I'll drive up to Chattanooga next week for another."

Diana leaned in, bright-eyed. "You've been close-mouthed about this one. Are you going to give me a synopsis now that it's out?"

Nathan flashed a grin. "Nope. But I'll give you a copy. You can read the blurb, but I'd rather you enjoy the surprises."

"Speaking of surprises, I got one at work today. I have to go to Phoenix for two weeks. Required training. I'm trying to rearrange my schedule. The people who plan these things fail to consider clients that can't go two weeks without help. I'm doing video conferencing sessions for some of them." She gave a theatrical groan. "I leave a week from Monday."

"Not a lot of lead time to plan."

"No kidding."

After dinner, Nathan drove Diana back to her Alpharetta apartment, joining the flow of bumper to bumper traffic. He parked in front of her building and got out to dig through a box in the backseat. "I have a copy of the book back here."

"No hurry, Nate. I'll have no reading time before I get back." She reached for his hand as they walked to her door. "Come in for a while?" She arched an eyebrow in question.

Nathan never went inside when he took her home. She wanted to move their relationship to a deeper level, but he kept it light. The further he got in, the harder it would be to end it. And it would end eventually.

They'd met eight weeks ago at Drake's home. A Memorial Day picnic with a few friends. Nathan suspected the chance meeting had actually been contrived by Drake's girlfriend. Diana was good company, but he didn't see that relationship going the distance.

"I have an early morning. I'll talk with you later this week but won't see you until you get back from Phoenix. I'll be in Greenville." He leaned in to give her a platonic kiss.

Diana turned his way with a pout and an audible sigh. She accepted the slight touch of lips and opened her door. "Good night, Nate. Thank you for dinner."

Nathan walked to his car. He wouldn't call her mid-week after all. Let it be the beginning of the decline.

~*~

The sun had not yet surfaced when Nathan awoke. Early mornings and late nights were his best writing times. He planned to get an hour or two in before Saturday morning basketball. The informal pick-up game consisted of whomever managed to make it out on any given Saturday. Nathan, Brian, and Drake were regulars, probably because they were the single ones.

With a steaming cup of coffee in hand, Nathan went to his desk. He pushed the laptop to the back, reached for the journal, and opened it to the first blank page. Handwritten journal entries had been the start of his writing career, a discipline he vowed to continue. His father's untimely death kept him from it, but he'd get back on track, starting today.

Two hours later, Nathan had completed his final edit, just six months after his last submission, a schedule that his publisher hoped to accelerate.

~*~

Grabbing his towel from the bleacher, Nathan wiped the sweat off his forehead, and took a long swig from his water bottle. Brian came up behind him and gave a thud to his shoulder. "Better luck next time."

A quick glance around told Nathan the new guy wasn't in earshot. "Yeah, you gave me a rookie against you and Drake."

"Ha. Throwing your teammate under the bus. See you next week."

"Hey, Brian." Nathan called to his retreating back. "Can you get me a book signing in Greenville? Have to appease my mother."

As his publicist, Brian worked with him to schedule signings and speaking opportunities. Nathan and Drake were both authors with McAllen Publishing House.

"That should be easy. Bookstores like local authors. I'll get back to you."

Bittersweet. Nathan wanted to see his mother, but once again, he'd need to brace himself to face the past.

2

Angie Hernandez took her seat beside her cousin, Elizabeth, at the table in the small office of The Herald Center. She reached to rub her cousin's shoulder. "Liz, you look tired today."

"I didn't sleep well last night. Too much going through my head." Elizabeth's brow wrinkled when she reviewed the papers in front of her. The job of Executive Director could be taxing at times.

Angie glanced at the clock, ticking rhythmically on the wall. "My dad should be here any minute. Has he seen the estimates?"

"Yes. Actually, he talked with the building inspector and got the estimates for us. He e-mailed everything to me but will brief you and Jonas this morning."

Angie's dad went above and beyond the scope of his role as Chairman of the Board for The Herald Center. Elizabeth had lost her mother last year, ten years after losing her father, and he kept a protective eye on her.

They both looked up when they heard the front door. Alex Hernandez walked in, briefcase in hand.

He poked his head into the office. "How are my girls this morning?" Angie recognized his forced attempt at cheerfulness.

"Good morning, Papi."

Elizabeth got right to business. "I'd like Jonas in this meeting. He's been managing this place for twenty-five years."

Alex plopped his briefcase on the table. "Yes, ever since the doors opened. He knows the history."

The titles sounded lofty. On paper, Elizabeth Garcia, Executive Director; Angie Hernandez, Director of Operations; and Jonas Coleman, Program Director. In reality, they all pitched in, worked together, doing what needed to be done.

Elizabeth stood. "He's in the back room. I'll get him."

Jonas lumbered toward the office, the massive black man a stark contrast to Elizabeth's slender form. Closing the door behind them, all four gathered at the table. The metal folding chairs were slightly too short for the surface of the scuffed wood table, but they had grown accustomed to the mismatch. A glassed enclosure adjacent to the multi-purpose room served as their office. It was beneficial when the room filled with teens. More eyes to supervise.

Elizabeth slid the papers across the table. "Uncle Alex, will you get us started?"

He separated duplicate copies of the documents and turned one toward Angie and Jonas. "These are the estimates to replace the roof and the HVAC system. We've gotten three estimates for each. The building inspector didn't mince words. Without the necessary repairs, they'll close our doors. We have sixty days."

Elizabeth watched in silence.

Jonas picked up the roofing quote and emitted a low whistle. "Ain't no way we can meet this in sixty days. Can we patch and repair instead of replacing the roof?"

Angie glanced at her dad as he shook his head. "I asked that. The damage is too substantial. Three roofers said they wouldn't touch a patch job. It needs to be replaced."

Angie's gaze followed Jonas's as he peered upward. Watermarks stretched across the ceiling even in this tiny office. The multi-purpose room had sustained worse damage. An air conditioning unit rested in a high window, running at full speed to help the faltering central air. Its noisy motor amplified off the hard gym surfaces. In a little while, that room would be filled with kids playing basketball. If the AC stopped, it would be stifling.

Jonas shook his head and reached for the HVAC estimate. "Guess that means we can't get the gym floor fixed." The warped section of water-damaged hardwood had buckled, creating a tripping hazard. Bright orange safety cones cordoned off that corner.

"Let's deal with one thing at a time." She turned from face to face. "Does anyone here think God's work at this center is ending?"

"No," they resounded in unison.

Angie joined the others in shaking their heads.

Elizabeth nodded her agreement. "I know there may be a day when He has other plans for this community, but as long as we all agree that God's call is still here, we have to believe that He'll supply all of our needs. God says to make our requests known to Him. I think we should do that and then make our needs known to the community. They've supported us through tough times before."

Jonas grimaced. "I always hate asking folks for money. Telling people we can't keep our doors open.

Folks around here mostly live on hard times."

Alex looked from face to face. "Folks around here may live on hard times, but we can appeal to businesses. And to the greater Greenville area. The Herald Center's work with teens helps everybody."

Angie rested her chin on her arm, thinking. After a long silence, an idea began to take form. "People need to know what we're doing here. Let's see if we can get a video with some testimonies and then launch a fundraiser. I'm sure I can talk Mr. Williams into doing some free videography."

When Jonas smiled, his gleaming white teeth stood in stark contrast to ebony skin. "Angie, you could talk an Eskimo into buying snow. I think we need your face on that video."

Angie shook her head. "Not mine. Elizabeth's. The Executive Director should do it."

Elizabeth agreed with Jonas. "No, Angie. You do have a gift of persuasion and a look of pure innocence. And right now, you're more hands-on with the kids. Let's script it coming from you."

Angie looked at her father. "I agree. And I have a friend at the TV station who I might convince to cover it for us."

Elizabeth glanced at the clock. "I have a parenting class to teach. Time is of the essence. Can we all gather our ideas and reconvene tomorrow at 9:00 AM? Come with suggestions about the video—who would be good for a testimony. Bring some thoughts about the direction of a fundraiser. We could do a fundraising dinner, a walk-a-thon, a fair. Think about the logistics of each and the time we have to work with. Let's set a timetable."

Ideas were already taking root in Angie's mind.

~*~

Once they started, everything moved at record speed. Darren Williams brought his video equipment. Two former student testimonies bookended candid shots of programs that the center offered, ending with Angie voicing their need and inviting all of the community to a fundraising jamboree.

Volunteers organized games, a craft show, a corn hole tournament, and an antique car cruise. Women from their church planned baked goods to be prizes for a cake walk. Angie's dad, true to his word, managed to get airtime as well as newspaper coverage.

Angie caught sight of her cousin standing before the picture of her father in the lobby, its gilded frame inscribed. Elizabeth, six months older, was more like a sister than a cousin.

Angie walked to the foyer, a closet-sized cubby separating the front door from the gymnasium. She draped an arm around Elizabeth.

"You OK, Liz?"

Elizabeth leaned into Angie's embrace. "I feel such a burden of responsibility to protect his legacy. He worked so hard to build this place. I can't lose it all."

"You won't lose it. You said it yourself—God has kept these doors open through tough times. He's able to do it again."

"Thank you for always reminding me of what I know. Sometimes I allow fear to hide my faith." She gazed again at the portrait. "I still miss him."

Angie grasped her hand. "He taught me so much. When I was a child, I once complained about some of the kids acting out. He bent down to my level and took my hands in his. He said, 'Angelina, look deeper. There's so much more to see. Some people have a lot of hurt inside. Maybe we can show them the answer to their pain.'" Angie could still hear his beautifully accented voice, his words slow and eloquent.

Elizabeth squeezed her cousin's hand. "Yes, he met each cynical, rebellious teenager with respect and grace."

"I try to remember that today when these kids come in with big attitudes and bad language. I remind myself to look deeper, just like Uncle Ramón once did."

3

Nathan merged his car with the traffic on 1-24 outside of Chattanooga. His phone rang. He hit the Bluetooth button and answered.

"Nate, it's your mother." She always identified herself, despite the caller ID.

Nathan turned off the car radio. "Hi, Mom. I'm in my car, so I have you on speaker."

"Are we alone?"

A tractor trailer passed on his left. "Yep, just letting you know in case you hear the whiz of traffic."

"I don't know what's going on, but I tried to transfer money from the business to my personal account, and it won't let me transfer. That's how your dad always paid himself."

His dad had run his own business, but his bookkeeping skills were lacking. He'd have to go over the business records and meet with the auditor.

Heavy traffic hemmed him in. He glanced in his rearview mirror, then his side mirror before easing over to the slower right lane. "Don't fret about it, Mom. I'll come down a few days early and see if I can straighten out the mess. I'm sure it's just a result of paperwork and signatures. Do you need me to put something in your account?"

"No, I'm OK for a week or two. When will you get

here? I'll make a nice dinner."

"I'll be there on Wednesday, sometime around noon."

~*~

When Nathan arrived in Greenville, he placed a call to his dad's auditor.

"Our firm doesn't keep your father's records. He always kept his own books. We were called in to audit from time to time, mostly when he needed government forms. Last year we identified some delinquencies, but he said he was prepared to pay those off. We can schedule an audit if you like, or you might want to talk with Tony Willis."

Scheduling an audit would take some time, and Nathan had no intention of remaining in Greenville any longer than necessary. "Who's Tony Willis?"

"He's a local attorney your father used occasionally."

Nathan hung up the phone and called to schedule an appointment with the attorney. He would see him the following morning.

~*~

Nathan located the attorney's office off of Stone Ave. The side street was once residential, but most of the small houses had been adapted for businesses. The frosted bubble glass window on the front door identified it with the stenciled lettering, *Law Offices of Anthony R. Willis, LLC.*

It felt awkward opening the front door to what otherwise looked like a home, yet it now served as a business. Nathan turned the knob and stepped inside. The entry held a desk and file cabinet within walls that were, no doubt, retrofitted to convert this home to a law office.

A woman looked up at him from behind her desk. "Good morning. Can I help you?"

"Nathan Drummond. I have an appointment with Tony Willis."

She rose from her swivel chair and ushered him through double French doors into another office space. Tony Willis stood and extended his hand to Nathan. "Have a seat, Mr. Drummond." A completely bald head showed signs of shaving the lower portion to match a balding pate. The only visible hair was a short, facial beard, snowy white streaked with gray. Bald head, trimmed beard, wire-rimmed glasses—he looked more like a psychiatrist than an accountant.

Nathan sat across from Mr. Willis, glancing at the photograph on his desk. Family surrounded him—a wife, two boys, and a teenage girl smiling through metal braces. Nathan peered into the kitchen area. Were they now seated in what was once a living room or dining room?

"It's good to finally meet you. So I imagine you're here about your father's finances."

"Yes. I spoke with my father's auditor. He indicated that I should start with you. We're trying to dissolve his business and move all funds to my mother's account. The auditor said they've been frozen. How can that be?"

The attorney poked a key on his laptop, calling it to life, then pulled up a file.

He made little *tsk tsk* sounds, shaking his head. "Yes, a shame it came to this. Seems that your father accumulated some heavy debts. Two vendors placed judgments against him, freezing all business assets. Your father's company was structured as a business partnership, with your mother named as a partner. Did she work with your father?"

"Minimally. She sometimes spent a day or two in the office keeping it organized and answering the phone."

"That's unfortunate because it places joint accounts at risk. The only funds not frozen are from the account that's solely in your mother's name. That can't be touched. It doesn't accumulate anything. Looks like an in/out account that she uses for daily expenses. Anything in your father's name or owned jointly between your father and mother is unprotected."

Nathan leaned back and crossed his arms. "Even her house?"

The attorney nodded stoically. "It's unlikely she'll lose it, but they've placed a judgment lien against it."

Nathan felt a tightening in his chest and immediately thought of his father's heart attack. He took a deep breath and slowly blew it out, easing the stress. "I'm rather baffled here. What debts? Who did he owe and how much?"

Another touch of the laptop preceded his response. "He distributed tools and building supplies to contractors. Looks like he neglected to keep up with the manufacturers. The largest debts are Fidelity Tools for $225,000 and Ellison Tool and Equipment for $209,000. Fidelity has filed suit."

Nathan's whole body tensed, catching his breath in his throat. He forced himself to breathe in and out.

"That's over $400,000. And there's a lawsuit pending? Why didn't my mother know about this?"

"They filed it two days ago. I suspect they learned of your father's death and wanted to make sure they were on top of the list when his assets were dispersed."

Nathan stood up and paced around the small office. He turned back to Tony Willis and adjusted himself in his seat. "I know my father's used your legal services in the past. Have you been hired by the two companies or by my father?"

The attorney leaned back, arms folded behind his neck. "I worked for your father when he needed me. Which wasn't often. He called when he received notice of the judgments. The tool companies each have their own legal counsel."

Nathan glanced at the clock and saw dollars signs. That meant he'd be billed for these minutes. "What can I do? How do I guarantee my mother won't lose her home?"

He bent forward and steepled his hands, elbows resting on the desk. "The surest way is to pay the debts. They'll lift the judgments and withdraw the lawsuit."

"I don't have that kind of money, and mother's house isn't close to that value."

"Your mother could file for bankruptcy. I suspect that's the only logical option right now."

Nathan fingered his collar, tugging to loosen its tight grip. "What does that do to her home?"

Tony tipped his reading glasses forward on his nose and looked over the top. "Chapter Thirteen bankruptcy will probably be the best option for keeping her house. That is, if she's not significantly delinquent on mortgage payments."

Nathan ran his hands through his hair, cradling the back of his neck. "I have no idea about that. Let me take a few days to check some things and think through our options." Nathan stood to end the ticking of the clock, hoping Tony Willis didn't round up. Every minute meant more law fees.

The attorney rose and extended his hand to Nathan. "Let me know if I can help. I've enjoyed your last few books."

Nathan left the law office and drove the short distance to downtown Main Street. He couldn't go back to his mother's right now. There were too many things to think through. He pulled into a diagonal parking space. Fishing through the loose change in his pocket, he fed the meter two quarters before walking toward the Liberty Bridge.

The crowd on Main Street consisted of shoppers and workers. At the moment, no one leisurely strolled the curved foot bridge over the falls. Nathan walked to the center and tried to make sense of all he'd heard.

His mother hadn't worked outside the home since he and Leah had been born. She'd allowed her teaching certificate to expire years ago and had no skills for the workplace. In her early sixties, it wasn't feasible to expect that drastic of a change. It would fluster her to know what had happened. She'd fret over her security and mourn over his dad's failure, blaming it for the heart attack. Nathan couldn't allow her to suffer that same level of stress.

Bankruptcy would humiliate her, even if no one else knew. Nathan considered all the areas where he could liquidate. He had equity in his townhouse, but nothing near the amount of the debt.

He could ask his mother to sell the house and

move to Atlanta with him. Even as the thought formed, he realized how selfish that would be. Leaving her home of thirty-five years, her friends, her church? No, that couldn't happen.

The practical solution would be for Nathan to sell his Georgia townhouse and move back to Greenville, eliminating rent for a year while plugging away at the debt. Could he do that? Could he return to the place he avoided except during brief visits? Could he live here and still hold the past at arms' length?

Nathan leaned over the bridge and peered at the river, his restless fingers clenching and unclenching repeatedly. A familiar pounding thundered in his ears. The summer heat beaded his forehead with perspiration. Water from the Reedy River Falls rolled downstream, trickling around the rocks, obstacles that defined the direction of its flow. Like the flowing water, he also had no real choice about his path. It would go where the obstacles required.

Moving would bring a logical closure with Diana. Their dating had never moved beyond superficial, so there should be no expectation of a long-distance relationship. He'd miss the proximity with his publisher and colleagues. And he'd have to find some basketball buddies.

~*~

Nathan returned home to find his mother flipping through a picture album, looking into faces of the past. She did a quick swipe of her eyes, but he could tell she'd been crying. Pulling a chair closer, Nathan lowered himself so they could look through the pictures together.

"Can we turn back a few pages?" He flipped to a picture of his parents' wedding. 'James and Jenny Drummond, June 2, 1979' stretched across the bottom of the page. The wedding picture displayed wide smiles and hopeful eyes from a young James and Jenny.

"Had I really been that slender? It feels like yesterday, but we celebrated our thirty-ninth anniversary two months ago."

Each turn of the page became the passage of time. A flip of another page showed Nathan as a newborn, his mother holding him from her hospital bed. He watched as she brushed her finger on the picture lovingly. "After nine years, we were starting to think it would never happen. Then you came, our little miracle." She smiled up at him. "And two years later," she flipped the page, "Leah."

Christmas pictures. Beach pictures. School pictures. The camera captured posed smiles and authentic ones, and years of laughter. Her sandy blond hair, fine and spilling over her shoulders next to his dad's thick brown hair. They were so young. Nathan glanced from the old photograph in the album to the shelf with a framed picture from last year. It showed his father's salt and pepper head, still full, while his mom's had become thin and streaked with gray. Each chapter of life alluded to its brevity.

"It went so quickly. I wish I had done less fussing over the house and laundry and had savored each precious moment."

"It's a life well lived. You and Dad gave us a great childhood." He leaned over and placed a kiss on her cheek. "And there's still plenty of life ahead. Dad's was shorter than we expected, but he'd want us to keep on living."

"I know. And I'll need to buy my airline ticket. Did you figure out what's wrong with your father's funds?"

"Just a few legal snafus. You'll have your airline ticket."

He needed to say more. Standing, he moved the chair back in position and sat on the ottoman. "Mom, would you consider signing a form allowing me to serve as executor of Dad's business, giving me power of attorney? It's more complicated than I realized, and I don't want you to have that kind of stress."

"Aren't we just dissolving the business? There's really nothing to sell—except his good name."

"Even dissolution isn't as easy as you might think. We have to settle accounts receivables and payables, sell off some assets, assess tax liabilities. And we all know that record keeping wasn't Dad's greatest strength."

She gave him a sad smile. "No, he loved working with people but hated the paperwork. You've convinced me. I'm out of my league. Can you do it from Atlanta?"

"Actually, I've been thinking about moving from Atlanta. What would you think about me moving back to Greenville?"

His mother lifted the album from her lap and placed it on the end table. Removing her glasses, she stared at him. He couldn't read her expression, but she didn't look thrilled.

"You think I can't be on my own? Nate, this is a hard time right now, but I'll be all right. I've taken care of you and Leah for close to thirty years. I'm not quite ready for you to be taking care of me." She replaced her glasses. "I don't want to feel like a burden."

Nathan chuckled. "Not the reaction I expected. I thought you'd jump for joy to have me back in Greenville. And, Mother, you'll never be a burden."

"Of course I'd love to have you closer. I just don't want you upsetting your life for me."

"There are a variety of reasons. Fortunately, I can work from anywhere. Would you be okay with me moving in here temporarily? That'll give me time to sell my townhouse and decide what I want to do."

She eyed him skeptically. "This is the last thing I expected, but it would be nice to have someone to talk to and cook for. Your room always belongs to you. Just do what works best for your own future."

~*~

Seated across from the notary, Nathan handed his mother the pen and documents to be signed. She took the pen and carefully scribed her name on the forms. The solicitor affixed a seal on each page. Now Nathan could begin to undo his father's mess without his mother's knowledge.

With that task finished, he made a day trip back to Atlanta to list his townhouse and liquidate his 401K. His stomach churned when he saw the penalty for early withdrawal. Nathan closed out the account with $107,000, losing ten percent. The amount transferred was $96,300, costing him $10,700. That was a lot of books. The new release needed strong sales, or he might find himself looking for a teaching position again.

Walking toward his car, Nathan clenched his hands. He got in and slammed the car door. *Way to go, Dad. Most kids get an inheritance. I have to bail you out.*

Guilt gripped him instantly. Laying his head against the headrest, he rubbed his temples in circular motion. He loved his dad. He didn't want to feel anger.

Just move forward. Nathan never wrote well with life distractions, but he had better get writing the next novel. Necessity would force him to overcome that dilemma.

Parking the car in his mother's driveway, Nathan went inside and entered his old bedroom. Very little had changed since his high school years: bed, dresser, mirror, and basketball trophies. Fresh paint in the same shade of blue had covered the putty-marked walls where he'd hung posters. Could he make this a bedroom, office, and writing room? He'd need a desk, and it allowed no room to pace. He definitely needed to pace when he wrote. This would never do. Taking the stairs up to the bonus room, he wandered around the area. A spacious living room, private bath, and bedroom. The ceilings sloped with dormer windows. Not a lot of natural light, but the six can lights on the ceiling cast sufficient light for writing.

Sparse furniture amounted to a recliner, an arm chair, one end table, and a TV. He envisioned the area with his furniture and writing desk.

Nathan bounded down the stairs. "Mom, what are you doing with the upstairs?"

She looked over her shoulder from the open refrigerator door. "Nothing. Your dad sometimes watched TV up there, but my hips don't take kindly to those stairs."

"Could I take it over for my writing room while

I'm here? Maybe move some of my furniture up there? There's plenty of room."

"You can have the whole upstairs if you want. There's an extra space for a bedroom, or it could be storage for your things. Do whatever you like with that space. We still have your bedroom and Leah's down here."

The townhouse wasn't large, but he had furniture and a fully equipped kitchen. He'd need to store everything, and money was too scarce to rent a storage unit.

"I'll keep my bedroom down here but use upstairs for storage and writing, if that's OK."

"That's fine with me." She closed the refrigerator. "Give me a list of some things you'd like for dinner this week and next."

Nathan laughed. "No, Mother. You're not going to cook for me every day. I've lived on my own for more than ten years. I'll do some cooking, and sometimes, I'll just grab a sandwich and keep writing."

She narrowed her eyes and frowned. "So how am I supposed to know when you want me to cook?"

"Let's make a deal. You cook Monday and Wednesday. I'll cook Tuesday and Thursday. Any other time, I'll be on my own. Does that work?"

She pursed her lips thinking through that. A mischievous grin emerged. "I think I like that plan. You do know it's Tuesday? I'm going in to read your new book. Call me when dinner's ready."

4

Nathan shook hands with Tony Willis.

"Good to see you again. Please have a seat." the lawyer greeted.

Nathan's phone vibrated as he sat. He discreetly pulled it from his pocket just enough to see Diana's name, a distraction he didn't need right now. He should have powered off before the meeting.

Nathan had no intention of engaging in small talk during his billable minutes. He slid a copy of the Power of Attorney across the desk.

Tony pushed his wire-rimmed glasses up and gave the form a quick perusal. He slid it into a file. "Have you made a decision about the bankruptcy?"

"Yes, we're not filing. I'm going to pay my father's debts."

Tony tipped his glasses to the end of his nose and looked over them. "Good. That's always the best solution. But you said you didn't have the funds? Has that changed?"

"Not exactly. I have $100,000 to make the first installment. I'm here to request that with my good faith effort, the two judgments be lifted and the lawsuit withdrawn. I'm working on getting the funds and plan to pay it in full, but it may take a while."

Tony scratched his forehead. "That's not my decision, but I'll take your request to the two companies. Are you looking to pay this installment to one or to split it equitably? That may make a difference." His chair squeaked as he leaned back.

Nathan squinted. "I hadn't given that much consideration, but I suppose it needs to be equitable. If only one lifts the judgment, we're still frozen. I'll have an easier time settling this if I can sell off some assets."

"That's true. Although your father's business didn't lend itself to many valuable assets. Just some office equipment and furniture."

"We're scraping here. Everything will help. And I need to empty his office so I can end the lease. I'll hold the first installment and hope to hear back quickly. If all are agreeable, I'll submit a payment of $50,000 to each. I imagine a certified check will be acceptable."

"When do you foresee another installment?"

"My townhouse in Atlanta is on the market. My equity should yield another $100,000."

Tony nodded, fingering his tapered beard. "That brings you halfway." He phrased it as a statement, but Nathan heard the embedded question.

"At that point, I may be able to take out a loan for the balance. I can't do that while I have a mortgage. My books sell well, but we all know, that's not a guaranteed paycheck. I'll have to find a lender that will work with me."

"Without collateral? Might be tough." A condescending smile accompanied a shake of his head.

"Mr. Willis, I'm doing all that I can. I will pay this debt. As you see, I have Power of Attorney, and my mother is not to know of this situation." He stood, hoping to end the billing meter.

"I'll get back to you as soon as I'm able."

Nathan left the office and went to his car. As he

closed his door, he reached for the phone that had vibrated during the meeting. He stretched his tight neck muscles and listened to Diana's message. "I'm back from Phoenix. Call me when you have time."

She still didn't know.

~*~

Nathan stayed busy in his writing room, although very little writing occurred. He organized his new space, checked social media and e-mails, and responded to blog comments. The aroma of garlic wafted up the stairs. Nathan rolled his neck from side to side to stretch the stiffness away and logged off.

Bounding down the steps, he saw the table set for two. "Spaghetti? I could smell it floating up the stairs."

His mother handed him a large dish and pointed toward the pasta. "Come fix your plate. I'll put the salad on the table." She opened the refrigerator and retrieved a bowl of chopped greens tossed with a colorful array of vegetables.

The TV in the next room could be heard. His parents often took their dinner in there. "Mom, it's OK if you want to watch news while we eat."

"Not with spaghetti. Too messy. Besides, it's nice to talk over dinner. Brings back good memories."

Nathan chuckled. "Yeah, like Leah and I squabbling over who had to do dishes or grabbing to get the first piece of chicken."

She shook her head with a smile. "You two did like to quarrel. No, I remember dinners when we talked about school work and plans for the weekend." A sigh escaped. "It doesn't seem so long ago."

"I know, Mom. But the calendar keeps turning. Good things are ahead, like that new baby."

They carried their plates to the table and said grace.

His mother's eyes locked with his. "How about you, Nate? I don't suppose you'd have left Atlanta if you had anyone special waiting there. You said it yourself. The calendar keeps turning."

"In due time. I've been too busy making up stories."

She shook her head. "Don't wait too long. It seems like a blink of an eye, and you're applying for social security."

Nathan needed a change of subject. "Did you see that I transferred money into your account?"

"I did see that. Thank you for taking care of that mess. If it's straightened out, I can handle my banking."

He didn't look up as he scooped a meatball from his plate. "That won't work right now. We're in the process of dissolving the business. Let me do that for you for a while longer."

She eyed him, frowning. "Are you managing to keep up with your writing while you have this extra work?"

Nathan twirled his fork to wrap the length of pasta. "The question is, are you managing to read my novel? I haven't heard you mention it."

She laughed. "Always looking for compliments. You can see my bookmark moving. I'm three quarters through and determined to solve the mystery before the book tells me. I have about three possibilities that I'm mulling over."

"Ah, but don't I typically surprise you at the end?"

"Yes, and I'm trying to stay one step ahead of you. I know how your mind works."

The TV droned on in the next room, and the newscaster's voice trickled into the kitchen. Nathan caught something about The Herald Center and twisted to see the screen. A familiar sense of panic fleeted through his chest when he heard the name spoken out loud.

His mother eyed him curiously. "Something you want to see?"

Nathan rose and walked toward the living room. He stood at the archway, distracted by the newscast. "Sorry. Give me a minute."

Returning to the table, he stabbed a meatball a little too forcibly.

His mother sent him a quizzical look. "I heard that at noon today. They're talking about a fundraiser at The Herald Center. Do you know someone there?"

He diverted his eyes. "No, just caught my attention. I'm looking for a place to play basketball."

"Oh, Nate, you don't want that place. It's mostly for inner city teens. There's a lot of trouble in that area. Try Parkwood Church. They have a large gym, and I've heard of others playing basketball there."

~*~

Nathan pulled his journal from the drawer and set pen to paper. With the time spent moving his things, he had neglected it all week. He'd leave the journal out and visible on his desk. That would remind him. It helped him through some difficult times in the past. Living in Greenville, so close to raw memories, he'd need an outlet to ease anxieties.

The TV downstairs continued to send its noise up the stairs, and Nathan felt a stab of guilt for not spending any time with his mother this evening. But he was way too distracted. At nine o'clock, he forced himself to walk down and chat with her for a little while. At nine forty five she headed to bed, and Nathan returned to his writing room.

He spent time looking at his empty plot map, a flow chart he'd used to make the first rough sketch. But he had no plot and couldn't commit words to paper. The eleven o'clock news came on, and Nathan hit record on his DVR, even though he intended ·to watch it live. It carried the typical segments. Local crimes, political entanglements, weather. Finally, they repeated the story from the earlier newscast.

"The Herald Center saved my life." This was a video of a young Hispanic man, well-dressed and articulate. "I was fourteen and making poor choices. My friends were joining a gang and encouraging me to follow suit. I wanted no part of the afterschool programs at the center, but Stephen, a volunteer mentor, never gave up on me. When I didn't show up, he somehow found me. He showed me that I had choices and those choices would follow me. I had never experienced anyone treating me with respect until I met Ramón Garcia." The video flashed to a portrait of the man. "The staff at The Herald Center helped me to succeed in school, to find funding for college, and still today, after all this time, Stephen stays in touch with me."

The video moved to scenes from the center. Then a young lady holding a baby began to speak. "I was seventeen and pregnant, headed for the abortion clinic.

Angie Hernandez talked me through the other possibilities. She took me to the doctor, went to birthing classes with me, and stayed by my side while I gave birth to my little girl. Angie helped me find an adoption agency that placed my baby in a good home where she's loved and cared for. That was six years ago. Today," she smiled down at the child she was holding, "I have a little baby that I'm able to keep and raise well. I'm so thankful that my two little girls both have mamas that can take care of them."

The camera shifted to its final speaker. "I'm Angelina Hernandez, the Program Director at The Herald Center." Nathan watched, transfixed by the young lady speaking. Her lilting voice held no trace of an accent, yet her Hispanic background was obvious—precise language and clear articulation—evidence that her parents probably learned the language analytically. The shine of dark hair, loosely bound and hanging over her right shoulder, stood out in stark contrast to the ivory complexion, despite the subdued shades of the TV. "This urban outreach has been changing lives for twenty-five years. You've heard two stories, but we have hundreds. Our volunteers work tirelessly to help the young people in our community. But sometimes the task is bigger than we can meet." The camera swept over damaged ceilings, a warped gym floor, and some peeling paint. She continued, her voice soft and rhythmic. "Please consider helping us while having a fun, family day at our jamboree." Her brilliant smile lit the screen before closing with a few details, the date and times.

As the video ended, the newscaster continued. "You may remember that Ramón Garcia, founder of The Herald Center," his picture appeared again on the screen, "was killed in a New Year's Eve accident ten years ago. Check their website for all of the jamboree activities."

Nathan hit the off button on his remote. The screen went blank, but the picture of Ramón Garcia stayed fresh in his mind.

5

"Hi, Diana. I got your message. How was Phoenix?" Nathan would have to deal with this sooner or later. May as well make the call and get it done.

"Hot and busy. Not a spare minute if I wanted to explore. How's the book tour?"

"Not exactly a tour. Just random signings. But a lot has happened since I last saw you. Some family issues that I need to help with. I've actually listed my townhouse with a realtor and moved back to Greenville." He waited through the silence to let that sink in.

After a prolonged silence, Diana spoke. "Permanently?"

Nathan paced around his new bonus room office. The tension found its way through the phone lines. "That's hard to answer. Let's just say, I'm needed here for now. I don't anticipate returning to Atlanta within a year."

Another lengthy pause followed. "Wow. Well, I guess I won't be seeing much of you."

"I'm sorry, Diana. You have family. I'm sure you know how those obligations go. I've got to be here for now. I'll check in with you when I'm headed to Atlanta."

"And if I'm free to make the drive there, would

you welcome a visit?"

Nathan hadn't anticipated that question. His hesitation in answering wasn't received well. He heard the exhale of air before she spoke.

"I see. Well then, I guess I'll say good-bye."

"Diana, wait. I didn't mean I wouldn't welcome you. I'm just thinking through some logistics. My mother isn't well and may be needing some surgery." The words were a stretch but not entirely untrue.

"All right, Nate. Call if you're ever around." The phone clicked with the disconnection.

That was uncomfortable, but it was done. With that behind him, it was time to see Sam. Nathan had avoided him every time he'd passed through Greenville. But he'd be living here now. Nine years had passed since he'd seen his old high school friend. They were once inseparable, but they'd grown apart during college. Perhaps they'd both grown up enough to restore their friendship.

He grabbed his car keys and headed for the door. "Mom, I'm going out for a little. I'll be back later—with dinner."

She stepped into the living room. "Have a nice day. Do you want me to fix dinner?"

Nathan raised an eyebrow before shooting a teasing wink. "Don't mess with the schedule."

Nathan didn't know where Sam was living, but he knew the insurance agency where he worked. He drove to the West End and found meter parking on Main Street. A jingle sounded as he opened the door and walked to the front desk.

A wooden nameplate on the desk introduced the receptionist as Margie Whitely. Her name matched her hair, which was devoid of color. She tipped her head to look over her eyeglasses and greeted him pleasantly. "Hello. Can I help you?"

"Is Sam Harper in?"

"Yes. Is he expecting you?" She glanced from Nathan to a desk calendar and back again.

"No. Just tell him it's Nate. He'll know me." Name recognition wasn't always a plus. For once, Nathan wasn't anxious to talk about his books. The receptionist punched his extension into the phone and announced him. Within seconds, Sam filled the doorway. He had always been larger than Nathan but now wore thirty extra pounds. His easy smile remained.

"Nate. It's been years." He extended his hand and when Nathan took it, Sam pulled him into a man hug, slapping his back. "I have a little time. Come on back."

As they sat in Sam's windowless office with the door closed, Nathan noted the lingering scent of cigarettes. An uneven stack of papers overflowed from a desk tray next to a half-filled mug of coffee that appeared to be stone cold. Nathan recalled Sam's high school book bag, always in disarray with wrinkled papers stuffed inside. Some things never changed.

Sam shook his head. His face was much fuller than Nathan remembered. "Man, it's been a long time. You're looking good. I see your face in all the bookstores."

Sam seemed oblivious to the low hum of a radio talk show on the floor by his feet. A glance down showed a mass of tangled cords. "How you doing, Sam? I hear you and Sarah had a baby."

"Two. Marissa's four and Chloe just turned a year."

"Girls? You're outnumbered. Better try for a boy."

"Ha. Our house is crazy enough with two. Hey,

come on over and meet them. Maybe we can head out for a beer and a game of pool."

Nathan's grin disappeared. He rubbed his brow. "You still doing the suds? I gave that up."

A hard expression fleeted across Sam's face, disappearing as quickly as it began. "I still get together with a few of the guys for poker. Why don't you join us? Bring some of those big bucks you're making on books."

Nathan grinned. "I think there's a misconception about how much authors make. I'd really like a pick-up game of basketball. Do you still play?"

Sam leaned back and patted his rounded stomach. "Do I look like I play? Skip the B-Ball and let us deal you in."

The years had moved their paths in separate directions. They wouldn't be spending evenings together. "We'll see, Sam."

He laughed out loud. "We all know what 'we'll see' means."

Nathan sombered. "Hey, do you ever think about…"

Nathan's words were halted by Sam's extended hand, fingers splayed open. His challenging eyes became steel. "Stop. Don't go there."

Sam had always assumed the role of ringleader, and Nathan had allowed himself to follow. The two sat staring each other down.

Finally, Nathan nodded. "I better get going. Looks like you have work to do." He motioned toward the stacks of paper on the desk. "Good seeing you, Sam."

"Hey, don't be a stranger."

Nathan walked to his car, the jingling office door announcing his exit. He sat in his parked car, remembering the years. Classes together, playing on the same little league team, and then moving to basketball in middle school and hanging out at each other's home. They'd grown up together, best friends. How was that possible when they were so different?

Nathan set his GPS before pulling into traffic, heading west beyond the downtown area. He followed the directions to The Herald Center with no intention of going in. Something compelled him to see where it was. Within a few minutes of the downtown area, he saw the center. It was definitely in a rundown area of town. Abandoned store fronts, boarded windows, and littered streets. The occupied houses had tiny yards with unkempt grass, toys overturned and forgotten. Two old men sat on concrete front steps, a glow blazing from the tips of their cigarettes.

Large letters above the door announced The Herald Center. The sidewalk had been swept clean, in contrast to the neighborhood. Nathan saw kids exiting a small bus and walking in the front door. The end of August. School was back in session.

Nathan steered his car into a parking space. A large man stepped out and flashed a broad smile, holding up his arm for the kids to give fist bumps and high fives. Even from this distance, Nathan could see the beads of sweat glistening on his dark skin. A few older teens walked while dribbling a basketball. They bounce-passed it off the sidewalk to the man greeting. He caught and returned it as the boys strolled in.

Nathan got out and leaned against his car, watching the teens, his hands itchy for the feel of a basketball—dribbling it, shooting it, passing it. When all of the teens had entered, he walked over and opened the door. No one sat at the small, wooden desk in the foyer.

In the adjoining room, students formed small groups, clearly divided by age. A half-dozen adults mingled and sent groups in different directions, giving order to the chaos.

Nathan glanced at the photo on the wall—Ramón Garcia was inscribed on the brass nameplate. It was the same picture that had been shown on the news. Nathan shrank under that gaze, moisture gathering on his forehead. Yet the man's eyes were soft. Welcoming. The words from the video resonated in his head. *Ramón Garcia treated each one with respect.*

As he stood staring at the portrait, the man who had greeted the kids walked over, extending his hand.

"Hi, I'm Jonas."

Nathan glanced at the large, sweaty palm before lifting his to shake it. "Nathan Drummond."

"Sorry. I was shooting around a little before the kids arrived."

Nathan returned the smile. "No problem. I like a good game of hoops myself."

"So how can I help you?" Every few seconds, Jonas glanced over at the crowd, but they all appeared to be moving to their designated spots.

How can you help me? Nathan had no idea why he stood here, or why he walked from the parked car and stepped inside. Maybe the time had come to stand face to face with his past.

"I wanted to see about volunteering. I don't know if you're looking for help."

"Son, we're always looking for help around here. Any particular area of volunteering that interests you?"

Nathan hadn't given this much thought. Actually,

he hadn't given it any thought. He just saw the place and walked in. "Well, I used to teach high school English. Do you need tutoring help?"

"Tutoring. Mentoring, Coaching. Have you looked at our website to see our programs?"

He shook his head. "No sir. I should have done that."

Jonas walked to the desk and opened its only drawer. He pulled out a stapled packet of papers and brought them to Nathan. "We need to do background checks. Shouldn't be a problem if you've taught school. I imagine you've been fingerprinted and vetted. Fill these out. Go to the website and see what we do. Download a volunteer handbook. Come on back in with your paperwork, and we'll get you set up."

~*~

Could he do this? Nathan scrolled through the website and looked over the programs. Mentoring. Tutoring. Coaching. A special section promoted the upcoming jamboree fundraiser. He had taught high school, so he had experience working with teens. White, suburbanite, upper class teens. The ethnic mix at The Herald Center couldn't be that much different— could it? Ramón Garcia had treated each one with respect. Surely, he could do that as well.

But could he walk past the portrait of Ramón Garcia every day? It had taken a long time to overcome the crippling guilt, the panic attacks, and nightmares of a jail cell.

6

A ringing cell phone halted Nathan's scrolling. Brian's name flashed in front of him. Nathan answered his phone, happy to shake off thoughts of The Herald Center for a few moments. "Brian, how are you?"

"Hey, Nate. Miss you Saturday mornings."

"Yeah. I may have to drive out there to play some hoops. I haven't connected here yet."

He sat back and stretched his legs up on the footstool. "But you surely didn't call to see how my basketball's going."

"Nope. Just touching base. I received your new manuscript. You should get the contract this week. Remember we talked about accelerating the schedule. I like to work ahead, so I'm checking the calendar."

It had been three weeks, and nothing was started. "A setback with my dad's funeral and sorting through his business finances. I'm a little behind. I'm getting it started now."

"That's understandable. Can we expect a draft in …let's say, three months?"

Nathan blew out a puff of air. "That's pushing it. And when did you become my agent? I expected her to start asking that."

"Anya? I saw her at the writing conference. She'll be calling you. I just like to touch base. You've got momentum right now. Let's try to keep it going."

Kathleen Neely

They ended the call and Nathan wheeled back to his desk. The Herald Center website glowed from the monitor. He reluctantly moved the cursor to the upper right-hand corner and clicked on the X. His home screen appeared. He had no work in progress. No file to open. No ideas streaming through his mind, begging to jump on the page. Nathan went to his word processing program and started a new file. He stared at the blank page but only saw Ramón Garcia's face.

With no plan in mind, Nathan began punching letters on his keyboard. Letters that became words. Words with haphazard thoughts connected to them. He had no idea where it would go, but at least he could say he had a work-in-progress file.

~*~

Angie set her chin on the chinrest at the base of her violin and supported the neck in the crook of her hand. She placed experienced fingers on the bow, curving her thumb at the indentation, careful not to touch the hair. After a few practice movements, her bow danced across the strings with the playful notes of Vivaldi's *Concerto in A Minor*. She knew it by heart. The tedious practice in fifth grade, repeating each measure in slow speed, then bringing it up to tempo, over and over until she mastered it. The rise and fall of eighth notes, sixteenth notes, laced with an occasional staccato. What was once grueling practice had now become a delight.

Her application to Julliard had included Bach's *Partita No. 3* along with Brahms' *Violin Concerto in D Major, Opus 77*. The two varying styles showed her ability to play a diverse repertoire—one a lively release, the other filled with emotion, tempo shifts, contrasting dynamics, and passion. Angie loved the passion of Brahms, but it taxed her musical abilities. Julliard would have alleviated that. But long ago, she stopped the what ifs. No good ever came from them.

The squeak of the front door startled Angie, and her gaze flew toward the clock. She had gotten lost in her violin, forgetting the time. The jingling of keys told her Jonas had arrived. She came to a good stopping place and lifted the bow. Taking up a lint-free cloth, she wiped down the chinrest, the strings, and cleaned any remaining rosin from the bow. Loosening the hair, she packed it carefully in its case, then moved it to her tiny closet where she stored her handbag. Both were far from the hands of the teens.

Jonas turned the corner into the office space. "Hey, Angie. Getting a little practice in?"

"Hello, Jonas. Yes, I have that program for local artists at the Peace Center. I use every spare moment to practice. Mornings offer a time of quiet solitude. We both know how long that lasts." She motioned toward the window as they heard the blaring of car horns.

"Starts now and gets worse through the day. But quiet comes back in the evenings after the doors lock again."

That thought brought a smile. "Bookends. God gives us a beautiful time of quiet to start and end the day. It supports what's in the middle."

He nodded. "Bookends. I'll remember that. Guess it's time to get ready for what's in the middle." He tossed his notebook down and reached for the coffee. An errant drip sizzled as it reached the warming plate. Jonas poured two mugs of coffee and held one out to Angie. "What do you have scheduled for today?"

She reached for the coffee and cupped the mug in both hands. "Thanks."

They sat down and pulled out their spiral notebooks to compare schedules. The front door creaked open with an accompanying knock, and they turned their heads. Jonas got up and walked to the lobby. A man stepped into the doorway and extended his hand to Jonas. They stood talking while Angie watched from the office. He had turned toward Jonas, allowing her to see his face. There was something vaguely familiar about him. Tall, dark hair, with an athletic build. His face looked familiar, but Angie couldn't place it. He handed some paperwork to Jonas and scanned what could be seen of the facility, stopping when his eyes reached Angie. He gave a slight smile and nod of his head. Angie returned the greeting with a warm smile, certain she knew him from somewhere.

Jonas saw the man out and returned to the office.

"Who was that? He looked familiar." Angie peered out the window as the man stepped into a silver Jeep.

Jonas took a long gulp of his coffee. "New volunteer. Nathan something. Can't remember the last name. All background checks are clear. He'll be back later today during roundup. We'll start him with some rec time and then hook him up with a tutoring group."

~*~

Nathan returned to his car, wondering what in the world he had just done. Brian's calendar showed the date for a new draft. He should be home writing, not driving across town to play with teenagers he knew nothing about. Their worlds were too different.

He skirted around the city on the interstate, pulling into his mother's driveway before ten o'clock. He'd take advantage of the writing time before heading back this afternoon.

The lady in the glass office had been Angelina Hernandez. He remembered her face from the video. Nathan was glad she didn't come out to introduce herself. He had stumbled over his words when they made eye contact.

His mother's quilting group met today, so he had the house to himself. A ringing cell phone delayed his start.

"Nathan, Tony Willis here. I've been in touch with both parties regarding the judgment."

Nathan stood, pacing. "What's the verdict?"

"They're both willing to lift the judgment but not the lawsuit. I believe they recognize your need to liquidate, and lifting the judgments will help with that. But Fidelity wants to keep the pressure on, so they refused to rescind the lawsuit. Both companies want to meet with you to discuss repayment options."

Nathan let out a puff of air. "OK. Do you have contact information?"

Tony Willis gave him the information, but Nathan wouldn't call today. He needed to talk with his realtor and start writing. A new book was critical.

He pulled out his laptop and opened the file, *Work in Progress*. It was always the name until the right one emerged. Rereading his haphazard words, he began to pluck away on the keyboard. He chose the name Aiden for his protagonist.

Aiden drove erratically, veering from lane to lane. The

lights ahead were concentric circles that blinded him, constantly moving, changing positions. He swerved to change with them.

The characters were flat, begging to be developed. The storyline sketchy. He knew the first half by heart, but wasn't sure where he would take it. Most storylines mirrored life experiences. He needed to plot this one in a different direction. But he had a beginning. The ending had to stun the readers. As thoughts took shape, his fingers flew over the keys.

At two o'clock, Nathan realized that he hadn't eaten lunch. He hit *save*, checked his back-up file, and logged off. Jonas suggested being inside The Herald Center before the students arrived. He grabbed an apple and a bag of chips, the quickest thing he could find, and ate on the drive across town.

As he drove, his mind was still on the new novel. He became Aiden and lived out each scene. It was easy for Nathan to immerse himself completely in this role, easy to feel the emotional impact. When he arrived at The Herald Center, Nathan's heart raced, pounding like a drum in his chest. His forehead was soaked in sweat.

7

Jonas waved as Nathan entered the multi-purpose room. He pointed Nathan toward a young lady with a clipboard. With her spiked hair and layered tank tops, she could have been mistaken for a student. As he approached, she set the chart down.

"Are you Nathan? Jonas told me to expect you."

"Yes, my first time here." Nathan scanned the room, glimpsing at four other volunteers.

"No worries. We'll get you placed. I'm Mayzie. I'm a volunteer, too, but Jonas has me coordinating the rec groups. He said you like basketball?"

"Yes, but I'll do whatever's needed."

"We'd like to give you a tutoring group and one assigned mentee, but today we'll keep you on the rec team—recreational. I like to clarify that 'cause sometimes it looks like a wreck team, if you know what I mean." She laughed at her own quip.

Mayzie stood at least a foot shorter. She spoke with her face upturned and hands on her hips, "You'll cover basketball with ninth through twelfth grade boys. Let them organize teams with your supervision. You're the final voice on any disagreements, the referee for any disputed calls. Make it fun. Teach them a little if you're comfortable with that."

Mayzie spoke and maintained eye contact the

whole time. Her tapered jeans clung tightly, and her scoop-necked blouse would have been far too revealing if it weren't for the layered tank top underneath. A butterfly tattoo peeked out from the strap of the tank top. Nathan glanced at her high heels with a raised eyebrow, bringing a laugh from Mayzie.

"I don't do a sport. I'll be doing creative writing with the middle school girls. They think the shoes are cool."

Nathan nodded his understanding. "Do you write?"

She picked up the clipboard. "Let's just say that I write better than middle school girls."

"Do you offer creative writing for the boys?"

That brought another laugh from Mayzie. "Are you kidding? The room would be empty." She stepped toward the adjacent doorway. "If you need anything, just whistle for Jonas. It's pretty open in here, so you're not really alone. Always someone you can call. Balls are over there. You have the whole court." She pivoted and made her way to another helper, as the narrow tip of her shoes clicked their way across the gym floor.

Nathan got a ball and cradled it as students started arriving. Jonas stood at the doorway greeting them. Mayzie organized them into clusters. Once the groups were divided, nine boys headed toward Nathan, eyeing him suspiciously. Uneven teams. The mix was diverse with Hispanics, blacks, and one short, scrawny white kid.

"Hi, boys. I'm Nathan and I'll be your coach today. Tell me your names, and I'll try my best to remember." Nathan looked at the silent group. The scrawny kid shifted from foot to foot, eyes focused on the floor. Most of the others stood waiting for someone else to start. One boy, the tallest in the mix, stood with arms crossed, his body rigid, and eyes narrowed, glaring at Nathan. He stood taller than Nathan's six-foot three with cornrows that jutted out in all directions.

Looking from face to silent face, Nathan pointed to the one closest to him. "Your name is…?"

"Chaz," he offered the one-word reply. Nathan pointed from one to the other as they all said their names. The scrawny kid continued to shift uncomfortably, mumbling his name without looking up. "Thomas." The last in line was the tall kid with a big attitude. "Del." He spit the word out through a pinched mouth. He challenged Nathan with his eyes.

Tapping his fingers on the ball, Nathan decided he better take charge. "OK, we're going to divide into two teams. Unless you have a method you typically use, I'll choose two of you to pick teammates."

Immediately, the group moved to form two clusters, one Hispanic and one black. Thomas stood alone. Nathan looked from group to group. "Uh, looks like we have all of the height over here. Let's balance that a little. He walked closer and wished he remembered all of the names. He started with one that he recalled. "Chaz." He flicked his arm, motioning for him to change places with the tall kid. "Del, let's move you here." He looked back to the group where Chaz stood unwavering. Another boy standing beside Chaz spoke in Spanish. "*No se mueven*." Blanking on the boy's name, Nathan touched his shoulder. "Let's move you…"

Before he finished his sentence, the boy placed two hands on Nathan's chest and shoved. "No *me toques*." He shouted as Nathan hit the floor, landing on his posterior. The boy stood over Nathan's stunned form and pointed a finger. "Don't never lay a hand on me."

Nathan balled his fists and leapt to his feet, neck muscles corded. As he stood, he caught sight of Angelina Hernandez hurrying toward them. *Control, Nathan.* He loosened his hands and softened his facial expression.

She came first to Nathan. "Are you all right?"

He brushed his wrinkled T-shirt. "Yep, all but my pride. He took me by surprise."

"I'm so sorry. That was unacceptable." She turned to face the boy who now stood down, a subdued frown on his face. "Carlos, please come with me."

Carlos pointed toward Nathan. "*Me empujó.*"

Angie's tone remained calm, her voice like velvet. "No, Carlos. I was watching. He didn't push you."

She motioned toward her office. Carlos followed obediently, not a word of protest. Nathan watched them walk toward a glass-fronted office and enter. Turning his attention back to the group, he noticed that they had put on the mesh scrimmage vests. The teams hadn't merged. The Hispanics were wearing the blue, and the African Americans were wearing the red. Thomas stood off to the side by himself. Well, that evened out the teams. Nathan tossed Thomas a blue vest.

The next forty minutes of chaotic play crept by with Nathan looking at the clock. The tall kid dominated. Other students touched the ball only to throw it in after Del's successful shot. He managed to steal it back immediately.

Nathan kept one eye on the office where Carlos and Angelina sat, her chair pulled close to his as she leaned forward in conversation. He imagined her soothing tones, her unruffled countenance correcting, guiding the boy.

At four o'clock someone blew a whistle. The boys whipped off the scrimmage vests and tossed them in the box, all except Del. He continued shooting, rebounding, and shooting some more. The others moved toward an adjoining doorway.

"Hey, Del, where are you supposed to be next?"

He continued dribbling the ball while he answered. "Nowhere. I stay here and shoot around."

Nathan watched Angelina take Carlos to the room where everyone else had gone. Then he glanced back and forth between her and Del, who still had a petulant attitude. It had diminished somewhat during the game but resurfaced during the transition.

"You're pretty good. You want a little one-on-one?"

With one eye narrowed and lips clenched tight, Del turned to face him. He looked him up and down and then thrust the ball toward him.

Nathan started to dribble and Del went into defensive mode. Nathan pivoted but couldn't get a shot off. Del went for the steal, palming the ball, but Nathan managed to sidestep and take the shot. As the ball slid through the net, Del retrieved it and their positions were reversed. He had at least four inches on Nathan, so defense was tricky. Del had mastered the art of the low dribble, denying Nathan space to get a hand on the ball. Then when he caught a moment's hesitation, Del sprang up, extending to his full height and took the shot.

Nathan nodded in admiration. "Nice shot."

Del formed the slightest start of a grin. "You ain't too bad for an old man."

Before play could begin again, Del's gaze moved past him, and Nathan heard the gentle voice. "Del, you need to be in tutoring now. They're waiting for you."

"Told you I'm quitting."

Angelina walked toward him and held her hands out for the ball. "That's a subject for another day. Today you're in tutoring."

Del handed her the ball, his tall shoulders slouching, and walked to the door. She watched as he kicked the door before entering.

Turning toward Nathan, she extended her hand. "I'm afraid we haven't properly met. I'm Angie Hernandez."

A subtle scent of honeysuckle reached him. When he met her hand, his felt large and awkward as it encased her tiny one. Despite his moist skin, he felt its softness. "I'm Nathan. It's my first day here."

"Yes, Jonas told me. Carlos has a tendency toward reactive behavior. I'm very sorry that you encountered that. He's in tutoring right now, but he'd like to speak with you before you leave today."

The sides of Nathan's mouth rose slightly. "Carlos would like to speak to me, or you're requiring him to speak with me?"

"Nathan, I encouraged Carlos to do the right thing, but requiring it would be senseless. My hope is always that these kids will examine their own behaviors, test their hearts and minds. Perhaps they will eventually begin to employ that process before actions and not after. If they do, their choices will begin to improve."

The melodic enunciation held him captivated. Once again, Nathan heard the blend of a native speaker of English laced with the beauty of her heritage. He suspected that her parents were not native speakers of English. Most likely, they would have learned it analytically and enunciated fully.

Jolted back from his focus on Angie, he realized there had been a lull in conversation. "I'll be happy to talk with Carlos. I'm just going to straighten this up." He motioned toward the box with pinnies and balls. "After that, I think I'm through today. Unless you have any other needs?"

"Jonas would know that better." She flashed a smile. "You seem to have connected well with Del. I applaud you for that. He doesn't accept everyone that quickly."

"We have a common interest." Nathan tapped the basketball. "He has some real potential on the court. Will he play for his school?"

Angie's smile disappeared. "No. His grades were too low at the end of last school year. He'll be on academic probation until he pulls them up. But, as you saw, he resists tutoring. He's talking about quitting school." Angie's eyes widened with a new revelation. "Perhaps you could help. Are you willing to tutor?"

Nathan nodded, amazed at the sudden change that filled her face. "Yes, I put that down on my form. I used to teach high school. Mayzie said that they would connect me with a tutoring group and someone to mentor."

Angie's face lit with vision. "No. No group. Just one-on-one tutoring. And mentoring. We'll just assign you to Del. Is that all right with you?"

"Well…sure, if that's what you need." He watched with amusement as a wide grin formed and Angie clapped her hands together.

"Oh, this is an answer to prayer. We've been

Kathleen Neely

praying for Del, even though we weren't sure how to pray. God knew exactly what he needed. You."

Nathan sobered. "Angie, I'm not sure I'm God's answer for anyone. Don't get your hopes too high here. I'll give it my best, but…"

"Yes, you give it your best, and God will do the rest. Oh, thank you, Nathan."

He hadn't curbed her excitement at all.

8

Angie couldn't get past the feeling that she knew this man. She planned to ask, but first the situation with Carlos had to be addressed.

"Why don't we walk through the area where tutoring occurs. You can see the set up, and we'll find a spot to talk with Carlos."

Nathan hurriedly tossed the pinnies and balls into their proper space.

Angie led him into a long hall with doors on each side. "These are our tutoring rooms. We're blessed to be able to separate the groups. It helps with the noise, and all doors have windows for safety purposes. Either Jonas or I will be in the hallway walking back and forth, checking in."

Nathan stretched his neck to peer into the occupied rooms. "You have some larger groups and a few with only three?"

"Yes, eight students are maximum for any tutor, but we try to group them according to their academic needs. Some are significantly delayed while others just need motivation."

Nathan nodded his understanding. "Where would you place Del?"

"Significant." Angie answered without hesitation. "I'm sure there are learning disabilities that were never addressed, but that's not our call. We don't diagnose."

"They have snacks while they work. Do you supply them or do they bring their own?"

"Oh, we supply an afterschool snack. If they brought their own, most wouldn't have anything. It's a big line item for our budget, but we get some help from a few venders." Angie slowed her steps. "Carlos is in here."

She stepped into the doorway. "I apologize for the interruption, but may I see Carlos for a moment?"

The teen walked into the hallway without a glance in Nathan's direction. Angie motioned them away from the classroom door. "Carlos, I told Mr. Nathan that you wish to talk with him."

He looked instead at Angie. *"Me disculparé, pero le has dicho que no me tocara?"*

She nodded her head and responded. "We will discuss that, but you must remember that Nathan is a volunteer. His time is a gift to you."

Carlos turned toward Nathan. "Me disculparé …"

Angie shook her head. "English, please."

He began again. "I'm sorry I pushed you. I don't like to be touched."

He looked like a small child in an oversized body. She glanced at Nathan and saw the same understanding, a gentleness in his expression.

"I'll try to remember that, Carlos. And I'll learn everyone's names. If I had remembered your name, I wouldn't have touched your shoulder. I'll try to do better."

Angie waited, but no further conversation occurred. "You better return to tutoring now."

Carlos made his way back to the room.

"Thank you, Nathan. We both know his action was unacceptable, but you allowed him to save face by accepting some responsibility regarding his name. That was very kind."

Nathan smiled, the first real smile that Angie had seen. "So, what was his question before that? I don't speak Spanish."

"He asked me to tell you that he doesn't like to be touched." Angie always had a protectiveness regarding Carlos. "He's not a bad kid."

"Has he been abused?"

He looked into her upturned face, and she quickly became aware of the nearness. She stepped back, creating space between them. "Why do you ask that?"

"Training sessions on how to recognize signs of abuse. Fear of touch is characteristic."

"Probably. If I saw physical signs, I'd have to report it, but I just see fragile emotions. His father has two domestic violence charges for injuring his mother, and now she has a restraining order against him. I have no way to know if he physically harmed Carlos as well. I feel certain that social services would have questioned him."

Angie touched Nathan's arm to indicate that they'd walk back to the multi-purpose room, away from the tutoring area. "You look so familiar to me. You said this is your first time volunteering?"

"Yes. I've never been here before this week." He answered while they walked but glanced her way while he spoke. Angie caught an amused light in his eyes.

She stopped walking and looked up at him. "So where do I know you from?"

"I don't know." His amusement grew.

Her head tilted to one side, squinting an eye. "I think you're teasing me."

Nathan laughed out loud. "Sorry. Do you enjoy mystery novels?"

She gave him a confused look. "Yes, what does that…" Then it came to her. "Nathan Drummond? I should have known."

A grin spread across his face. "I never know who's a reader. Some people wouldn't know my name or picture. Others recognize me immediately."

"I should have been one of the latter. I've read most of your writings. I'm very pleased that you've come to our center. Perhaps we could have you speak about writing to those who are interested."

"I'd be happy to. Anytime." They continued walking and entered the foyer. Nathan's eyes turned toward the portrait of Ramón Garcia, his expression growing somber. He quickly looked away.

"What days will you be here?"

"I've signed up for Monday, Wednesday, and Friday. Does that work?"

"We're blessed to have any time you can spare. Some volunteers can only give us one day a week, so three is very generous. I look forward to seeing you on Wednesday."

Angie stood by the scuffed glass of the front door and watched him walk to his car.

~*~

The tip of the pen rested on the journal as Nathan sat thinking. A cold sweat gathered on his forehead as he relived the scene. Somehow it had more clarity ten years later than it had that night. Setting the pen aside, he paced circles around the room. A burn rose in the back of his throat. Sometimes there weren't sufficient words to capture all that needed to be communicated.

Returning to his desk, he picked up the pen and stared at the thin blue lines where sentences should be. Then he began moving the pen, writing just a single word—*If*. Nathan stared at the emptiness. Finally, he began filling the space between parallel lines. Reaching the bottom of the paper, he read what he had written. But *if* was an act of futility. He ripped it from the threaded seam, and crinkled it into a ball, flinging it across the room. Then he ran to retrieve it so no one would ever read his words. He took a lighter to the paper and watched as it was reduced to ashes.

While he had fought for adequate journal entry words, the discipline prepared him for the story in progress. When he opened the file, his fingers flew over the keys. Thoughts came faster than he could capture them. It would require some serious editing, but words flowed.

9

The sunlight from Aiden's window sent shooting pain to his eyes. He pulled the bedspread up to cover his face, holding the assault at bay. Details of the party came back to him. Old high school friends, now scattered to colleges across the nation, all home for Christmas. The beer, the music, the laughter. But something else? What was it?

The car! Aiden bolted upright with the memory. The red car. It had spun to avoid hitting his truck when he turned for the ramp. He darted to his laptop and pulled up the website for the local news station. There it was. The wreckage on Pleasantburg Road right before the 385 on-ramp. "New Year's Eve wreck takes the life of a Greenville man." Jose Mendez, forty-five years old.

Aiden felt the nausea rising to his throat. Sweat soaked his forehead. He wouldn't make it to the bathroom. Grabbing the trashcan, he emptied the contents of his stomach, the sour taste burning his throat.

He texted Dan, asking him to meet at the school. It was closed for the holiday so no one would be around. Aiden drove around the back of the school to the baseball field where Dan sat on his car's back bumper waiting. It was now January, but still a sweatshirt day in South Carolina. Dan's Clemson orange shone bright in the sunlight.

Aiden had stopped by the grocery store and picked up a newspaper with a picture of the mangled red metal and the damning headline. He held it out to Dan, who pushed the paper away.

"I saw it." Dan's eyes were bloodshot with dark circles beneath. "Listen, last night didn't happen. We weren't there. Never, ever breathe a word to anyone."

"Dan, a man's dead. We can't pretend that didn't happen. Did you read it? Someone saw a white truck driving recklessly."

"Half the trucks on the road are white. Listen. We didn't go home that way. We went up Wade Hampton instead. We were nowhere near Cottonwood. Don't go all Boy Scout on me now. You want to go to prison?"

Aiden's stomach roiled again with the thought. How could a kid like him, good family, scholarship to Auburn, eighteen years old, how could he end up in prison? Dan was right. That's exactly what would happen. Beads of perspiration gathered on his forehead, and his hand shook as he wiped them away.

Aiden looped his arms behind his head, lowering it to his knees.

"Look at this." Dan reached for the paper. "This guy lived over by the urban center. You know that's filled with druggies. Guy was probably a dope head. Had to be some kind of low life to live in that scrapyard. Mendez—probably an illegal. All you have to do is keep your mouth shut. Forever. Never tell this to anyone. Not your parents. Not a girl. Not your wife or kids in years to come."

Aiden paced around the parking lot like a caged animal. His chest constricted, making it difficult to breathe. He couldn't think through the pounding of his ears. Fists clenched open and closed until his knuckles turned white.

Dan jumped up from the bumper of the car. "Hey Dude, tell me you aren't going to do anything stupid here. I mean it, man. This is serious."

"Don't you think I know that?" His voice held controlled anger, spoken through clenched teeth. "I'm the one who was driving."

Dan's hands separated, palms down. "Then let's just calm down, go get a coke, and never mention this again, even to each other."

Aiden stretched the tension from his neck and shoulders. "Get your own coke. I'm going home."

Dan grabbed his shoulder and turned him around, stepping into his space until they were nose to nose. "I'm not kidding, Aiden. Don't mess up my life!"

Lifting his hands chest height, Aiden shoved Dan backward. "I don't see that I have much choice."

Panic filled Dan's eyes. "Which choice? You turn us in, I swear I'll kill you."

Aiden hopped in his white truck and spun his tires as he left the parking lot.

10

Names were changed, but the story lived in him. An avalanche of words raced from Nathan's brain to the page, adding 3,500 words before the deluge slackened. Too many details could be dangerous. Nathan moved his cursor up and changed the location of the accident. He moved toward the sofa and collapsed onto it, experiencing the release of tension that had been building all day. He wasn't sure when sleep claimed his body, but he woke on the sofa at 2:00 AM.

~*~

The emotional exhaustion of writing his story under the guise of Aiden caused Nathan to sleep like the dead.

At nine-twenty the next morning, he sat on the side of his bed, running a hand over his bristly face. Soft tones from the television reached him as he made his way to the bathroom. One look at his bedhead and scrubby face sent him to the shower to help him wake.

Twenty minutes later, alert and refreshed, Nathan made his way to the kitchen. Popping a coffee pod into the single serving coffeemaker, he called into the living room. "Sorry I slept so late."

His mother came through the doorway, holding an ice pack on her hip. "I know you were up late last night. It was around two-thirty when I heard footsteps coming down the hall."

"Sorry if I woke you."

"Did you hear your phone this morning? It rang twice." She made her way to the freezer and exchanged the ice pack for a fresh, cold one.

"I vaguely remember hearing it. I'll check in a few minutes. What's with this? Bad day?" He pointed to the ice as she limped back to her chair.

She shrugged her shoulders. "Some days are worse than others. It may be the humidity."

Nathan's brow furrowed. "Or it may be time for surgery."

"I've told you, I'll know …" His mother crossed her arms, her tone sharp.

Nathan finished the statement for her. "I'll know when the pain is worse than the surgery will be."

She nodded. "So if you remember that, why do you keep pressing me?"

Nathan carried his cup to the table. "Sorry, Mom. I just worry about you. The hip's not going to get better."

"Let me worry about my hip. Are you doing dinner tonight?" She eased back into her chair.

He gave her a wink and a grin. "Of course. It's Tuesday."

~*~

Nathan saw two missed calls and one voicemail

from his realtor. He hit *play* on the voicemail.

Nathan, we have an offer on the townhouse. I'll e-mail you the details. Get back to me as quickly as you can.

A few clicks of his iPad opened the e-mail. The offer was twelve thousand less than asking price. His realtor thought it was a fair offer, but the difference would come from his equity, reducing cash flow. He needed to think about that and decided not to return the call just yet.

Next, he opened his publisher's site and logged into his author page. Book sales were strong for the new novel. The bigger surprise was a boost in sales for his previous novels. Sometimes that happened. A new one would spark interest in prior works. That was a good thing since he'd established an ambitious repayment plan with both of his dad's creditors. Book sales were crucial.

He logged off, fixed an egg and some toast, and took them upstairs to his writing desk. He was on a roll and needed to keep the energy in motion.

His new character would be Maggie, short for Marguerite. He could see her clearly, her long, dark hair smooth as silk, her melodic voice, and her wide smile. Nathan typed a chapter and brought Maggie to life. He paced in his upstairs writing room trying to decide what would happen next. Would Maggie be a key player? He wasn't sure how, but it was his story to invent. And he definitely wanted Maggie around. He went back to his laptop and typed. *Aiden couldn't stop thinking of Maggie.*

11

Nathan opened his realtor's e-mail and hit reply.

Can you get them to come up in price? Townhouses in my complex are hard to come by.

Arriving at The Herald Center an hour before students, Nathan hoped to get some specifics on Del's academic needs. He couldn't prepare for a tutoring session until he knew what to focus on.

Closing the door behind him, he stepped in from the foyer. No one in sight. The door hadn't been locked, so someone must be there. Nathan wasn't sure if he should call out or go on a search. He moved further in and caught a glimpse of Jonas in the hallway.

"Hey, Nathan, come on back here." He waved a large hand, motioning in his direction.

Jonas pushed a cart with snacks as he delivered apples and cookies to each tutoring room. "Hi, Jonas. You need help?"

"I never turn down help. Look at the names on each door and count out that many for the room. Just leave them in the basket on the table. Jonas pointed toward the box of latex gloves. "Gotta wear those. Department of Health."

Nathan pulled out a pair of gloves and began sorting snacks. "I came early hoping to get some insight into Del's tutoring. I don't know how to prepare."

Jonas laid his cluster of cookies in a basket and returned to the cart. "That boy needs just about everything. Biggest problems are reading and math. I suspect that reading is the real reason for everything else failing. Boy's just like I was."

Nathan raised an eyebrow. "You had trouble in school?"

"Ha. Couldn't read to save me. It made me an angry kid, ready to pick a fight with anyone that crossed me." Jonas stopped his task and stood facing Nathan. "You know, when you fail at everything, you search for something you can do well. For me, it was fighting. I became a scrapper, trying to prove my worth. You see I'm a pretty big guy. Didn't take much for me to win a fist fight. For Del, I suspect it's basketball. But that ain't going nowhere unless he can make it in school. NBA won't look at a dropout."

Nathan nodded. "So what got you out of the fighting stage?"

"Prison."

Nathan's gaze shot up.

"Prison and Ramón Garcia," Jonas continued. "He was one special man. Ramón believed in me, told me I was better than a fighter, that I was created for a higher purpose. He was the first person that ever said anything like that. Other folks just called me stupid. Said I wouldn't amount to nothing. Ramón told me that honorable living didn't depend on reading."

Jonas resumed counting out snacks. "Sad, sad day when we lost that man." He moved his head back and forth, like he still felt the heaviness. "I can't tell you how many lives he changed. That's what we try to teach these kids, how to live with honor, not the kind that gangs talk about, but the kind your heart tells you."

Nathan remained silent. He didn't trust his voice to speak through the thickness in his throat. Prickles of gooseflesh raised on his arms. He scanned the hallway so he wouldn't have to look at Jonas.

"The Lord took Ramón Garcia way too soon if you ask me. We still got lives that need changing. But it ain't my place to be second-guessing what God decides to do."

Heat climbed Nathan's face, and he carried his basket toward a tutoring room.

"Hey, Nathan," Jonas called after him. "You forgot the cookies."

Nathan turned back and quickly counted out the cookies to add to the apples. "Sorry. Guess my mind's on tutoring. I have some things I need to get ready."

"Last room on the left. That's where you'll be with Del. You can work in there if you want."

Nathan shuffled down the hallway to the last room. He lowered himself into a chair, the legs scraping as it moved back. His heart began beating wildly, and he had difficulty getting a breath. He forced himself to breathe deeply, diaphragmatic breaths from deep in his abdomen. He exhaled slowly, counting to ten, until he could think clearly without seeing a red car crushed against a tree.

The erratic heartbeat fell back to an even rhythm. Nathan forced himself to refocus. He opened his backpack filled with books for tutoring. Reading or math? He'd start with math. It was logical and easier to tutor without prepping. He had no idea what form of math Del would need. Clearly it wouldn't be the same as most college-bound seniors. No calculus or trigonometry. He'd have to wait for Del and take his lead from him.

He checked his phone for an e-mail. The one he looked for waited in his inbox. "Sorry, Nathan. They said that's their top offer. I think you should take it. If not, it might be a while before we have another buyer."

Hitting the off button, Nathan flung his phone into the backpack with too much force. Maybe he should just move back to Atlanta. He had a good life there. He could forget The Herald Center and let his sister worry about their mother for a change.

The sound of voices reached Nathan, along with the clicking of footsteps in the hallway and the rhythmic thud of someone bouncing a ball. Taking a deep breath, he put a check on his anger and made his way back to the front room to the cluster of boys that had been in his basketball group.

Del was the one bouncing the ball, dribbling while other kids chatted. Thomas slouched and shuffled. Carlos eyes darted back and forth. Jonas's words came back to him. "Teach them to live with honor." Was he the right person for that task?

Teams were uneven. Thomas stayed where he had played two days ago, with the Hispanic team. It proved to be an uneventful forty-five minutes. No one knocked him off his feet or swung punches. He needed to correct a few expletives and some unruly elbows. Del monopolized, and Thomas never touched the ball. Changes would come slow.

At the sound of the whistle, students began moving toward the hallway door. Del continued shooting. Nathan allowed it until everyone else had cleared out of earshot.

"Del, did they tell you I'll be working with you in

tutoring?"

"Ain't going." He kept shooting baskets.

Nathan stepped in and rebounded a shot, cradling the ball in his arm. "Give me a chance here. I used to teach school. I think I can help you."

Del stared him down. "You think you can help me act like a good little white kid?"

Nathan took a deep breath. "No, Del. I think I can help your reading and math so you can get back on the basketball team. You're too good not to play."

"I'll play. I'm gonna get up to Charlotte and see the Hornets, see if they'll look at me."

"They won't." Nathan spoke to Del's retreating back as he walked toward the ball cart and retrieved another basketball. He began shooting again. Nathan, with one ball cradled in his arm, swatted the other ball out of play.

He repeated his words. "They won't, Del. They aren't allowed. New signing policies are in place. Come on back with me, and let's talk about how to get you to the NBA."

"You lying." Del kicked at the post and started walking toward the hallway door.

Nathan put the balls away and followed Del to the small room. He was already seated, his lanky frame in the small chair, eating his snack. Del's textbooks sat on the table, but Nathan decided against diving right into math. He'd be trying to teach a brick wall. Instead, he pushed a piece of paper and pencil across the table. "Time for a quiz."

Del bit into his apple. "Ain't taking no quiz."

"Humor me. First question. What's the average height of an NBA player?"

Del stopped chewing and looked up suspiciously.

He pulled the paper toward him and wrote.

"Next question. What's the average starting salary for an NBA rookie?"

Del marked something on his paper.

Nathan continued. "What's the average salary of all NBA players?

Del looked up at him. "I don't know, man. It's like millions."

"So, take a guess."

After Del scribbled some numbers on the page, Nathan continued.

"How many players did the NBA draft last year straight out of high school?"

The questions kept coming.

"What university sent the most players to the NBA last year?"

"Do you believe you have the talent to play in the NBA?"

Del rocked his chair back on two legs and stared at Nathan.

"It's a yes or no question, Del."

He held Nathan's eyes for a moment before writing.

"Last question. Are you willing to work hard to get there?"

Del answered quickly and set the pencil down. Nathan swiveled it so both could see. The writing was barely legible, but this wasn't the time to pick that apart.

"You said average height is six-foot seven. You're spot on. How tall are you?"

Del allowed a slight lift to the corners of his mouth. "Six-foot-seven. I heard that before. It was easy to remember 'cause that's my height."

"Good. Rookie salary—you said a hundred thousand. It's almost five times that. The average rookie salary last year was approximately $490,000. Average overall salary—you said five million. You're pretty close. It's almost six and a half mil."

Del took a final bite of his apple and shot it, basketball style, into the corner waste can.

Nathan went back to the answers. "Players drafted right out of high school? You said about ten or twelve. The answer is zero. Zero!" Nathan looked up to see Del's expression. His lanky arms folded in front of his chest. "New drafting policies prohibit that. You must play college ball for at least one year."

Nathan moved his finger down the paper, pointing to the next question. "What university sent the most players to the NBA last year? You said University of Kentucky. I see that you watch the draft. UK's a powerhouse. They sent the most last year and consistently for the last few years."

"Yeah, I watched the draft, and I seen the Wildcats on TV a few times."

Nathan leaned forward. "Del, I'm looking at your paper. You said you believe you have the talent for the NBA. I haven't spent much time with you, but from what I've seen, I believe you do, too. The real question is the last one. You claim that you're willing to work hard to make that happen. Here's where the work starts." Nathan tapped the table where they sat. "Not out at the hoops. That's not work for you because you love it. This is where you have to put in the work."

"Man, I ain't never getting into no college." He leaned back and spread his long legs in front of him.

"Why do you say that?"

"I can't even play on the high school team. This

stuff's too hard for me." He shoved his book across the table.

"Del, I believe I can help you if you're willing to do your part. You don't have to be an A student. You just have to pass. Colleges like UK will make things happen if you're trying." He turned the paper toward Del and pointed to his final answer. "Are you ready to start working?"

A sigh escaped Del's mouth. "Yeah. I guess."

"*You guess* isn't good enough. I'll put a lot of time into helping you. I need your promise that you'll do your part. This only works if both of us are committed."

Del looked at the books he had shoved to the end of the table. He pursed his lips. Nathan watched him sizing up the enemy. Del's long arm reached and drew the books back to a stack in front of him. "Yeah. I'll do my part."

"And that's a promise?"

"Yeah. That's a promise."

"Good. Show me where you are in this math book."

Tutoring time ended before it had barely begun, but the time spent had been valuable. When they stood up, Nathan peered up at Del's face.

"We have a covenant here. I'll do all I can to help as long as I see you trying. Bring me all of your test and quiz results. Bring me any homework that you have on a Monday, Wednesday, or Friday. We have to split our time working on math and reading. I'm going to give you my phone number. Call me if you're working on something and get stuck."

He handed Del a business card. Del turned the card and read it slowly, his struggle evident even with those few words. Eventually, understanding dawned.

"You an author? Do you like, have books that people buy?"

Nathan smiled. "Yeah. Some people buy them."

"Are you like, rich or something?"

Nathan laughed out loud. "No, I'm not rich. But when you're in the NBA, you will be. I've got some time. You up for a little one-on-one?"

12

Angie couldn't stop thinking of Nathan. Was it the fact that he was a best-selling author? She didn't think so. She had never been easily impressed with fame, but she had learned to appreciate talent.

She watched for him as the tutoring broke up. Some students left and others stayed for music lessons or art workshops. Angie stood outside the office door saying good-bye to students and watching for Nathan.

He walked out with Del, and turned toward the ball rack. They began shooting hoops at the far end of the court. She wouldn't interrupt them. This was so good for Del.

Angie sat in the office, watching through the glass wall. They played at full speed and looked equally matched, even though Del had the height advantage. When play halted for a moment, she would catch Nathan glancing in her direction. About twenty minutes passed when they tossed the ball back in the rack.

Angie stood, determined to catch Nathan before he left the building. He saw her and gave a wave.

"Nathan, have you got a minute?"

He said something to Del and then turned in Angie's direction.

"Come sit for a moment. I have something to ask

you."

They walked into the small, enclosed space and sat across the table from each other.

"I'm going to be forward and ask you for something. I feel like I can be bold on behalf of the center and the children. Would you consider donating an autographed copy of your new novel to be part of our silent auction at the fundraiser? And would you consider attending and signing books for readers?"

Nathan answered without hesitation. "Yes to both. Just designate the book signing to about a two-hour time frame. That's about all I can handle."

Angie clapped her hands together and released a little squeal. "Yes. Thank you so much. It'll be a welcome addition. Having a celebrity always helps to draw people."

"I'm not sure how much of a celebrity I am."

"Our fundraising goal is substantial. Everything we can add to the jamboree will help."

Nathan squirmed in his seat. "I think I need to say something here. I know that the center has some financial difficulties right now. Many people have a misconception about the income of authors. I'm one of the fortunate ones that I've been able to make a living from writing. But only the superstars get rich from it. The ones who get movie deals and go international. The rest of us just get by."

Angie's mouth dropped open. "Nathan, I never had an expectation about any help financially. We're so happy to have you helping here."

"I know, but I just wanted to explain. On top of that, my dad died a little more than a month ago, and I discovered that he had some serious debts. I'm trying to take care of that without my mother's awareness. No sense her worrying about her security."

Angie felt a familiar ache in her chest. "I'm so sorry. The loss of a loved one can be devastating."

A shadow crossed Nathan's face. "I shouldn't have shared about my father's debts. Please keep that in confidence."

"What I hear in confidence, I keep to myself. And I'm sorry for your loss. I'm blessed to have my parents, but my cousin lost hers. We're very close and those were such hard days."

Silence hung between them for a moment. Angie saw pain carved on Nathan's face. "You must be a very good son to have such kindness toward your mother."

He shifted his chair back and stood up. "I should go."

Angie stood when he did. They began walking from the office. "Oh, Nathan. There's, Liz, my cousin. I told her about your work with Del. Do you have a moment to meet her?"

Nathan turned toward the lady approaching from the hallway off of the multi-purpose room.

"Sure. I have a few minutes."

They changed directions and walked to meet her.

"Liz, I'd like you to meet Nathan Drummond. He's the volunteer who's working with Del."

Elizabeth extended her hand, and Nathan reached to accept it. "Mr. Drummond. I'm pleased to meet you. Angie's been telling me how nicely you and Del have connected."

"Thank you. I hope I can be some help to him."

Elizabeth flashed an apologetic look his way. "And I hear that Carlos gave you a less than hospitable welcome."

Nathan laughed aloud. "No harm done. I've

taught school before. I know how teens can be." Nathan looked back and forth between the two cousins. "Easy to see that you're related. I might have mistaken you for sisters."

Angie's eyes remained fixed on Nathan's. "I told you we're very close. Our mothers were sisters, and they bore a strong resemblance. You wouldn't be the first to mistake us for siblings." Elizabeth's short, dark hair framed her face while Angie's hung long, tied and pulled over her right shoulder. "Before Liz cut her hair, some people mistook her for me."

"I have an appointment, but I'm pleased to meet you," Elizabeth excused herself. "My cousin spoke very highly of you."

Heat radiated into Angie's face. Why had Elizabeth said that when she barely knew the man? Perhaps she had spoken of him too much Monday evening. She needed to counter that remark.

"It's been hard to reach Del. I'm thankful for all of our volunteers."

Nathan nodded his understanding. "Speaking of Del, is it possible for me to speak with his teachers? I'd need parent permission."

Angie tried to remember if she'd ever met his mother. All phone numbers were in the registration. "I'll try to arrange that. I'll give her a call this evening."

Nathan glanced at the clock. "I better go. I've got the date of the jamboree. Let me know when you have the details."

~*~

Even before Nathan opened the front door, he

knew something wasn't right. A smoke detector shrieked from somewhere inside. As the door opened, a burnt odor hung heavily in the living room. He pushed the front door closed and bounded into the kitchen with swift movements. A smoky haze filled the air.

"Nate." The barely audible plea came from the adjoining pantry where his mother lay sprawled on the floor.

Nathan pulled the blistered pan from the stove top and ran to his mother.

"I can't move, and I don't have my phone."

"Shh. Don't try to talk. Stay still, and I'll get help."

Nathan grabbed his cell phone and dialed 9-1-1. They answered as he yanked the cover off the smoke detector and pulled the battery to stop the shrill screeching. "I need an ambulance at 3573 Pacific Street. My mother had a fall. She can't get up, and I think she may have broken a hip." When he hung up, he lifted the kitchen window to clear the smoke, and then he ran to the front door. He opened it and made sure the screen door wasn't locked. Hurrying back to the pantry, he knelt down beside his mother and took her hand. "Help's on the way. Where's the pain?"

Her voice was barely above a whisper. "My hip. And my wrist took the weight of my fall."

Nathan looked at the wrist positioned on her abdomen. He touched it gently, feeling the bones. "I don't think it's broken, but they'll check it out."

He heard the siren, followed by the call from the front door. "We're back here."

Two paramedics hurried in and took over, checking vitals and immobilizing her neck. Nathan grimaced as he heard his mother's cry of pain when they lifted her onto a stretcher. The driver turned to Nathan before closing the door. "We're going to take her to the main hospital downtown. They're better equipped if she needs emergency surgery."

"I'm right behind you." Nathan jumped into his Jeep Cherokee and kept pace with the ambulance.

~*~

Nathan sat in the crowded ER waiting room while his mother underwent numerous tests. He jumped up when he heard his name being called.

With three long strides, he reached the nurse with a clipboard. "How's my mother?"

"The doctor will go over everything with you. I'll take you up to him."

They went up the elevator to the third floor, to an empty patient room. "They'll bring your mother to this room, and the doctor will be in to talk with both of you."

Again, Nathan waited. After fifteen minutes, an orderly wheeled his mother in, and he and a nurse transferred her from the gurney. Nathan watched her twisted expression as they shifted her to the waiting bed. He sat beside her and took her hand. "Did they give you something for the pain?" His eyes strayed to the dripping IV.

"I think so. Everything's a little fuzzy right now." Her voice held no strength. A few minutes later, the doctor arrived.

"I'm Dr. Hastings, an Orthopedic Surgeon with Ryland Orthopedics." He clicked a few keys on his laptop and some images of her hip came into view.

"Mrs. Drummond, your right hip was compromised before the fall. You can see right here." He pointed to the area in question. "You suffer significant osteoarthritis, limiting your ability to move that hip. These two bones were rubbing, causing the pain. When you fell, you fractured the upper portion of the femur." He pointed toward the white line indicating the fracture.

"We're looking at a total hip replacement. It will address both the pain from arthritis and the fracture."

Nathan's mother nodded. "I guess it's time."

Nathan nodded toward the doctor. "When can you schedule it?"

"Tomorrow morning. Seven a.m."

Her small voice interceded. "How long's recovery?" Her eyes filled with tears. "I have to fly to California."

Nathan explained for her. "Her first grandchild will be born in a few months."

"Short-term recovery is four to six weeks. Long-term, expect up to six months. I see no reason why you can't be on that plane."

She turned her eyes toward Nathan. "All right. Let's get it done."

13

Nathan called Leah in California to let her know that the surgery went well. He hadn't told her about their father's financial mess. Her husband's residency status and student loans would place them somewhere near the poverty level. No sense stressing her during pregnancy. At least their mother's health insurance was still intact. Now they just needed to get through recovery. It meant home health care for two weeks, then outpatient PT. Nathan couldn't let Del down, and Angie had announced his presence at the jamboree next week.

Nathan left the hospital after the surgery and stopped by The Herald Center. Thursday wasn't his volunteer day, but he wanted to touch base with Angie or Jonas. Music reached him as he walked in the front door. Stepping from the foyer, he saw Angie, alone in the glass-enclosed office. She held a violin to her chin and played a sweet, familiar melody. She hadn't seen him as she played with skillful abandon. Nathan intruded on her privacy, but the music drew him like a sweet caress. Just like her voice. Something united the sound of her voice and the beauty of the violin. Both had the ability to soothe, to captivate. For a moment, gone were the financial worries, the concerns over his mother's rehab, the struggle to teach Del. Nothing matched the draw of the music. The music and Angelina Hernandez. Her eyes were closed, and her silky hair draped over her right shoulder, opposite of where the violin rested.

So lost in the moment, he startled when the melody stopped abruptly. Their eyes met, holding that glance for an instant. Angie's face reddened as she set her violin on the table and walked out to meet him.

"Nathan, I didn't hear you enter." She fidgeted with her hair.

"I'm sorry. I found myself fascinated." He sucked in a quick breath and gave a disbelieving shake to his head. "You play beautifully."

A radiant smile replaced her awkwardness. "Thank you. I love to play. Please, come in."

They walked into the office where Angie proceeded to pack up her instrument.

"Please don't stop on my account. I'll only be a minute, and then I'll be on my way."

She continued to place each piece in the case with great care. "No, I'm done for today. I need to pry myself from the violin to do tasks that await me." She flipped the metal closure and placed the case in the closet.

"So what brings you by today?" She pulled out a chair and sat at the table.

Nathan slid into a seat across from her. "My mother had emergency surgery this morning. She fell and fractured her hip. They did a complete hip replacement. I thought I should let you know."

Her hand flew to her chest. "Oh, Nathan, I'm so sorry. What can we do for you?"

"Nothing. Everything went well. I'm hoping that I can get our neighbor to help her on my days here with

Del, but I wanted to let you know just in case anything interferes. She won't be released until Saturday, so I'll definitely be here tomorrow."

"I understand. We meet for prayer later today and will ask for God's healing and peace."

"Thank you." Nathan's eyes darted toward the closet where she had placed the instrument. "So where did you learn to play violin?"

Angie placed her elbows on the table and leaned forward. "I started lessons at a young age. Five years old."

"How long did you study?"

"My first teacher stayed with me until I was fourteen. Then she recommended someone more proficient. My new instructor played with the Charlotte symphony, and my mother drove me an hour each week for my lesson."

"Angie, all those years? Did you have dreams of a musical career?"

Her eyes dimmed and she offered a sad smile. "I did. But real life changes dreams. Julliard accepted my application, but my uncle died suddenly. At the same time, my aunt was severely injured. She never walked after that. Elizabeth needed me."

"Julliard's a big deal. Not many people can make their cut. Couldn't someone else have helped? You sacrificed your life's dream after all those years of practice?"

The sad smile returned but carried a little more light to her eyes. "Your mother needs you. Would you turn that over to someone else right now? Did you turn your father's financial difficulties over, or did you sacrifice to help?"

"But I didn't give up writing to help. It's

just…you're so gifted."

Angie reached and touched his hand. "I needed to ask myself the 'why' question. Why did I want to attend Julliard? Why did I want to become a concert violinist? The answer to those questions had nothing to do with God or family. They had everything to do with me. It was a dream to give recognition to myself. I had to relinquish that."

Nathan could only think as far as his hand. Her touch lingered. Everything in him wanted to turn his hand over and enclose hers inside. She removed it before he had the opportunity. "Do you think God's the one who gifted you? Did you ever consider that you could use that gift for Him?"

"Yes, I have thought that. But at the time, I chose correctly. My focus was on myself. And Nathan, do you remember when you asked me to keep a confidence regarding your father's indebtedness?"

He nodded, not fully understanding the connection.

"Well, please keep this in confidence also. Elizabeth does not know that I received an acceptance from Julliard. She didn't need to feel guilt on top of grief."

Something they shared. He didn't want his mother to feel guilt on top of grief.

Angie walked to the door with Nathan. "Oh goodness. I almost forgot to tell you. I spoke with Del's mother, and she has sent notification to the school providing her permission for teachers to speak with you regarding his academic needs. I will send you an e-mail with his school information."

"Thank you. I suspect he's dyslexic. I want to see if any testing's been done."

~*~

Nathan stopped by the school at three o'clock hoping to catch Del's homeroom teacher when students dismissed. He signed in at the office and received a visitor's pass. They placed a call and ushered him down the hallway, past lockers and a school day's-worth of litter. The old building paled next to the Atlanta school where Nathan once taught English. The sage-green lockers wore scratches and dents, a few with doors that hung awkwardly on broken hinges. His escort pointed toward the room and left him.

Nathan walked into the sizable classroom to find a large woman with an artificial shade of red hair. Her handshake matched that of a man—strong and dominant.

"Judy Lockhart. So you're Del's tutor. Well, you've got your work cut out for you. He's the underachiever of the century."

Nathan bristled. He had taught school. Start every conference with a positive. Every kid has something good that can be shared. Nathan would do that since she didn't. "Del's a great kid. Real potential on the basketball court, and he's working hard for me." A little stretch, but all indications were that he would be working hard.

"Well, if you say so. I haven't seen it here." She walked behind her desk and sat down.

"I suspect that Del has some learning challenges, possibly visual processing issues. I wondered if any testing's been done. Has he been identified for special services?"

She pushed back in her swivel chair, arms folded behind her neck. "Del's just lazy. He's unmotivated and refuses to do the work."

Nathan took a deep breath, reminding himself to keep her on his side. "Maybe, but I've seen kids that use that to cover their inabilities. If everything is too hard, they shut down." He repeated his question. "Has any testing been done?"

"Just standardized testing. His ability index is extremely high — 137. He just refuses to work."

Three short dings preceded the static of the intercom system. Mrs. Lockhart rolled her eyes at the disruption as someone droned on about the change in location for the faculty meeting. Nathan, still standing, motioned to a student chair within reach. "May I sit?" She waved her hand for him to sit, showing her annoyance that he spoke while she listened to the announcement.

He pulled the molded plastic chair in front of her desk and sat, waiting until the intercom clicked off. An ability index generated from a standardized test didn't provide a clinical IQ but typically served as a good indicator. That score would place him in the gifted range. Yet, as an educator, they should know that a diagnosed learning disability could coexist with high intelligence.

When the final click told him the intercom had been silenced, he attempted to phrase that thought without sounding condescending. "Typically, a wide gap between ability and achievement is indicative of a learning disability."

The teacher shrugged her shoulders. "He's a senior. Too late for that. It takes a while to schedule. By the time testing occurred and we organized a team meeting, we'd be nearing the end of the school year."

Nathan would get nowhere in this system. They had failed Del, pure and simple. They allowed him to fall through the proverbial cracks without providing for his needs. He'd do what he could, making his best assumptions of Del's challenges.

Nathan left the school and placed a call to a former colleague. She taught elementary school, but that might be where they needed to start. "Can you give me some strategies for teaching a dyslexic to read?"

14

On Friday afternoon, one extra boy joined them for rec time. He self-grouped with Del's team. The teams would have been even if Carlos had shown up. When a ball went out of play, Nathan made every attempt to toss it to Thomas. Del would typically have possession within fifteen seconds. Those were the only times when Thomas touched the ball. He never went after it on his own.

A shrill whistle ended play, and they all headed back for tutoring. A yellow Post-it note stuck to the table beside Nathan's backpack. *Nathan, please stop by the office before leaving today.* It wasn't signed but contained a flowing, feminine script.

Nathan set the note aside and pulled out four flash cards with high-frequency words. Del held his phone and began plugging letters in his text box. With a swift movement, Nathan snatched it from his hand.

Del's long arms attempted to take it from him. "Hey, that's mine!"

"Phone-free zone." Nathan powered the phone off and handed it back. He watched as Del rolled his eyes, much like his teacher had done. Nathan ignored the look and turned the first index card toward him. It contained the single word, *because*. Instead of asking him to read the word, Nathan read it, pointed to the print, and then proceeded to ask him a series of questions.

"What's the starting letter?"

"What's the first vowel?"

"What two vowels are blended?"

"Which comes first?"

"What vowel is used twice?"

Nathan placed the card face down and turned three more to be analyzed. When they had finished, he put the cards away and looked at Del's failed math test. While perusing it, he said, "Spell *because*."

"What for?" Del's tone was defiant.

"Because you can."

"B-E-C-A-U-S-E." Del slowed at the blended vowels.

"Great." Nathan slid a paper toward him. "Here's a list of a hundred high-frequency words. Analyze them like we just did with these." He tapped the stack of four index cards. "Until you can spell each. Then you'll readily recognize them when you read."

Del leaned back and extended his long legs. "Come on, man. This whole list?"

Nathan pulled out the quiz he kept in his folder and pointed at Del's response to the last question. "You said you were willing to work hard." Nathan set the math down and put his elbows on the table, leaning forward. "Here's what's happening. Your brain uses so much energy decoding—sounding the words out—that you lose comprehension. You finish a passage in your history or science book and don't remember what you read. Once you can read fluently, you'll be able to put your concentration on the meaning of the words. Start here." He held up the word list.

Del silently placed the list in his folder.

"Next—do you learn better when you read about it or hear about it?" Nathan knew what the answer would be, but Del needed to recognize it for himself.

"I guess when I hear."

"Great. When you study, read out loud. If you struggle over words, work through the words. Then go back and read the passage again aloud. Do that until you read it fluently."

Nathan opened a passage in Del's history book and walked him through the process. They analyzed words, re-read a sentence, and then put it all together by re-reading the paragraph. Each time Del's frustration began to surface, Nathan said, "This is the road to the NBA."

There was so much to accomplish, and their session went too quickly. They ran out of time before reviewing the math, but Nathan pulled out a tablet of gridded paper and gave it to Del. "Look at your work. You started aligning numbers then ran crooked. Use this and rework a few of these. Call me at the number I gave you if you get stuck. I jotted answers on the back. You can self-check."

Del laughed. "You think I won't look?"

Nathan squinted. "You can look at the answers if you're not willing to work for it. I guarantee you won't find the answers on the back of your real test." He reached in his bag and pulled out two more things, handing the first one over to Del, an elementary reading book, *Salt in His Shoes: Michael Jordon in Pursuit of a Dream.*

Del picked the book up and looked at the front cover, turned it over, and tossed it down. "This is a little kid's book."

"Hey, Michael Jordan's story doesn't change. You can read it here or read it in a three-hundred-fifty-page biography. Your choice."

Del slid the book into his pack.

Nathan handed him the next item—an audio book. "John Steinbeck. *Of Mice and Men.* Have you read it?"

Del shook his head, eyeing it suspiciously.

"Do you have a CD player?"

He nodded. "My mom does."

"Great piece of literature. Listen to it, and we'll discuss it next week."

Del slid it in his pack.

"Those are from the public library. Don't make me pay for them. They're due back in three weeks." Nathan leaned back, his voice softened. "Del, you've got to learn to work your strengths. You can enjoy great literature through reading it or listening to it. Right now, your strength is listening. Know your strengths and weaknesses. Reading's a struggle, so don't pick books that tax you. Pick ones that are easy to read, but keep working to build that. Reading a children's book will help. Keep doing that, and you'll soon be reaching for books at higher levels. If you're not reading anything, you're ignoring the problem. Sometimes you have no choice, like in your history class. That's when you've got to bite the bullet and get disciplined. Work the problem. You can do this.

"I can't say with certainty, but I suspect that you have a visual processing disorder."

"You mean, like, I need glasses?"

"No. Not like that. If I'm right, your eyes see things well, but your brain scrambles that information. You need some strategies to stop your brain from doing that."

Del nodded slowly. "Guess I need to keep telling myself this is the road to the NBA."

"That's right, buddy. This isn't your fault, but it is your problem. Keep your eyes on the goal. You're a smart kid."

Del's gaze shot up. "Now that's something I ain't heard before."

Nathan felt an ache in his throat. He had grown up with affirmation from both of his parents. Where would Del be now if someone had helped him and encouraged him? If teachers hadn't ignored a problem? No wonder he wanted to quit school.

"Believe it, Del. It's the truth. Let's go shoot some hoops."

~*~

Angie had left a note on the tutoring table for Nathan. When tutoring dismissed, she wasn't surprised to see him head to the gym with Del. A smile formed as she watched the two of them fiercely competing under one hoop.

Nathan glanced her way and caught her staring. She pulled some files before her that needed no attention. It would be better to appear focused on something besides Nathan Drummond.

She glanced up from the file and caught them putting the ball away. Nathan pulled a towel from his pack and wiped his forehead. He and Del exchanged a few words before Nathan headed toward the office. He poked his head in the door.

"Nathan, come in. How is your mother?"

Nathan strode in, taking the chair across from

Angie. "Surprisingly well. She'll have a journey of therapy ahead, but they're releasing her in the morning."

"Wonderful. Elizabeth and I prepared a meal for you. You can use it when she returns tomorrow, or freeze it for a day when it's needed." Angie walked to the mini-fridge and pulled out a shopping bag. "Sancocho—a Puerto Rican stew. It's thick and hearty—a favorite in our family." She pointed toward the bread. "Garlic bread. It's good for soaking up the broth."

Nathan opened his mouth to speak but closed it again and tilted his head to the side. He released a breathy, "Thank you," not more than a whisper. He reached for the bag that Angie held out to him. "Puerto Rican? Is that your family's roots?"

Angie sat back, welcoming the time for conversation. "Yes, my parents were both born there. My father attended the Universidad de Puerto Rico de Rio Piedras. He then accepted employment with Reglan Enterprise. They're an international company and offered him a transfer to the states. They already had citizenship because of the Jones Act. It gave US citizenship to all Puerto Ricans."

"And Elizabeth?"

Angie smiled. "My Aunt Elena couldn't bear the separation from my mother. They followed a year later. And what about you, Nathan? Do you have siblings?"

"A sister. Leah's two years younger. She's living in California now while her husband completes his residency. He's a med student at UCLA. I'll be an uncle in a few months. They're expecting their first child."

Angie clapped her hands together in glee. "How wonderful. But so far away."

"Hopefully that's temporary. Eventually they'd like to be on the east coast." Nathan glanced at the clock. "Hey, any word on why Carlos wasn't here today?"

Angie frowned. "I wondered that as well. I called his home but no one answered. Hopefully, he'll return on Monday."

Nathan rose to leave. "Thank you for this." He held the bag up. "And please thank Elizabeth. I've worked out our schedule so I won't be missing time with Del. I'll see you Monday, and I've got the jamboree secured for next Saturday."

"Good. *Buen Provecho!*" When Nathan gave her a puzzled look, Angie smiled. "The Spanish version of bon appetite. Enjoy your meal."

~*~

An e-mail alerted Nathan of his latest royalty check. He logged into his bank account to view the direct deposit. Very few checks were written by hand, but Nathan wanted a strong paper trail. He addressed two envelopes, one to Fidelity Tools and the other to Ellison Tools and Equipment.

His realtor informed him that they lost the sale. He needed that townhouse to sell. Perhaps he should have taken the offer. Too late now. He'd keep plugging away at the debts until then. The lawsuit would come into play in about thirty days if nothing substantial happened.

Nathan opened the journal and began to write immediately. The time spent at The Herald Center provided so much to journal about. When he finished with his handwritten journal, he opened the desk drawer and found his mason jar. He crumpled the page and dropped it inside before reaching for his lighter. After he watched it burn, he logged onto his Work in Progress file. Words came easy.

15

Aiden tore a perforated sheet of tablet paper from a notebook. He sat at his desk and wrote.

"I can't speak these words to anyone—ever. But if I don't, I think I'll explode with the guilt. So I'll write them. No one will ever read this. I'll destroy it when I'm done." He went on to write what he remembered of the night before.

Aiden finished writing and re-read his words before crushing the paper into a loose ball. Loose enough to burn quickly. He emptied a mason jar that he used for a catch-all on his dresser and placed the paper inside of it. He lifted the window a few inches and reached inside the jar with the long nose of a candle lighter and lit the paper. It charred and dissolved to ashes. As the last remaining sliver of paper singed, he put the lid on and tightened it. The captive smoke blackened the jar with a sooty residue.

Sitting on his bed, holding the ashes before him, Aiden changed his plan to flush the contents and discard the jar. For some unexplained reason, he needed to keep those ashes and to continue writing. He would purge his soul and feed the jar. It held the memory of his sin and of Jose Mendez's life.

16

A ringing cell phone jolted Nathan from his concentration. Anya. He had been expecting his agent's call. He shook his head, attempting to clear his mind of the story details.

Nathan answered the phone. "Writing as we speak."

Anya gave a throaty laugh.

"And hello to you, too. Glad you're writing. Sales are strong."

"I saw that. The previous works picked up as well."

There was a suppressed excitement in her tone. "Are you sitting?"

Actually, he was pacing. "I can be."

"Well, please do."

He started to lower himself into a seat.

"Drumroll …" She made little repetitive syllables. "We have a possibility of a movie deal."

Nathan sprang up again. "You're kidding? What book?"

"Number four. *Secret on the Bayou*. Not kidding. It's on the table for discussion. They're talking $300,000 signing, but I think I can talk them up."

"They approached you?"

"Of course not. I'm always working for you, Nate.

I sent a couple of inquiries. Don't get too excited about the money. It would be split 50/50 with whomever is hired to write the screenplay."

Nathan mentally factored Anya's fifteen percent but didn't mention it. She earned her money. "So what do we do now?"

"The ball's in their court. I hope to hear from them within two weeks. Oh, and if it becomes a made-for-TV movie, that reduces the signing dollars. If you're a praying man, pray for the big screen. If this flies and does well, it opens up a whole new world. You'll be a household name. And the signing bucks will increase with your popularity."

Nathan paced again when he hung up the phone. This would settle the financial dilemma. He could easily handle the remaining debts if he had this and his townhouse equity. He could get his own place again. Maybe move back to Atlanta.

That immediately brought thoughts of Diana. She'd make a good match for someone, but it wasn't him. Angie's smile flashed before him. Her hand touching the top of his while it rested on the table. He had taken Diana's hand many times, and it never affected him the way Angie's touch had done.

Perhaps a townhome in Greenville would be better.

17

Nathan pulled his car into the garage so his mother would be close to the back door. It had only one small step up. The physical therapist had shown them how to best maneuver steps. Nathan positioned her walker inside the doorway. Leading with her good leg, his mother used her arm strength to step up into the house. They stood in the kitchen for a moment while she regained her balance, and then Nathan helped her into the living room where he had rearranged furniture to make her movement easier.

His mother's face contorted as she lowered herself into the closest chair and exhaled. "Thank you, Nate. You've been busy." She looked around the room, her eyes landing on the basket beside her. It held her reading glasses, TV remote, tissues, cell phone, and a book she'd been reading.

"I'll bring you some water and your pills. Anything else right now?"

"No, but we have to talk. Come sit down when you get those."

Nathan placed her water on the table and her pills in the basket. He made a quick trip to the car and brought in the flower arrangements which had been sent to the hospital, placing them on different tables. He leaned back on the recliner and kicked the footrest up, stretching his legs out in front of him. "You've done well. A few weeks and you'll be back to your normal routine. What do you want to talk about?"

"I'm glad you're here, but surgery wasn't as bad as I had anticipated. I don't want you upsetting your routine. I've made some arrangements for help."

Nathan crossed his arms. "Mom, that's what I'm here for. Even before I moved, I told you I'd come and take care of you after the surgery."

"I know. That's why we need to talk. Your help will be great in the mornings and evenings, but I have friends, too. People from church and from the neighborhood have been calling. I have someone coming every day for the next two weeks. I suspect some meals will arrive as well."

He looked at her sallow complexion, wrinkles forming on her forehead. "That's good, but those are visitors. I can help with other things. You can't have several people divvying out medicine."

She set her jaw and drilled him with determined eyes. "It's my hip, Nathan. Not my brain. I can handle my own medicine. There are some things that a son should not do for his mother. I've arranged for help."

He answered with a small nod, understanding dawning. "OK, I get it. I'll back off, but please let me know what you need." That brought the meal to his mind. "That reminds me, I have a meal for tonight if you're up for something a little different. Some friends sent it."

"Different?" A puzzled look crossed her face.

"Puerto Rican. She said it's like a stew."

His mother lifted an eyebrow in question. "She? I know you've been going out playing ball, but you never did tell me where."

Nathan had dodged the conversation after his

mother's advice to avoid The Herald Center. But he wouldn't dig a well of deceit. "I've been volunteering some time at The Herald Center. I get to shoot some hoops, and I'm serving as a mentor to a high schooler."

She studied him, wordlessly for a long moment. "The Herald Center? You just be careful over there."

"To answer your question, two of the ladies that run the center sent a meal. Just let me know what time you'll want to eat."

"What I want right now is to close my eyes."

Nathan kicked the footrest down and stood up. "Then I shall leave you to rest. Holler if you need me." He placed a kiss on her cheek and went upstairs to his writing room.

~*~

Nathan skipped church so his mother would not be alone. The visitors began around one o'clock. As friends stopped by, the refrigerator began overflowing. Nathan politely excused himself and disappeared into his writing room. The company was good for his mother and freed him to write.

His cell phone alerted him to an incoming text. He didn't recognize the number but opened the message. "Hey, it's Del. I can't figure out this stupid math and there's a test tomorrow."

Nathan typed a question. "What type of math?"

It took a few minutes for the reply to come through. "I guess it's like algebra or something?"

This wouldn't work by texting. Nathan hit the call back option.

Del was quick to answer. "Hey. That you,

Nathan?"

"Yeah. I need more information. What else can you tell me?"

"I don't know. It's all this stuff about rational equations and coefficients and stuff like that."

"Del, give me an example. I need to write it down to see what you're dealing with."

"It's like, all stacked up—like a big fraction but with letters and signs."

That visual alone would be a challenge for Del. "OK." Nathan sent a quick prayer that he could help. He was an English teacher. Without a book in front of him, some of the math taxed his memory.

"Hey, tell you what, I can't be much help without seeing it. Can you meet me later, maybe at a coffee shop? What's close for you?"

They made arrangements to meet at a diner in Del's neighborhood at four o'clock and ended the call. Nathan shut down his work-in-progress and searched for examples of algebraic equations. He'd known this stuff once, but today it was all new math. He had to find current methods used to solve the equations. He had time for a two-hour refresher.

~*~

"Del." Nathan slid into the booth and greeted him. The scattering of customers all turned his way, the one white face among them. Del's empty glass and open math book indicated he'd been there a while. Nathan's eyes scanned the little diner with sports photos scattered throughout. Two TVs with two different football games were muted.

Heads turned again when Del walked up to the counter. It was probably hard not to glance at someone six-foot seven with cornrows adding three more inches of height. He returned with his refilled Coke and ice water for Nathan.

Nathan swiveled the math book a quarter of a turn so they could both see it. "I have to tell you, I needed a quick refresher before I came. It's been a long time since I've done this."

Del's eyes narrowed. "You said you taught school."

"English. Not math. I've done this, but it's not something you remember when you don't use it."

Del slouched over the table. "Then why do they make us do it?"

"Because they do."

"That ain't no answer."

Nathan flipped the page. "It's the only answer I have. Let's get busy."

They worked through a few algorithms following the formulas. When Del had correctly worked three of them, Nathan nodded his approval. "You've got this. All you need to do is remember the formula and take it step by step."

"But I don't get it. I can do the steps, but I don't know why it works that way."

Nathan leaned back, the start of a smile in his eyes. "That's a question that mathematicians ask. Me—I just followed the formula. Here's something I'd never have told my students. When it comes to higher level math, don't ask why. Just do it."

~*~

Rain fell on Monday afternoon as Nathan dashed from his car to The Herald Center. He took care to protect the card in his pocket. His mother's thank you note included her beautifully scrolled signature and his hastily scribbled name, an acquired disadvantage of signing his autograph. He placed it on the table in the empty office.

Nathan saw a familiar face and walked toward her. "Hello, Mayzie. I haven't seen you around."

"I think our days have crossed. I was here Tuesday and Thursday last week. My schedule at work keeps changing."

Today's shoes angled to a severe point in front of the stiletto heels. Her hair had gained a few red streaks through the spikes. "What's your work outside of here?"

"I'm a hair stylist. EconoCuts. They schedule me different days each week."

Nathan nodded. Ten-dollar haircuts with chains in strip malls. "Well, it's good to see you. How's middle school writing?"

"Ha. You neglected to tell me you're a writer. Jonas told me last week. Is that why you asked about a boys' writing class?"

"Just curious. I'm quite satisfied doing basketball."

Mayzie swiveled around with the sound of students entering. She flicked her hand toward Nathan, waving. "Here come the troops. Talk to you later." Holding her clipboard, she went into action, moving each one to their assigned group.

Nathan wanted to ask Del about the math test but decided that wouldn't be a good idea around his peers. Best to wait until tutoring. He was glad to see Carlos back, but he gave a quick scan to see if any bruises were visible. There were none. The restraining order should eliminate that threat.

Thomas stood waiting until Nathan tossed him a blue pinnie. With slouched shoulders and no eye contact, Thomas looked like this was the last place he wanted to be. A skinny frame and slender arms exposed a disparity to the developing bodies of his peers. Nathan had a growing determination to include him more in the game. When they were ready to begin, he motioned for Thomas to take the ball. Thomas passed it to Chaz and never went after it again. No teammate efforts were ever made to include him. The rec time ended without Thomas touching the ball again.

The crowd of kids converged and headed toward the hallway of tutoring rooms. Nathan walked near the back of the line. He couldn't help but see how Del's head and slouched frame stood out among the others.

"So, how was the math test?"

"Won't know 'til Wednesday." Del reached for the basket with a granola bar and a single-serving applesauce.

"You won't know your score, but how did it feel? Did you feel confident?"

A small grin formed on Del's lips. "Man, you teach that stuff better than Old Man Hayes. I did what you said—just did the steps and hoped it worked."

Nathan suppressed a grin. It helped when you just finished a two-hour crash course yourself. "Good. I'm glad. And I'm proud of you for calling me. That means you're really trying."

Del tossed the Michael Jordan book and the Steinbeck audio on the table. "Done with these."

Nathan reached in his bag. "Great. Here's another book." He tossed a children's book toward Del. *The NBA: A History of Hoops: the Story of the Charlotte Hornets.* Del picked it up and looked at the front, turned it over and read the back-cover blurb. With a slight nod, he placed it in his backpack.

"You ever been to a Hornet's game?" Nathan hadn't planned to ask the question. It just came out.

"No. Ain't never been to Charlotte. Ain't never been nowhere but Greenville."

Unbelievable. Charlotte—an hour north and Del had never been there. "Bring me your first test with a B, and I'll take you to a game. With your mother's permission."

Del's eyebrows rose. "You kidding me?"

"Nope. I enjoy watching a good game. Bring me that B." Nathan reached into his bag and pulled out another audio tape. "*Treasure Island.* A great classic by Robert Louis Stevenson. It was one of my favorites when I was your age. What did you think of the Steinbeck book, *Of Mice and Men?*"

Del crossed his arms in front of his chest. "They treated Crooks like the ranch animals, making him stay in the stable and not letting him in the bunkhouse."

"Do you think Steinbeck was a racist or do you think he attempted to show the unfairness of racism?"

Del leaned his chair back on two legs. "Curley's wife said she'd have him lynched. I guess Steinbeck used that to show how bad those times were. And Crooks was an honest worker. He didn't take charity, so Steinbeck made him look like a good guy."

Nathan rested his elbows on the table. "Even though he scared Lennie, telling him George would leave him?"

Del shrugged. "Man, that was weird how Lennie was so fascinated by the puppies and liked stroking furry things. I didn't expect George to go shooting him like that. He didn't really mean to kill that lady."

This was the part of teaching that Nathan missed—analyzing characters, emotions, and motives. "And yet, he did kill her."

"Couldn't they just teach him not to be so rough?"

"Ah, the argument between punitive and reformative."

A puzzled look crossed Del's face. "I don't know what that means."

"Never mind. Do you think unintentional actions should have consequences?" As the question passed through his lips, a familiar twitch throbbed in his jaw. He clenched his teeth to still the erratic movement.

"I dunno. I guess, but shooting him? That don't seem right."

Anxious to move on, Nathan reached for the history book and opened to the sticky note that held the page. World War II. "We better get busy."

He wouldn't drill the facts. Kids hated it, and it proved to be the lowest level of learning. Critical thinking skills didn't come from mnemonic memorizing. Certain that Del could hold his own, Nathan began a discussion of the war.

Del leafed through the book, looking at pictures of concentration camps. "So if there were, like millions of Jews, how come they couldn't just fight back?"

"Good question. When do they start to fight? When it affects their businesses? When transports begin? When they're in the work camps?"

"I don't know. I guess when they start to take them to the camps."

The teacher in him surfaced. Always answer a question with a question. "So how would they organize that effort? How do millions of Jews get together and form an army in cities filled with Gestapo?"

Del shook his head. "No. I guess maybe when they were in the camps they might have a chance to organize."

"They did try. Prisoners in Auschwitz revolted."

Del's eyebrow shot up. "What happened?"

"What do you think happened?"

"Nazi's probably killed them."

Nathan nodded. "They did. It was too late. They were starving, sickly, and had no resources. I'll look for a book about the revolt. I think you'd like reading about it."

"So how did the Americans beat Hitler?"

Nathan leaned back, enjoying the banter. "Who said the Americans did?"

"OK. You know, I mean the allies."

"There was another huge factor in the fall of Nazi Germany. The Red Army."

Surprise crossed Del's face. "You mean, like Russia? I knew they were in the war, but weren't they like our enemy, too?"

"Have you heard the old proverb, 'the enemy of my enemy is my friend'? At that moment in time, we shared a common enemy. Hitler was dangerous. The Red Army defeated Germany in many battles. If they hadn't weakened them, we might be looking at a different outcome."

"So how come the German people believed Hitler?"

The questions went on and on. Had Del's school

ever moved beyond "read the textbook and test"? Nathan doubted it.

18

When tutoring ended, they entered the gym. Mayzie stood with her clipboard as students left or transitioned to another activity. Nathan walked over to see her.

"Can I ask you a question?"

"Sure. What's up?" She gave an exaggerated tilt of her chin to look him in the eye.

"What other activities are offered for high school boys? I have one that doesn't seem to enjoy the basketball."

"There's an art club. They do some acrylic painting and some pottery. We have a cooking class that boys can join, but none do. Who are we talking about?"

"Thomas. He's out of his element with the athletes and doesn't try. I attempt to include him, but he shrinks back. Who's his mentor?"

Mayzie pursed her lips. "Joey. He's only here once a week, so I'm not sure how much Thomas gets to see him. Why don't you talk to Jonas or Angie?"

"I guess I'll do that. I haven't seen Angie." He surveyed the room. "Someone said she's busy with details for the jamboree."

They both turned as the office door flew open, and a wide-eyed Elizabeth dashed toward them. "Mayzie, I have an emergency with Renee and her baby, and I don't have my car. Can you ride me over there?"

Mayzie shook her head. "I took the bus. No car here."

"I'll take you."

"Thank you." She bolted for the door, and Nathan followed.

When he pulled the car onto the road, Elizabeth explained. "Renee is a new mother. She has anxiety issues and once shook her baby when he wouldn't stop crying. She realized what she was doing and put him down before he was hurt. But she's terrified of losing control and harming him. She called to say he won't stop crying. I heard him screaming in the background. I told her to put him safely in his crib and walk to the front door. Stand outside where she won't hear him as loudly but don't leave the house. I said I'd be right there." She pointed toward the upcoming red light. "Turn left and she's down one more block."

They turned onto the street, and Elizabeth motioned to the house. "That's her."

A woman stood outside with her hands covering her ears. Nathan pulled toward the curb, and Elizabeth jumped out and ran to Renee. When Nathan parked and reached the door, she had crumbled against Elizabeth. Honey-blond hair, limp and scraggly, flowed to cover her face.

Elizabeth looked over her shoulder. "Nathan, can you see to the baby?"

His mouth opened, but no words came. He glanced from her to the house and back again. "I…uh …"

"You'll be fine. We will just be a moment."

As Nathan walked into the house, the scent of urine and cigarette smoke assaulted him. The baby still shrieked. Nathan reached into the playpen where the infant squealed, tiny hands clenched into fists, face red from the rampage. He was soaked clear through his diaper and clothing. Nathan glanced toward the door and realized he was on his own with the child.

How hard could it be? He saw the changing table and extra diapers. Stripping the child, he found a crimson rash covering his diaper area, prickly splotches blistered on tender skin. He used a wet wipe to clean him as much as possible. There was nothing in his reach to ease the sting of the rash. The child still screamed, flailing his feet, toes clenched tightly. Nathan looked at the diaper. Which was the front? He made his best guess and slid it under the child. Pulling snuggly, he adhered the tape to one side and then tugged the backing off of the other tape. By the time it was fastened, he'd lost the snugness. The clean diaper sagged loosely, but at least it was dry. Elizabeth and Renee walked in as Nathan completed the diaper.

"I think he needs a change of clothes." Nathan stepped aside, his hand never leaving the thrashing baby.

Renee reached below the changing table and handed him a one-piece garment. She made no attempt to take over the task. Instead she sat on the sofa and slipped a cigarette from the pack on the end table. As she picked up the lighter, Elizabeth removed it from her hand. "Remember, we talked about the smoke. It's unhealthy for Connor."

"Look how I'm shaking? I need a cigarette." Renee's voice rose.

Nathan glanced over for his first real look at the mother. The turned-up nose dotted with freckles may have once been charming, but now her face was weary, her eyes dull. Renee couldn't be much more than a teenager.

Elizabeth handed the cigarette back. "Then take it outside, please. When did Connor last eat?"

"I think it's been a few hours." She turned and walked out the door.

Nathan watched as Elizabeth shook her head, a bitter smile showing her disappointment. She went to the kitchen as Nathan struggled to get the kicking feet of a screaming infant into the legs of the onesie. Elizabeth came back with a bottle.

"Nathan, do you mind? I should go out to talk with her." She extended the bottle toward him.

He reached for it and sat down on the rocking chair. The baby immediately began to drink. The stiffness melded into softness as he drank in earnest. Angry red cheeks softened to a creamy ivory as they sucked nourishment from the bottle, his cheeks moving in and out. Nathan had never changed or fed a baby before today. A rush of protectiveness overwhelmed him.

What would happen to this child? So helpless and innocent. Would he grow up hard and take to the streets? To drugs or gangs. Possibly to prison. Nathan had an unexplained desire to take him and run. Run far from this neighborhood, from an unfit mother. Where was the social service system? Why weren't they protecting Connor?

Renee and Elizabeth walked back inside. Elizabeth took her hand. "You did the right thing when you called me. But, Renee, it's my hope that you'll be able to handle the problems. Connor only wanted to be changed and fed. Is he getting enough formula?"

Renee's eyes were pools of liquid, tempering the

hardness of her face. "I'm trying to make it last. We all have to do with a little less. He'll have to learn that too."

"No, Renee. Connor cannot learn that lesson. He's an infant with growing bones. Everything inside him is growing rapidly. He cannot be without his formula. You need to call me if you can't afford it. Tonight, you give him whatever he needs. I'll be here tomorrow with more."

Renee nodded. "Thank you. If you can help, I'll be going to the store. I can pick it up myself."

Elizabeth shook her head. "I don't have cash. I'll bring the formula by tomorrow."

Nathan caught her eye and motioned toward his pocket. She raised her eyes and gave a quick shake of her head.

Elizabeth got up and moved toward the child's playpen. The plastic pad was covered with a wet sheet. She removed it, found a disinfectant spray to clean the plastic, and lifted it to enclose the plastic in a clean mattress cover.

Connor now slept on Nathan's shoulder after devouring the full bottle and burping all excess air out of his little tummy. Elizabeth reached for him and laid him gently on his back.

"We must go. Remember, all he wants is to be cared for. Keep him dry and well-fed. I'll see you tomorrow."

When they reached the car, Nathan turned troubled eyes toward Elizabeth. "Why doesn't social services take that child? She's not fit to care for him."

Elizabeth reached into her handbag, finding a pack of tissues. She pulled one free and dabbed Nathan's shoulder where Connor had spit up. "It has to be much worse than that for social services to remove a child. Renee hasn't abused him or abandoned him." She patted his arm and removed her hand. "Oh, and Nathan, you never, ever leave money. We have no assurance that it would be used for formula. If we're called to help, we have to supply what is really needed."

Nathan merged into traffic and turned right toward The Herald Center. "How do you do this, day after day?"

She shrugged her shoulders. "It's the way I was raised. People are hurting, and they need to know Christ. They may only see Him through the actions of others."

Nathan had no response. They rode in silence. He tried to reconcile Renee's needs and Connor's safety. Nathan pulled in front of The Herald Center to let Elizabeth out.

She took a long look at him before speaking. "Thank you for taking care of Connor. I couldn't have done this alone."

He saw the depth in her eyes. Eyes so much like Angie's except for the light. Elizabeth carried a heaviness where Angie had joy. "You're welcome." Even as he thought of her, Nathan caught sight of Angie standing inside the center.

She sprinted out to meet them. "Is everything OK with Renee?"

They got out of the car, and Nathan stepped to the sidewalk.

Elizabeth glanced at Nathan. "Yes, everything is fine. Nathan can tell you about it." Elizabeth gave him a wink, the heaviness in her eyes suddenly replaced by a perceptive gleam.

Beauty for Ashes

119

19

Three weeks until the hearing on the lawsuit. If Nathan couldn't convince them to drop it, his mother would have to be told. He had paid Fidelity $62,000 from book sales and from liquidating his 401K. That left $163,000. Even if he signed the movie deal, he'd never have the money in time. But perhaps it would help him secure a loan. Nathan zipped off a text message to Anya. *Any news on the movie deal?*

A ding sounded quickly with her reply. *Patience, patience. These things take time. Could be months.*

He opened his computer and started a search on unsecured bank loans. He didn't find concrete information, but by definition, a loan of that type was based on the borrower's creditworthiness. He had good credit. He'd visit the bank today.

Nathan went to his DVR and pulled up the news clip from three weeks ago. He forwarded to the section where Angie spoke. Then he hit play. Mesmerized, he watched intently—every movement, every expression. The luxurious shine of her hair, the light that flickered in her eyes. He focused on the movement of her lips, imagining what it might be like to kiss them, to feel the softness of her cheek against his. Her smooth voice suddenly sounded like music from a violin. Nathan hit pause, freezing a picture of Angie on the screen.

But was there was a reciprocal connection? Sometimes he sensed it. But at the center Angie was everyone's sweetheart. She spoke to all the volunteers as well as to the kids. Why would he presume to be different? And if he dared to ask her out? This wasn't like Diana—someone he could see casually then move on. Diana was worldly. She'd shake it off and find someone else. But Angie? Nathan sensed an innocence, a naivety that could easily shatter. He had a few days to think about it. With the jamboree approaching, Angie wouldn't have a moment to spare.

~*~

Seated across the desk from the loan officer, Nathan couldn't help but hope she read mystery novels. A little recognition would be in his favor. He sat quietly while she reviewed his application. Her thick blond hair, perfectly styled and stiffly unmoving, sat like a helmet curving below her ears, never moving an inch when her head turned. She looked up and removed her glasses.

"You're a writer? What do you write?"

So much for wishful thinking. "I write mystery novels. I just had my eighth one published."

She grimaced. "I guess I should have recognized your name. I don't get much reading time."

Nathan smiled. "No problem. I'm not a household name. Some people know me. Many don't."

"Mr. Drummond, your credit's excellent and your income has been inconsistent but strong for the last few years. The problem is, we don't grant any unsecured loans for this amount. From what I'm seeing on paper,

I suspect we could get one approved for $30,000, possibly $40,000. Definitely not more than that."

Nathan ran his hands through his hair. Would that be enough to convince Fidelity to drop the lawsuit?

"OK. Can I amend this application or do I need to complete another? And how long will it take?"

She reached for a pen and slid it to Nathan. "Make the changes here and initial them. I should have an answer for you by tomorrow."

Nathan scratched his original amount and wrote $40,000 in its place.

~*~

Dynamics of the basketball game hadn't changed. Thomas retreated into himself, and Del dominated. At least Nathan had made Jonas and Mayzie aware. Del was his mentee, and that's where his attention needed to stay. Although in truth, Nathan's attention was far more focused on Angie than anything else.

The whistle blew and everyone headed to tutoring. Angie came out of her office and spoke to the students as they walked past. When Nathan approached, their eyes met, and they exchanged a smile. "Hello, Angie. How are the preparations for the jamboree? I hear they're keeping you hopping."

Her face glowed. "Yes, I never imagined myself to be an event planner. It's more than I bargained for. Stop by later, and I'll give you your time and location for the book signing."

"I'll do that." Nathan held her eyes for a moment before moving down the hallway. Yes, it just might be reciprocal.

Del sat stretched out in the small chair, legs bent awkwardly filling the space below the table. He crunched on chips from the individual-sized bag in the snack basket. A math test had been placed in front of Nathan's chair.

Nathan picked it up as he began to sit. "C-. Not bad. That's an improvement." He nodded his head in approval.

"Ain't a B." Del's words didn't mask his pleasure.

"Yet. Let's get to work and make it a B. How was the history test?"

Del's mouth tightened. "Don't know. Old man Hayes takes forever grading them."

Nathan drilled Del with what he hoped was an intense stare. Time for more lessons. "Don't you mean Mr. Hayes?"

Del raised one eyebrow. "Everyone calls him that."

"You're not everyone, Del. You're going to be a star basketball player for your school and an NBA player in a few years. That holds a big responsibility. You'll be an example for others, good or bad. Don't be afraid to make a positive stand."

Del stretched his arms behind his neck and leaned back. The corners of his lips rose ever so slightly. "Mr. Hayes," he emphasized the name, "takes a long time grading, but it felt pretty good. Might be my B."

"Good. I'm ready to see a game."

Del worked as hard as Nathan had ever seen, applying the analysis techniques while decoding words. When their time was up, both Del and Nathan were exhausted and needed the physical release of the basketball. As they walked past, Nathan glanced to make sure Angie was still in her office. Then they played full throttle one-on-one for twenty minutes.

Sometime during the twenty minutes, Angie and Jonas had come out, sat on the floor, and watched. Angie's knees were pulled up with her arms wrapped around them. She rested her chin on her knees and watched every movement on the court. When they finished, Nathan leaned over, hands on knees, catching his breath. Del passed him his water bottle and towel, giving a friendly shoulder bump with it. Jonas stood and reached a hand to help Angie stand.

"Remind me never to get on a court with you two." Jonas shook his head. "Makes me tired just watching you."

Angie stepped toward them. "Del, you truly are gifted. It's my prayer that you get back on the team."

"Thanks, Miss Angie. I'm thinking they'll take me back after this report period."

Angie answered Del but glanced at Nathan. "Well, you must have a very good tutor."

Del grinned. "Yeah. He's OK for an old man."

Nathan reached out his hand, poised for a fist bump. Del hesitated before meeting him fist to fist. "Man, I gotta teach you the dap!"

Nathan threw a blank look his way.

"The dap, Man. You gotta learn the dap." He held his hands out wide in front of him, palms up, before turning toward the door.

Nathan and Angie watched him exit. They turned toward each other and laughed.

Nathan squinted. "The dap?"

Angie's shoulders lifted in a shrug. "Don't ask me." She glanced out the window as Del walk down the sidewalk. "Nathan, I can't thank you enough for your work with Del. It's evident that he respects you.

That alone is quite an accomplishment." They sat across from each other at the scarred wooden table.

"Can you tell me anything about his home life? Is his dad in the picture? Any siblings?"

"Just his mother. I believe there was a boyfriend living there for a while but don't think that lasted. As far as I know, he's never known his dad. His mom works in a hotel at their front desk and has a swing shift schedule. She's gone many evenings, sometimes through the night."

Nathan shook his head. "That leaves him alone way too much. It's a wonder he hasn't gotten into trouble."

Angie reached out and patted Nathan's forearm. "You're good for him. God's provision." Then she rested her hand on the table.

Their eyes locked, filled with unspoken meaning.

"Thank you, Angie." They no longer had to dance around the attraction. They had shared a look that spoke volumes. The only thing remaining was how to move forward.

"The jamboree—do you have details for me?"

Angie opened her folder and handed him a page she had prepared. It had a map of the layout and his signing time—nine-thirty to eleven-thirty. "Does this work for you?"

"Yes. It's perfect. I'll be there a little early to set up." He could feel the warmth of Angie's smile, see the hope in her eyes.

20

A voicemail informed Nathan that his loan had been approved. The following morning, he went to the bank, signed the papers, and had a certified check made to Fidelity Tools. He drove to their offices without an appointment.

It only took thirty minutes. Nothing compared with face-to-face. The lawsuit had been withdrawn with a manageable repayment plan and the promise of a signed copy of his new release. The company president cooperated when he saw the potential. Nathan's townhouse would eventually sell, and a movie deal remained a strong possibility. The debt remained, but now his mother wouldn't need to know. His dad's good name stood firm.

~*~

Angie and Elizabeth arrived at the park two hours before the jamboree was to begin. Meteorologists predicted that the crisp early morning air would make way for bright sunshine. Jonas was already there, and Angie's parents, Alex and Adrianna, would arrive a short time later.

Balloons danced with the breeze, clusters of bright

colors tethered to the signpost at the park's entrance. Stations were identified with signs, big, bold, and colorful. Hopefully, in just a short while, the park would be filled with generous donors. They needed to reach their goal by the end of the jamboree. Without the new roof and HVAC, there would be no Herald Center.

Angie walked to Nathan's table and carefully displayed the copies he had donated. Once the silent auction began, the books would join the other items. Angie turned a book over to see his picture. He looked at her with a slight smile and eyes that held a secret. She had seen the fullness of his smile and the humor in his eyes. Studying the picture, Angie noticed the square jawline with the slightest dimple. His posed picture provided a glimpse of the man she had come to know.

Nathan cared for her. She could sense it. They had shared a moment, one of those intimate glances that revealed what hadn't been spoken. Angie held the book to her heart, eager to see what was ahead for them. There were subtle ways to let him know of her interest without being forward.

Replacing the book on the table, Angie joined her parents, along with Elizabeth and Jonas, and clasped hands for prayer. The future of The Herald Center depended on this fundraiser. They couldn't rely on their own strength to make this happen.

~*~

The park filled with families. Children with all varieties of face paint played with cans of silly string, running and laughing as only children could. Amplified music resonated from the stage area as a choral group performed. Different musical groups played every hour throughout the day. Angie anxiously awaited her scheduled time to play her violin, purposely slating it during the interval when Nathan would be here. She'd play festive selections to match the mood of the day.

Their paths hadn't crossed when Nathan arrived, and Angie couldn't manage a free moment to walk over. She stole glimpses of him as he signed books, smiling and talking to each person. Even in jeans and a sweatshirt, he looked striking. His gaze roamed the park but stopped at her. He gave a wave and continued to sign books. Surely there would be a pause in her activity, allowing her to go over and say hello.

Angie turned at the touch of a hand on her shoulder. Elizabeth followed the track of Angie's eyes and grinned. "I see that Nathan's a big hit. His smile could melt butter."

Angie blinked, returning her eyes to the book-signing table. "Yes, it certainly could."

"I'm detecting that it's melted more than that?"

Warmth welled up inside her.

Elizabeth turned her attention from Nathan to scan the park. "Angie, you've done such a great job pulling this together. I know you took the lion's share of the work. I'm sorry I wasn't available to help more."

Angie squeezed her cousin's hand. "No worries, Liz. Your class has been hard." Angie recalled the day Elizabeth quit school. She had completed her first semester in college. That New Year's Eve changed everything.

"It was a big step going back. I had forgotten how

much study time it takes."

"A big step, but a good one."

~*~

Angie lifted the violin from its case, reaching for the soft cloth behind it. The violin had been properly cleaned of rosin buildup before packing, but Angie wanted it to shine. Careful to avoid the fragile bridge, she used the cloth to buff the maple surface, removing any smudges. After checking the pegs, she began to rosin the bow.

She rarely played for an audience. She pressed a hand to her fluttering stomach, reminding herself that she would be background music. Everyone would still go about their business, laughing, talking, and having fun. Everything was ready—shined, rosined, tuned. Her sheet music in order, ready to place on the music stand. Bach's *Partita No. 2 in D minor*, Vaughan Williams' composition of *The Lark*, an arrangement of *The Bittersweet Symphony*, interspersing contemporary songs of praise with classical pieces.

She stepped out onto the small wooden stage, tucking her chin on the violin. Holding the neck, Angie lifted the bow and started with the most familiar piece—Bach's *Partita No. 2*.

~*~

Nathan moved his pen to complete his hastily inscribed autograph. As he handed it back to a waiting fan, he heard the first hums of the violin. All activity seemed to cease around him as heads turned toward the sound. Nathan craned his head to see. A crowd began to gather in front of the stage.

Angie stood center stage, her violin poised on her left shoulder, her head tilted against the chinrest. She had changed from jeans to a flowing skirt. Even from this distance, Nathan could see the shine of her long hair elegantly tumbling across her right shoulder, her eyes lowered toward the movement of her left fingers vibrating on the strings.

Nathan got up and took a few steps forward, shifting so he could see through the crowd. Her hands fascinated him, one gliding the bow gracefully over the strings, the other pulsating over the same strings bridged on the neck. Her face, so serene, brought a stab of envy. Had he ever experienced that level of peace?

The hour ended too quickly. As she lowered the violin and dipped into a slight bow, the crowd erupted into applause. Nathan's eyes followed her every movement, from the bow to the graceful exit at the stage door, before moving back to his table, realizing that an hour had passed without an autograph.

~*~

Excitement bubbled within Angie, and she couldn't wait to see Nathan. Behind the stage, she hurried to clean and pack the violin, and then she ran it to the trunk of her car before rushing back into the park. The stage amplified the voice and guitar from one of their volunteers.

She hurried over to see Nathan. "Nathan, this is the first I've gotten to talk with you. It looks like you've been busy."

"Yes, but I'm not the one who stole the show. That was incredible."

"Thank you. As soon as I began playing, my nervousness went away."

Nathan's face turned serious. "That was so clear, every eye turned toward you. Your skill is amazing, and your eyes sparkled while you were playing. Angie, you were born to play violin."

"Thank you." A flush crossed her cheeks. "Your time slot is almost over. Remember that we'll be recognizing our volunteers at noon. You'll be called on stage with the others."

"That's not necessary. I've gotten plenty of recognition this morning."

Angie put her hand on his arm. "That was a different kind. We just want to say thank you. You'll be among many others. It's important to show the community how many people sacrifice for these kids. How else can we expect them to sacrifice by donating?"

Nathan's gaze moved beyond Angie, and she swiveled to see where he looked.

"Papi!"

Her father rushed to embrace her. "Angelina Grace. That was amazing. Simply beautiful."

"Thank you. It was so fun to play for an audience." She tugged his arm and drew him into the circle with Nathan. "Papi, I want you to meet Nathan Drummond. He volunteers at the center and is an accomplished writer. Nathan, this is my father, Alejandro Hernandez."

Her father extended his hand. "Call me Alex. Pleased to meet you. I don't read much fiction, but I hope to read one of your mysteries. My wife and

Angelina Grace both tell me they enjoy them."

Angie shook her head, but the smile never left. She hooked her arm with her father's. "For most children, when a parent uses their full name, it means they're in trouble. For me, he uses my full name when he's pleased. Anytime he has been upset with me, it's *Angie.*" She mimicked a stern voice.

Her father laughed. "Our angel of grace. How could I use that name if I were upset?"

"It's a beautiful name." Nathan's smile turned toward Angie.

Alex added, "Yes, a beautiful name for a beautiful young lady. Don't you agree?"

Nathan nodded. "Yes, I agree."

~*~

Elizabeth tilted the microphone, freeing it from its stand as Angie and Jonas stood beside her.

"We'd like to thank everyone for participating in our jamboree today. Many hands made it possible. Your generous donations will allow us to continue to serve the community, enrich the lives of children, and provide a safe place after school. The only three employees are the three standing before you. The real work is done by those who sacrificially invest their time in the lives of young people. They're the heart and soul of The Herald Center. It's my pleasure to introduce you to our team of volunteers."

One by one, Elizabeth called the names. When Nathan heard his name, he walked to the front and stood with Mayzie and others. They looked out at the faces of those applauding.

Elizabeth's voice quieted the crowd. She forged an empty space between two of the volunteers. "Do you see this gap in our lineup? Perhaps it's for you. We always have room for one more. There is no shortage of needs at The Herald Center. If you'd like to join our team of volunteers, see Jonas." She waved a hand in his direction. "He will be happy to help you connect."

When Elizabeth dismissed the volunteers, Nathan could have taken off. His writing lagged way behind schedule. But after standing at his book signing table for two hours, it was nice to walk around and watch the activities. He stopped by the food vendor truck and purchased a hotdog, taking it to a vacant bench near the stage. He sat, listening to the last performing group of the day—a teenage band featuring a drummer, two guitars, and three amateur vocalists.

"Got room here for me?" Jonas came from behind the bench, taking Nathan by surprise.

Nathan shifted over. "Of course. You must be exhausted. At least it's a nice fall day."

"Yes, sir. This would be brutal in the summer. My old legs are ready for a rest."

They sat listening to the scratchy electric guitar tones. Nathan plopped the last of his hotdog in his mouth. "You need any help before I go?"

Jonas gave a hearty laugh. "Son, I believe I told you once before, I never turn down help. This ends in an hour, but we can begin breaking down some parts."

Nathan nodded. "Just show me what you need."

~*~

Angie and Elizabeth joined in the cleaning as soon

as the last of the families left the park. Mayzie was headed out of the park when she did an about face. "Angie, do these boxes go to the car? I'll take them."

"Wonderful. One less trip for us. You can put these in Elizabeth's car. It's unlocked. Jonas's truck will be for the tables."

After taking them to the car, Mayzie came back into the park and made three more trips. Elizabeth went to all of the trashcans tying the bags for Nathan and Jonas to remove. Angie cleaned off the stage and checked the adjoining room for any litter. Alex had taken the cash and checks to tally up the success.

The five exhausted workers stood in a circle. Elizabeth thanked each one. "Many hands make the tasks lighter and much more pleasant. Thank you for staying to help."

Jonas was the first to leave, but the other two helpers lingered. Angie hoped to have a moment alone with Nathan without appearing too obvious. That didn't happen. Mayzie called him to come over to a picnic table where her bag waited. She reached in her tote bag for a pen and handed it to him along with a copy of his book. Nathan opened it and wrote inside. They stood talking until Angie had no further excuse for lingering. Nathan occasionally glanced her way, a trapped look in his eyes.

Angie began walking from the park and passed close enough to hear Mayzie's question. "I'd love to hear how you go about planning a novel. Do you have time to stop for coffee?"

Nathan glanced toward Angie. "Actually, Mayzie, if I don't get home to my writing, I may not have a publisher for long. They're waiting for my draft."

She threw her head back and laughed. "Well, save

me some time on another day. Come on. I'll walk out with you."

Suddenly, Nathan knew what he would do. He'd invite Angie for coffee so she could tell him more about the complexities of playing classical violin. That would be far less intimidating than asking her out on a date. He'd ask her on Monday.

21

When basketball ended, the boys headed down the hall for tutoring. Del pulled the history test out and flung it toward Nathan. The red *B* was boldly printed across the top. Nathan picked it up, grinning and nodding his head as he looked over the essay questions. Thankfully, his teacher didn't deduct points for grammar and punctuation. The concepts were all there.

"Well done, Del. I guess I better get those tickets. He lifted his hand for a high-five.

"Man, I told you. I gotta teach you the dap."

"The dap?" Nathan smiled. "And what might that be?"

"It might be dignity and pride. Look here. Put your arm out like this. Slide down 'til you reach my hand." Their arms moved in unison. "Now, slap with four fingers, grip fists, slap four fingers again." Del demonstrated the tap. "Next, turn your arm and bump the outside of my arm with the outside of yours. Now do a regular fist bump and let your hand fly away like the last bump brought a little explosion."

Nathan followed step by step, repeating each movement Del made.

"OK, now faster." Nathan attempted to come up to speed, but mixed up when to slap and when to grip.

After four repetitions, he had it. Hopefully, he'd remember it next time they met.

"All right, Del. You've sufficiently used up ten minutes of our tutoring time. Let's get to work."

Del stood at his full height. "It was tutoring. I was teaching you. And you better work on that this week." He jabbed a finger toward Nathan. "That's your homework."

They sat down, ready to work. While Del worked through a math problem, Nathan pulled out his phone and began scrolling.

Del reached and snatched it from him. "Phone-free zone. Remember?"

Nathan reached up to reclaim the phone, only to find Del's swift movement extending high, out of his reach. Nathan shrugged. "I thought you'd want me to check the Hornet's schedule."

Del immediately lowered the phone and held it out to him. "Guess we can make an exception."

After scrolling through the schedule, Nathan peered at the math problem, checking Del's steps. "They play at home next Saturday. Does that work for you if your mom gives the OK?"

"That's good. My mom won't care."

"Nonetheless, I need her permission."

Their hour always ended with more to be done. But they had worked hard, and a game of one-on-one had become their routine. Work hard then play hard.

Angie watched as they played. When they finished, she walked out of the office and across the gym floor.

"Hello, Del. Nathan. How was tutoring today?"

They looked from one to the other, and Nathan gave Del a playful jab. "You tell her."

Del attempted to minimize his grin, but it shone through his eyes. "Got a B on my history test. Nathan's taking me to a Hornet's game."

Angie clapped her hands together. "Del, that's wonderful. I'm so proud of your hard work. And a Hornet's game will be so much fun."

Del picked up his backpack to leave. "Gotta go. I can't join the team 'til report cards, but coach wants to see me to talk."

Nathan nodded. "Great. See you Wednesday."

Del's tall, lanky frame walked toward the door, his cornrows jutting out in all directions, pants sagging low on his waist. "Oh, Nathan. I'm so happy to see how things are working for Del. It's so nice that you're treating him to a Hornet's game. Thank you for all you've done."

"Del's a good kid. And he's smart. Too bad no one took time with him. He's easy to teach." He watched the foyer door close behind Del. "Hey, you did a great job on Saturday. Everyone had a nice time. And the weather, sure glad it wasn't like this." He motioned toward the door where the fine drizzle fell.

Her soft hand landed on his arm, which was sweaty from the game. "Thank you. And how is your mother?"

"Mom's doing well. She's traded her walker for a cane."

Angie pulled her hair to one side, cascading down her shoulder. "So how many autographs do you think you signed?"

Nathan shook his hand out as if it were cramped. "Plenty. It was pretty nonstop, except when every eye turned toward the stage."

A smile flickered across her face, but she shifted

the attention from herself. "It must be so fascinating to make a story come alive. Planning out your mystery like you do. I don't think I could ever pull that off."

He remembered Mayzie's question from Saturday, and replicated it with Angie. Much less vulnerable than asking her to dinner. "Let's have coffee someday. I can talk about writing, and you can talk about playing a violin."

"Oh, that would be so nice." She responded immediately.

~*~

Angie sat on the sofa in the home that she shared with Elizabeth, legs tucked under her, a book face down in her lap. She fingered the frayed upholstery. The threadbare furniture carried over from Elizabeth's childhood. Her parents lived simply and meagerly, and Elizabeth was reluctant to change anything.

Angie's family always had more financial means. Not opulent, but comfortable. Her parents wanted Elizabeth and her mother to live with them when Uncle Ramón died, but they needed the familiarity of their own home. When Aunt Elena died last year, they tried again to convince Elizabeth to come to their home. When she refused, Angie moved in with her. Her parents fretted about that decision. They worried about two females living in this part of town. But Angie wouldn't allow Liz to be one female alone.

She looked at her book and realized she hadn't read a word in the fifteen minutes that it rested there.

"Liz, what do you think of Nathan?"

Her cousin sat in the recliner, taking notes from a

textbook.

She turned toward Angie and arched her eyebrows. "I think he's nice looking. We know he's a good writer. He's been responsible with Del." She touched her finger to the side of her chin. "Yeah, I like him. Why do you ask? Do you think he likes me?"

Angie remained silent, staring at Elizabeth.

Elizabeth burst into laughter. "What I really think is that I've never seen you quite so smitten with a man. From the way he looks at you, I'd say it's reciprocal."

Angie leaned forward, her heart racing. "Do you think so? We're going to meet for coffee next week." Turning in her seat, Angie moved the book to the end table. "He's only been coming to the center a little over a month, but I feel like I know him so well. He's easy to talk to."

Elizabeth smirked. "He's easy to look at, too."

22

Del didn't want to be picked up at his home. He waited for Nathan at the same coffee shop where they'd met to review for the math test. Nathan had set a few ground rules for the trip to Charlotte. Dress well. No pants hanging down on the hips. No questionable logos on his shirt. Dress as if you're meeting a college scout. No yelling at refs. No inappropriate language or gestures.

Del walked to Nathan's car door and stood, arms out at his side, doing a 360-degree turn. "So, do I pass inspection?"

He wore a collared polo shirt and khaki pants, neatly belted. The shoes were white sneakers encrusted with grime, but they hadn't talked about footwear. Other than the shoes, Del looked good.

He walked to the passenger side and climbed in. "You want, like, gas money or something?"

"No, but thanks for the offer. I told you it's my treat. Buckle up, please."

When they got close to the stadium, Del's gaze roamed over the landscape. Charlotte was a bona fide city, skyscrapers and all, while Greenville remained a small town.

Nathan shook his head. It was hard to believe that, at eighteen years old, Del hadn't been outside of

Greenville.

They parked and joined the crowd in motion, heading toward the Spectrum Center. The Hive, as fans affectionately called it, was a circular stadium that dwarfed Greenville's smaller venue. The 76ers were in town, and Nathan was thankful that good seats were still available. They sat in section 105, center court, just a dozen rows back.

The buzzer sounded, and both teams went into action. Del leaned forward, elbows on his long legs, and never blinked. His head moved up and down the court, following each play, only looking away long enough to check the roster.

"Man, I wanna be out there so bad."

"You've got the goods. Keep on working for it. I expect someday I'll be sitting in the seats watching you play pro."

At intermission, the crowd moved about, and Nathan stood to stretch. "Hey Del, I see an old friend. Take a walk with me."

"Nah. You go talk. I'm good here."

Nathan towered over him. "Be polite and walk with me."

Del rolled his eyes and stood. They made their way out of the row and down toward the front.

"Marcus. It's been a long time." Nathan held out his hand.

Marcus shook his hand and turned his attention toward Del. He extended his hand and introduced himself. "Marcus Conroy."

"Hi. I'm Del."

Marcus looked up. "You got a last name, Del?"

"Yeah. Jefferson. Del Jefferson."

"Pleased to meet you, Del." Marcus turned back

toward Nathan. "So, I see you in all the bookstores. Looks like you're doing well."

Nathan chuckled. "We can't all make a name playing ball. I did the next best thing."

"Well, I'm glad you called me." Marcus turned his attention back to Del. "Nathan tells me you're pretty good on the court."

Del turned from Marcus to Nathan and back again, confusion etched in his eyes. "Yeah, I guess."

"Marcus is a scout for Kentucky. I wanted him to meet you."

Del's eyes opened wide. "Uh …um … thanks. You go to schools? I mean, like high schools?"

"Sure do. That's about the only way to scout. That and some films. I'd like to see you play. Nathan sent me your school's name and address. I'll check out the schedule and stop in sometime."

A dazed expression filled his face. "Which game?"

Marcus threw his head back and laughed. "Hah. That's always my secret. Play every game like I'm sitting in the stands. I promise you this—I'll be there sometime to watch you. I trust Nathan's instinct. When we played college ball, we could read each other's mind on the court."

Del's head swung around to Nathan. "You played college?"

"Yeah. Emory. Smaller basketball venue, but they gave me a scholarship."

"Did you want to go pro?"

Nathan shook his head. "I was near the top of the game in high school. When you play college ball, the level of competition increases. I was mediocre there."

Marcus jumped into the conversation. "That's an understatement. He was good. Problem was, we were in a small school. The big competitors had the advantage."

Del shook his head. "Man, I didn't know you played college."

"My buddy here played in the big leagues." Nathan motioned toward Marcus.

Marcus laughed. "And that's an overstatement. I was drafted and saw the court a half-dozen times. I couldn't cut it. At least it opened the door for scouting. So, does Kentucky interest you?"

"You bet. Don't they, like, send lots of players to the pros?"

"Yeah, we do. That's because of my exceptional scouting!"

Nathan shook his head. "Still not afraid to pat yourself on the back."

"Good to see you, Nate. Don't be a stranger. And don't go calling other scouts to compete with me." He pointed toward Del. "Come on up to Kentucky sometime. Bring this big guy to see a game."

Marcus went back to his seat, leaving an openmouthed Del. "Man, I can't believe that just happened." He turned toward Nathan. "Nate? Is that what people call you?"

"Some people do. I answer to either. Come on. Let's get back to our seats."

~*~

When Nathan parked outside The Herald Center, he saw the roofer's vans in front. Four workers were stripping old shingles and getting ready to pound the new roof. A dumpster sat outside, receiving the discarded shingles they tossed off the roof. Jonas and Mayzie waited by the door, steering kids away from the debris.

Angie sat at the table in the office, working at her laptop. She looked up as Nathan entered. "Nathan! Hello. I hope it won't be too loud in here."

His eyes strayed upward, the source of the constant thuds. "I guarantee you we can make more noise than the roofers. So, did you net what was needed?"

She closed her laptop and pushed her hair to one side. "Above and beyond. We will be able to replace both the roof and the HVAC. City officials extended our sixty days." She tapped the table. "Please, have a seat."

"I can't. Kids are coming in. I just wanted to check on Wednesday. Are we still meeting?"

"Yes. I'm looking forward to it. I'll meet you at Falls Park, right by the bridge?"

"I'll be there at one o'clock. If it's nice, we can sit outside. If not, there's a café close by."

Nathan sprinted over where his basketball kids were already gathered. They played until tutoring time. When he and Del finished, they headed back to the gym for their one-on-one. Mayzie was still there and made a beeline over to Nathan, her shoes clicking off each step.

"There you are. I've been waiting for you."

He chuckled at the stilettoes. "Mayzie, don't you ever give your feet a rest?"

"Only when I'm home in my slippers. The heels bring me up to a full five-foot two." As proof, she craned her neck upward to talk with him. "So, I wondered if we could schedule that time for coffee."

Nathan hesitated long enough for her to follow it with a question.

She tilted her head. "You are single, aren't you? There's no Mrs. Drummond?"

He enjoyed her bluntness. Mayzie held nothing back. "Yes, I'm single."

Her hands rested on her hips. "Do I hear a 'but' coming? Is there a lady in your life?"

"Let's just say, there's a budding relationship."

She snapped her fingers in disappointment. "Well, if those buds don't burst open into bloom, give me a call." She tucked a business card from EconoCuts into his shirt pocket.

~*~

The new novel was taking shape. Nathan's fingers flew over the keyboard. Anya would be surprised by the changed style. She had advised him against being too predictable.

Aiden avoided Greenville, coming only when necessary. He never went in search of Dan. Their lifelong friendship had unraveled. After graduating, he settled near his publisher, a comfortable distance from his childhood home.

This was dangerous territory. Someone could put the pieces together. Hand journaling hadn't been enough therapy. A jar of ashes didn't come close to touching the guilt. Volunteering at the center, passing by the foyer picture did more to feed the guilt than heal it. Would this novel finally give him closure?

His cell phone chirped, relieving him of his confusing thoughts. "Hello."

An excited voice skipped the formality of *hello*. "We have a buyer." The sing-song voice belonged to his realtor.

"Is it a good offer?"

"Full price, if you'll cover half of the closing costs."

It was bittersweet. It's what he wanted. It would help the debt significantly. "I guess it's a 'yes.'"

"I'll fax you the agreement. They want to close in thirty days."

So it was done. Now what? Would he really return to Atlanta when he paid off the debts? Could he leave and forget Angelina Hernandez? The relationship was just beginning, but he wanted to see where it would go. He could imagine a future with her, and that had never happened with anyone he dated.

Nathan forced his thoughts back to the manuscript. He needed to stay on track. Anya and Brian would be pressing him for a draft.

23

Angie stood on the Liberty Bridge overlooking the falls. The leaves were showing the first signs of changing. Fiery-red and pumpkin-orange peppered the landscape under the bridge. The sun stood directly overhead, illuminating the water running over the rocks. Despite the sunny day, the air was crisp. Last week had reached eighty-one degrees, compared to today's sixty-four. How typical for South Carolina.

Nathan walked toward her, still indistinct in the distance, but she knew it was him. The dark hair, neatly trimmed, the relaxed stride of his long legs, the muscular build. He sauntered down the sidewalk not appearing to have seen her. She studied each step anticipating the moment when his eyes would meet hers. Gray, mysterious eyes, like they held amusing secrets.

Angie walked back to the end of the bridge as he approached. Nathan's face brightened when he saw her.

"Hey, you beat me here."

"I couldn't resist being outside today. Autumn is short and too beautiful to miss it." She wouldn't tell him how eager she was to meet.

"Would you like to bring our coffee out here, or is it getting too cool?"

She fell into step alongside him. "I think the wind is picking up. Perhaps we should sit inside."

They walked into the coffee shop and ordered pumpkin lattes and scones. "Another reason why I like autumn—I love anything pumpkin. It's the only time of year to get it." They waited while the barista prepared their coffee, topping each with foamy cream and a sprinkle of cinnamon.

Angie slipped into a booth, placing her coffee on a beverage napkin. Nathan slid onto the seat across from her and took a tentative sip of his coffee, testing the temperature.

Leaning forward with her elbows on the table, Angie rested her chin on her hands. "So, tell me about your new book."

Nathan picked up a piece of his scone and ate it. A shadow crossed his face for just a moment. He set his fork down before answering. "Well, it's different from my typical style. Maybe my publisher won't even want it."

"I doubt that. Are you going to tell me about it, or do I have to wait?"

A lopsided grin answered the question. "I think you're going to have to wait."

"How do you build your stories? You always have a way of drawing me in, like everything is real. Do you always know the ending when you start?"

Nathan leaned back. "Yes, I always know the end. I know the end before I know the beginning. Otherwise, I couldn't foreshadow or create red herrings."

"Red herrings?"

"Those are people or situations that a writer plants in a story to throw the reader's attention away from the real culprit. Think of a foul-smelling fish. That gets your full attention and distracts you from other things."

"Oh, like Jacob's brother in your last book. I was sure he stole the jewelry. How do you make your characters so lifelike? When I read, it's like they're real people."

A slow smile began. "They are real people. I have to make myself become them. My mind lives out each scene. What would they feel? How would they react? I'm an actor playing a role, except that I have to play each role, each character. I immerse myself completely, then find words to capture it."

He tipped his coffee cup and took a long gulp. "But what I could never do is to make music come alive. How can four strings and a bow create such a wide range of sound?"

"Ah, that's the technical side of playing. Chords, scales, keys. But music isn't completely different from writing. Just like spinning words to create a feeling, music uses rhythm, rhyme, and cadence. It has to touch something deep inside."

He nodded his understanding. "Well, you've mastered that well. But I've watched you play without any scripted music. Do you ever forget the notes?"

"I did that often when I was younger. Now I've learned that the music doesn't come from here." She tapped her temple. "It comes from here." She laid a hand over her heart. "When you know the piece and feel it in your heart, you just play it.

"There's such a difference when a musician plays something that is technically correct, and when they play from the soul. You must first learn the technique and master it, but magic occurs when something from deep inside surpasses the technique. I remember when it first happened—like I was transported and became the music."

Did she sound foolish? Could anyone understand if they hadn't experienced it?

Again, Nathan nodded. "I don't know if it's the same, but I feel that way when I get a flow of story that begs to jump from my head to the page. I get lost in it and can't stop the current." He reached across the table and patted her hand. "The difference is that I get to enjoy my gift every day. You, Angie, need to be playing for an audience."

Excitement bubbled up inside her. "Oh, Nathan, I almost forgot to tell you." She reached inside her purse and pulled out a flyer. "I'll be playing at this." She pushed the paper across the table.

He raised his eyebrows as he read. "The Peace Center. That's impressive."

"Yes, it's an afternoon program with local artists who are not professional. We all have other jobs. The director has worked with many of the others and wanted to put together an event where we could all perform. A friend told me about it, and I had a chance to audition. We've been rehearsing for many weeks."

"So, is it open to the public?"

Angie's stomach fluttered. She had hoped he would want to come but didn't want to be presumptuous. "Yes, the public is invited. If you're interested, I can get you a ticket. It's this Saturday."

"I'd love to come." Nathan glanced at his phone to check the time. "Two thirty. We better get back to the center, or Jonas will be playing basketball with my boys."

"This has been so nice. Thank you for meeting me.

And for sharing about your writing."

~*~

"Hey, Nate!" They were no sooner out the door when Nathan heard the familiar voice calling his name.

He turned. Sam headed in their direction. "Hello, Sam." Nathan shifted uncomfortably.

Sam's eyes studied Angie suggestively. "And who's this lovely lady?"

Anger swelled inside Nathan, and he moved closer to Angie, his hand on the small of her back.

She offered Sam a brilliant smile, her innocence oblivious to his ogling grin. "I'm Angie Hernandez. And you must be a friend of Nathan's?"

Sam took her hand in his and held it far too long, his lips forming a wolfish grin. "Nate and I go way back." He glanced at Nathan. "Don't we, buddy?"

"Way back." Nathan's tone was flat as he lifted his arm to Angie's shoulder, turning her way. "And we should go. We don't want to be late."

"So, where are you two headed in the middle of a workday?"

Nathan opened his mouth to brush Sam off without offering any information, but Angie spoke before he could get a word out. "The Herald Center. I work there, and Nathan volunteers."

An immediate transformation hit Sam. His gaze darted toward Nathan, filled with question marks before narrowing to mere slits in his fleshy face.

Nathan turned to Angie. "We both have our cars here. Why don't you head back, and I'll see you there."

She extended her hand to Sam. "It was so nice

meeting you." Sam took her hand, but this time he released it immediately.

Nathan watched Angie until she turned the corner toward her car.

"What are you thinking, spending time over there?" He spewed the words through clenched teeth.

"I'm thinking there are teens who need help. I tutor and mentor. What do you do that's not for Sam Harper's enjoyment?"

"So, you're still the boy scout. Go tutor someone in your own neighborhood."

Nathan crossed his arms over his chest. "Look, it's been ten years. It's over. And aren't you the one who swore off this subject?"

Sam poked a finger at Nathan's chest. "Is she his daughter?"

Nathan laughed. "Hernandez. Does that sound like his daughter?"

"You think I remember his name?"

Sam didn't even remember his name. The name that Nathan swore he'd never forget. Taking a step forward, inches from his face, Nathan's eyes drilled Sam's. "Ramón Garcia." He slowly enunciated each sound, emphasizing the importance of the name.

"So? He was Hispanic. She's Hispanic. Both at The Herald Center. There must be a connection."

"Check the statistics. Roughly twenty percent of our population is Hispanic."

They stood at an impasse, glaring. "Goodbye, Sam. I've got to go." Nathan turned on his heel and walked away.

24

Angie laid her black dress on the bed before stepping into the shower. Her violin was ready and she knew the music perfectly. She'd played for audiences before, so why was she so jumpy? Yesterday's practice had been a dress rehearsal with a practice audience of music majors from a local university. Today was it the larger venue, the full orchestra, her family in the audience, and Nathan. It all came together to increase her nervousness.

All of the musicians were to wear black. Nothing should detract from the music. Yet she wanted to look her best. Angie finished dressing and looked at herself in the full-length mirror. The square-cut neckline allowed enough of a contrast with her ivory skin, adorned by a teardrop pendant with a ruby and tiny diamonds, a graduation gift from her parents. With her hair clasped tightly in the back, her jawline and cheekbones created a sophisticated profile that pleased her. A polar opposite of how she felt. Slipping her heels on, Angie gave thanks that she would be seated for most of the performance.

As Angie stepped out of her bedroom, Elizabeth gave her an appreciative look. "Perfect. You look stunning."

"Maybe on the outside. Inside is a bundle of

knots."

"You'll be great. Let's go. Did you remember that I'm not coming home right away after the concert? Will your dad drive you back?"

Angie nodded. "I'm sure he will." Or Nathan. Maybe.

~*~

Saturday afternoon always saw a crowd in downtown Greenville. People liked to walk the sidewalks, viewing the historical statues of prominent figures in Greenville's history, window shopping and enjoying the activity. Benches and sidewalk tables supported the unhurried ambiance.

It wasn't a typical time for a concert, but this one featured local amateurs. That same stage would be used in the evening for a professional production. Nathan found a parking space and walked a few blocks. An usher looked at his ticket, identifying his row. As he approached, he saw Elizabeth along with Angie's parents. Why hadn't he anticipated that? Of course, they would be here. He squeezed past a few people in the row to reach his seat.

Elizabeth patted the empty space next to her. "Nathan, we were looking for you. Angie said you'd be here."

Before sitting, Nathan greeted Alex, who then introduced him to Adrianna. It was easy to see where Angie got her looks. Slender with classic beauty—a refined look.

"Mr. Drummond, I've been anxious to meet you. Angie speaks so highly of you." Perfectly spoken

English with an accent.

"Thank you. I've enjoyed meeting your family."

Elizabeth made small talk while the tuning and testing echoed from the stage. Finally, the lights dimmed bringing quiet to the room. With the lifting of the conductor's wand, the momentary anticipation, and his sudden circular hand movement, music filled the auditorium.

Adrianna pointed to show Alex where she had spotted their daughter. Nathan's gaze landed there as well. Even with the space between them, he could sense her elation. This is where she belonged, before an audience with her chin resting on a violin.

A few solos and duets were included, often embedded within a larger piece, including Angie's duet with a pianist. Angie stood, the orchestra entered a decrescendo and faded completely. Then there was a pause, and with perfect timing Angie and the pianist played the bridge—softly at first, then rising in intensity before the full orchestra joined them in a powerful conclusion. The audience erupted with applause. Angie and the pianist bowed and then took their seats.

A fifteen-minute intermission allowed everyone to stand and stretch. Alex stepped toward him. "What do you think of my little Angel?"

Was he talking about her music? "She's amazingly talented. And I think she loves what she's doing."

"Yes, she does. She'll be on an emotional high when she comes off that stage. I've made dinner reservations and hope you'll join us."

Nathan's gaze moved from Alex to Adrianna. "I don't want to intrude."

"It'll mean a lot to her. And it's within walking

distance."

Elizabeth piped in. "You best plan on coming. My aunt is anxious to talk with you about your books. Her book club read one of them, and I think she wants to go back and boast that she had dinner with you."

Adrianna playfully swatted her hand. "Don't tell my secrets." Then she looked up at Nathan with eyes so much like Angie's. "Will you join us?"

There was no other answer but yes. "I'd love to."

~*~

When the concert concluded, Nathan waited in the back of the auditorium with Angie's family. When she came into view, she bounced toward them, a spring in each step. It was, as her father had predicted, an emotional high. She hugged her father first and then each one in the small group.

Alex motioned for them to start toward the door. "I have reservations at Graziani's Steakhouse. Nathan's coming, too. Elizabeth, are you sure you can't join us?"

"Thanks, Uncle Alex. I have some plans this evening."

Angie wore a sly grin. "She has a big date tonight."

"It's not a date. Just a friend." She shot Angie a look of mock annoyance.

Angie wasn't deterred. "A mighty handsome male friend."

Elizabeth ignored the comment. "Will someone take Angie home? We rode together."

Alex turned toward Nathan. "I'm sure Nathan will want to take her home. Isn't that right?"

"Uh ... sure."

They left the auditorium, and Elizabeth went toward her car while the others turned to walk in the opposite direction. Angie still carried her instrument case. She stopped short. "Wait. Papi, I need to take this to the car. I don't want to have it in the restaurant."

"You two young ones can do the walking. Your mother and I will go get our table."

Nathan stopped to turn around. "My car's back this way." He reached for the case. "Can I carry that for you?"

Her eyes cut to the violin case, and her head tilted in question.

He couldn't help but laugh at her expression. "I won't drop it. Promise."

She handed him the case and hooked her arm through his. Angie was as happy as he'd ever seen her.

They walked past the bronze Poinsett statue on Main Street as a brightly colored trolley went by. Nathan shortened his longer stride to match Angie's.

"What do you think of my parents?"

Nathan guided her around a slow-moving couple. "They couldn't be nicer," he answered. "I think you're a very lucky young lady. And I think you're a daddy's girl."

She chuckled. "Guilty. He has pampered me. My mother always had to be the stern one."

They reached Nathan's car, and he opened the hatchback. "I can't imagine you doing anything that required them to be stern."

An alarmed look crossed Angie's face. "Will my violin be visible? I always keep it in the trunk of my car."

"Not to worry, my dear." Nathan lifted the flap

covering a storage area in the back of his Jeep. "I told you that the instrument was in good hands."

He secured the violin in the storage compartment and locked the Jeep. "Are we good here?"

"Yes, thank you. I know I obsess a little, but it would be awful to have something happen to my violin."

"Angie, I know I said this before, but I hope you realize what a gift you have."

She reached for his hand. "Thank you. God has gifted us both so differently. I hope you enjoy my craft as much as I enjoy yours."

Her eyes radiated happiness. He could get so lost in them. Sliding his arm around her shoulder, they walked to the restaurant where her parents waited.

As they approached the table, Nathan noted the bottle of wine. Alex and Adrianna held glasses glowing with red, while two empty ones waited their arrival. As they sat, Alex began to pour. "Is Merlot all right? I can order another if you like?"

"Thank you. I'll just stick with water for now."

"But we have a toast. A toast to my little musician. Here's just a toast's worth. Hah, I think I just made up a new word." He poured an inch of the red wine into Nathan's glass and filled Angie's.

Nathan picked up the glass. Tonight was her night, and he'd toast to her talent.

Alex held his wine glass high. "To Angelina Grace, angel of grace. A beautiful young lady, a talented violinist. And to Angelina and Nathan. May your friendship grow into something beautiful." His eyes flitted toward Adrianna, alluding to a comparison between relationships.

They clinked their glasses and sipped their wine, a

rare moment for Nathan. He hadn't had a drink in ten years. Tonight, he'd stop after his toast's worth.

Graziani's was legendary for their steaks. The ladies ordered first and both selected a filet, so Nathan followed suit. Alex, last to order, made it unanimous. "You can't go wrong with their filet. It's the best around."

Angie touched Nathan's arm. "Nathan, my mother is somewhat of a writer as well."

Nathan looked to his left where Adrianna sat. "Really? What do you write?"

She shook her head. "It's too much of a stretch to call me a writer. I've done a few magazine articles."

"Well, that's still writing. What topic?"

Angie answered for her. "Mother's such a wonderful cook. She's written some cooking articles for Southern Cuisine and some decorating articles for Good Housekeeping."

Nathan nodded. "That's impressive. Two well-established publications."

"Well, I love to cook. I read those magazines, so I had an idea of what kind of articles they like. I enjoy writing, but I don't think I could ever write fiction. I do better with things I know." She spoke eloquently.

Alex took his wife's hand and raised it to his lips. "Both of my ladies are beautiful and talented. I'm a blessed man. Nathan, you have to come to Sunday brunch. See for yourself what a cook my wife is."

Angie clapped her hands together, her sign of excitement. "Yes, you'll love my mother's brunch."

Alex broke in. "Then it's decided. Tomorrow following our nine-o'clock church service. Brunch will be served around ten thirty or eleven.

Nathan wanted to be included, to step deeper into

Angie's life. He was a stranger to her parents, yet he had a sense of belonging that he hadn't enjoyed for so many years. A fleeting sadness gripped him. His own family had scattered, even before losing his father. His mother would love to have everyone gathered for Sunday dinners.

He looked toward Adrianna. "Are you sure it isn't too short notice?"

"Not at all. I prepared food today for brunch tomorrow. We'd love for you to join us."

"Thank you. I'd be happy to."

When they finished their dinner, the waiter left the check. Nathan reached for his wallet, but Alex stopped him.

"My treat tonight." Nathan started to protest, but Alex wouldn't hear of it. "There's something you can do for me instead." He leaned forward conspiratorially. "I don't like Angie living in that part of town. Tonight, she'll be going into an empty house since Elizabeth is out. Please take her in and check her house before leaving her."

"Papi, I'm fine. You worry too much."

Nathan agreed with Alex. It wasn't good for two young ladies to live alone in that area. "I'll definitely do that." He turned toward Angie. "Why do you and Elizabeth stay there? It only takes about fifteen minutes for me to get there from the suburbs."

"I would be happy to live elsewhere, but I won't leave Elizabeth there alone. She's resistant to leaving her childhood home."

"Nathan?" Adrianna asked. "Would you talk with Elizabeth? Make the suggestion? We've tried, but she thinks we're old worrywarts. Maybe she'd listen to someone younger."

He didn't want in the middle of a family disagreement. But it wouldn't hurt to casually mention it. "I'll see what I can do."

25

Angie laid her head on the headrest as Nathan drove back to her home. It had been a perfect day. "Thank you, Nathan."

"For what?"

She lifted her head and looked at him. "For being here. For coming to dinner and taking me home."

"You're welcome."

Angie focused on his face, the profile from the side view. He appeared to be suppressing a grin. He must have enjoyed it as well. "My parents really like you."

He drove without comment. She lifted her chin and continued. "You'll love Sunday brunch. Remind me to give you the address."

Angie's home—Elizabeth's childhood home—was a block from The Herald Center. Uncle Ramón had always insisted on living among those to whom he ministered. Nathan parked in front of the house and stepped toward the porch, his hand on her shoulder. When she didn't move with him, he looked at her with a question in his eyes. "My violin?"

"How could I forget? I'm sworn to its protection."

"Are you teasing me?"

"Yes, but affectionately." He opened the back of the jeep and the storage compartment.

"Angie, it's gone!"

"What!" A panicked looked gripped her.

Nathan laughed. "Oh, wait. Here it is."

She gave him a playful swat and took her

instrument case.

They walked to the house with his arm touching her back. With Nathan beside her, Angie's awareness of her home heightened. The concrete steps with a weathered, flaking surface, a screen door repaired with clear tape over the torn screening, noise from a pub on the corner, just three doors away. She retrieved her key, and they walked inside. The room was tidy, but worn. The frayed carpet had stains that refused to come out, despite their best efforts. She wished her father hadn't insisted on Nathan coming in. And yet, it allowed her a little extra time with him. She'd make the most of it.

"I'd love a cup of tea. Would you like some? Or perhaps coffee or soda?"

"Tea sounds good." He surprised her by accepting.

Nathan followed her into the kitchen where she put water on the stove to heat. She reached for two mugs, placed them on the table, and set a container of tea bags beside them. "I have black tea or herbal. You can look through them and select." Angie put honey and lemon on the table as well. "Or do you like English style, with cream?"

"No, this is fine." He fingered through the selection of tea bags and opened a spiced orange herbal packet.

They fixed their tea and went into the living room. Angie took a seat on the sofa, kicking her dress shoes off. Nathan sat in a chair facing her.

"So your parents want me to talk Elizabeth into moving. What's the chance of that really happening? I don't want to overstep."

Angie held her mug, allowing the warmth to seep

into her hands. "Everyone grieves differently. I think for Liz, part of the grief process has been keeping everything about her parents' life the same."

"So that suggestion might be offensive to her?"

Angie pondered that. "Maybe not. As time goes on, she lets go a little at a time. It was a huge step when she returned to school to finish her degree. Dating is another good sign. It shows that she's healing." Angie breathed deeply, the steam rising from her tea. "The center is important to her. I believe that she would be open to a move if she felt it wouldn't detract from its success. That's why I started spending so much time there when she returned to school."

"Has she ever considered that the center can be healthy and thrive without either of you actually working there? Jonas knows the program, and a good director could be hired."

Setting her cup on the coaster, Angie gave him a puzzled look. "You don't think I've been a good director?"

Nathan leaned forward in his chair. "That's not what I meant. You're the best. Those kids respect you, and I can promise you, respect doesn't come easy. You have a special touch with them."

"So why wouldn't I continue to serve as Director of Operations?"

Nathan regarded her silently for a moment. "You know why, Angie. You know what you were born to do. You said you made the correct decision back then. Perhaps the time has come to revisit it."

She gave him a sad smile. "Julliard isn't likely to be offered twice."

"Julliard isn't the only road to becoming a professional musician."

Angie picked up her cup and sipped. They sat in contemplative silence. Nathan finished his tea and stood. Angie assumed he was preparing to leave, but instead, he walked over and sat beside her, his arm stretched across the back of the sofa.

"Tell me your greatest dream. What would it look like?"

She looked upward, choosing her words carefully. "I would be a first chair violinist playing in Carnegie Hall." She turned her gaze toward Nathan. "And I would have an opportunity to travel to Vienna and play in Musikverein." Angie chuckled at the absurdity of that. "Of course, I'd have to play something by Mozart if I visited there."

"Have you ever been to Europe?"

"No. My only visit outside of the continental United States has been to Puerto Rico to visit my grandparents. Have you been to Europe?"

"I did a semester abroad in Brussels. It gave me the opportunity to visit a few places."

He stretched out his arm on the back of the sofa behind Angie. She faced him, aware of the closeness, conscious of her black dress, the teardrop necklace and earrings. "Vienna?"

He shook his head. "No. I never made it there."

"What's your dream, Nathan? I told you mine."

With his elbow propped on the sofa, he reached his hand forward and brushed her cheek. Her hair remained gathered in the back, and his hand followed her jawline, brushing the back of his hand down its length, cupping her chin. "I'm not sure I have a dream."

Angie's senses heightened at the touch. "Everyone has a dream."

A shadow passed his face, and he moved his hand back to the sofa. "My dream would be to go back in time and do some things differently."

His response puzzled her. "Ah, but we're not afforded that opportunity. Would you still write?"

"Yes, I'd write. Without question," he answered. "Maybe my dreams have been fulfilled."

"Oh, but here's the cycle of dreams—there's always another waiting in the wings."

There were the eyes from the back of his book cover—steely-gray, intense with mystery. Nathan again touched her chin, drawing it closer as he leaned forward. His lips touched hers. They felt as soft as rose petals. The kiss ended far too quickly.

"Chase your dream, Angie." Nathan moved back, lifting her hand. "I better go." He stood, still holding her hand as she rose to join him. They walked to the door and lingered, facing each other.

Nathan looked at her upturned face with a question in his eyes. "Did I overstep?"

Angie wished she hadn't kicked off the heels. She reached up and placed her hand on his cheek. "No. You were a perfect gentleman."

Their lips met again, soft and sweet before he left.

~*~

The new novel almost wrote itself. Nathan plucked at the keys all day on Sunday after returning from his brunch with Angie's family. And then for half the day on Monday he worked again. Each stroke of his laptop clicked the story to life.

Aiden was falling in love. Maggie affected him in a way

that no one ever had. Now that he had kissed her, touched the soft, shiny hair, and held her close against him, how could he stop? When he wasn't with her, she was on his mind. When he was near her, he couldn't take his eyes off her.

When he reached the end, he'd have to go back and begin first-round edits. Way too much to accomplish in the timeframe they had discussed. Brian would act upset, but he'd get over it. Nathan would still be on target for two publications this year. Three might not happen.

The chirping of the phone perfectly matched the ending of the chapter he just finished.

Anya. He saw her name on the caller ID.

"Well, there's good news and there's bad."

Nathan stretched his back in the desk chair, turning his neck to relieve the stiffness. "And I'm sure you're going to tell me both."

"The good news is we've got the movie deal. They're ready to send a contract. The bad—it's a made-for-TV with a smaller signing bonus. They offered $100,000 but I talked them up to $120,000. That will be split 50/50 with the screenwriter."

"That's good news. The big screen was a reach. I didn't really expect it to happen."

"Well, I wouldn't rule that out for the future. But this is a good start."

"So how's this work? Who hires a screenwriter?"

"They want to use someone they've worked with before. I insisted on a contingency of our approval to any edits on the storyline. You don't want your name on it if they make drastic changes." She spoke rapidly, catching her breath in-between sentences. "Half of the funds will be an advance. The other half will be dispersed upon completion. So you'll see $30,000 minus my percentage, as soon as all of the paperwork is sent in."

A lot less than expected, but a nice chunk on the debt. "I'll sign and return as soon as I get it."

"And you will get it …" he heard the clicking of her computer, "now. I just hit send."

"Great. Thanks, Anya. This has been a nice surprise."

"Return it ASAP. And you'll soon be sending your next draft as well. Correct?"

He laughed out loud. "Only if you want it without an ending."

She mocked an exaggerated sigh. "Nathan. Nathan. Let's keep it going."

He needed to share his news. His mother busied herself in the kitchen. Other than tiring quickly and some residual joint pain, she had full mobility. They assured her the pain would subside.

Nathan bounded down the stairs, the scent of cinnamon reaching him. The oven door stood open as his mother reached for the mitts. He took them from her hands. "Let me get that." She patted the trivet that she had ready for the pie. "Smells good. But I came down because I have news. I just hung up with my agent."

She pushed the oven door closed. "From the look on your face, it's good news. New York Times best seller?"

"Not yet. This one's a first for me. They're making one of my books into a movie for TV."

Her mouth fell open, an incredulous stare. Then she squealed with delight. "That's wonderful. How exciting. When will it be on?"

"Ha, a long, long time from now. I'm just signing

the contract. Then a screenwriter has to rewrite it. No doubt the whole process will take over a year."

"Oh, Nate. I'm so proud of you."

He could hardly wait to tell Angie. She had asked about his dream. He didn't think about the movie deal, but this suddenly felt like a dream come true.

26

Angie was nowhere to be seen when he arrived. Jonas leaned against the office table, talking on the phone. When he hung up, Nathan made a point to walk over and say hello. Angie might be back by the file cabinet, out of his view.

Jonas wasn't fooled. "You looking for Miss Angie? She's out shopping for supplies. Should be back any time now."

The boys arrived and basketball flew into full swing. Nathan saw Angie returning, her arms full with plastic bags from the grocery store. Afterschool snacks, he surmised. He waved on his way back down the hall toward the tutoring room.

Del reached in his backpack and retrieved a piece of paper, passing it over to Nathan.

"I'm back on the team."

Nathan picked up the eligibility form and scanned it. "That's great news. That was our goal." He extended his arm. It took Del a moment to realize why, then he grinned, met his arm and went through the motions. Slide, slap, grip, slap, arm bump, fist bump.

"Yeah, one problem with that—I'll be starting afterschool practices in two weeks. I won't be here after that."

Nathan leaned back, thinking through the

ramifications. "Think you can keep the grades up?"

"I hope so."

"Del, there can't be any hoping. There has to be assurance. You have some new tools in your tool belt, but you'll have far less time to use them. If you don't, you'll be off again by mid-report period."

His shoulders slouched and his arms crossed at his chest. "Man, I worked hard for this. Don't go getting all down on me before I even have a chance."

"Sorry, Del. You have worked hard. I know that. What's your position?"

He relaxed his arms. "Point Guard."

"Good for you. Listen—call me anytime you feel like you're slipping. You've proven that you can do this." Nathan tapped the school papers that sat on the table. "If the schedule gets too crazy, call me. We'll work through it together. In the meantime, we have two more weeks. Let's make the most of it."

They studied for the science test much the same way they had done for history. If he didn't have to read the material, Del had great reasoning and logic skills. They talked through it competently.

When he had finished with Del, Nathan stopped by the office.

Angie closed her laptop as he walked in. "How was tutoring today?"

"Good. Del's back on the team."

"I'm not surprised. He's a different kid since you've been here."

"The downside is that he won't be here when practices start in two weeks."

Alarm crossed her face, much as it had with Nathan earlier. "Can he make it without tutoring?"

"I think so. He has some new strategies, and more

importantly, he recognizes his ability. I'm sure he always thought he was dumb. Now he knows better. And," he placed both hands, palms down, on the desk and leaned forward, "I do have a dream."

Angie grinned coyly. "You do? And what would that be?"

"I'd love to see one of my books made into a movie."

"Oh, that would be special."

"And," he shot her a mischievous grin, "it just so happens that my dream's coming true."

She shot up out of her seat. "Nathan, that's wonderful. What book? When will this happen?" She looked like she was about to run and throw her arms around him but practiced restraint. She sat back down.

"*Secret on the Bayou*. I just got the contract, so it will be a while. And it will only be for TV."

"You must be so thrilled. I'm proud of you." Joyfulness radiated from her as though it were a light in the room.

He shook his head, but the smile never left his face. "Angie, are you ever not happy?"

"Not if I can help it. I don't understand why people are gloomy. It's a choice. I choose joy." She turned toward something behind him. "There's Liz. Let's tell her."

Angie stretched her head toward the office doorway. "Liz, can you come here?"

Elizabeth jaunted over, a lightness in her step that he hadn't seen before. Her short hair bobbed with each step. Aside from the hair, she looked so much like Angie, especially since Elizabeth had a new light in her eyes. Perhaps this was due to the friend she was seeing.

"Nathan, tell her your news."

"I just told Angie I've signed a contract for one of my books to be made into a movie."

Elizabeth's reaction mirrored Angie's except that she reached over and hugged him. "That's wonderful news." He shared the details, eyeing Elizabeth's attire. She was dressed professionally, a gray business suit softened by a floral scarf. A nametag told him she must be headed to a business meeting of some sort.

As his eyes grazed over the nametag, he stopped short, mid-sentence. Elizabeth Garcia. A rush of adrenaline jolted through him. He caught himself stuttering as he continued. Garcia? He had assumed it was Hernandez. Nathan found it hard to breathe, blood pulsing through his head.

Angie stood and walked toward him. "Are you OK?"

He pasted a smile on his face but sat in the chair that remained pulled out. "Yes. I guess I played a little too hard out there."

Angie wordlessly went to the refrigerator and brought a bottle of water.

Elizabeth took that opportunity to exit. "I have a presentation at school. Great news, Nathan. Angie, I'll be home around eight o'clock."

Nathan sipped the water and recovered from the surprise. He had to know the truth. "Elizabeth's nametag said Garcia. I thought it was Hernandez."

"No, our mothers were siblings, not our fathers."

He tried to sound nonchalant. "So is that Garcia, like the founder? Are they related?"

"Yes, I told you about her father. The accident that killed him."

Sam was right. There was a connection. "You told

me he died, but I didn't know it was an accident. And I didn't know it was Ramón Garcia."

Angie blinked rapidly, frowning. "I'm sorry. I feel sure we talked about this. It's the same accident that injured her mother. I told you how close we all were— my family and Elizabeth's. Her parents were so special to me. The loss was great for all of us." She exhaled deeply. "I still miss them." She came around to stand in front of Nathan and stooped down, her hands resting on his knees. "That's why this center is so important to Elizabeth. I apologize if I didn't make that clear."

He looked at her upturned face, heart-shaped and so angelic, silky hair draped over her shoulder. He studied her lips, remembering the softness. Lips that were off limits to him now, that one brief kiss all they'd ever share. There could be no future with anyone from the family of Ramón Garcia.

He lifted her hands from his knees and drew her upright. He stood, reluctant to release her. Once done, he wouldn't hold them again. "I need to go." He freed her and reached for his backpack.

Angie matched his pace and stepped to the front door with him. They turned toward the portrait at the same time. Angie's eyes held nostalgia, while Nathan battled the image of a red car, spinning and crashing.

As they stared, Angie hooked her arm with his. "He would have loved you. Loved the way you work with Del. He never met anyone he didn't think could be redeemed. No one beyond forgiveness."

Nathan looked toward the door. He patted her hand and removed it from his arm. "I'll see you on Wednesday." With that, he walked out the door and to his car without a backward glance.

Kathleen Neely

Nathan drove home forming a new plan. He needed to get out of Greenville. He had known better than to move back here. Did he really think he could ease the guilt by volunteering at The Herald Center? Like putting a Band-Aid on a gunshot wound.

Two more weeks with Del. Nathan couldn't leave him now. Couldn't have another person fail him. He laughed cynically as he compared himself to Del at that same age. Del lived in a single-parent home in a distressed part of town. He spent long hours alone while his mother worked. No father or male role model. Nathan grew up with all the advantages of a solid home life with two involved parents. Why was he so easily influenced by his peers? He had been smart in school but made stupid life choices. Del put him to shame.

In two weeks, Del was back on the school's basketball team, and Nathan was done. He'd stop volunteering, forget The Herald Center, forget Angelina Hernandez, and move back to Atlanta. He needed to begin writing in earnest.

Nathan swung the Jeep into his mother's driveway, still numb. When he opened the front door, he could smell the aroma coming from the oven. With a hasty apology, he took his plate upstairs. "I'm fighting a deadline. I've got to keep going."

His mother looked at him skeptically. When he left the house earlier, he'd been elated about the movie deal. "Sorry, Mom. I'm just behind schedule."

With his journal open, Nathan squeezed the pen, scribbling deep indentations on the page. Anger coursed through his fingers. Angie. He'd cost her Julliard. He changed the course of her life, Elizabeth's life. Her mother—she was injured in the same accident

176

that killed her husband. She never walked again. The newspaper hadn't told him that. The consequences reached far beyond what he'd ever known. Shame exploded through him.

Angie was the first person with whom he could imagine a future. It was the first time someone reached that deepest place inside him, and he couldn't pursue a relationship. She was off limits. She'd hate him if she knew.

Nathan threw the pen across the room. It wasn't enough to satisfy his anger. The imprints on the paper mocked him. He ripped the scribbled page from the journal and tossed it as well. Then he paced, like a caged animal in a confined space. He turned toward the TV and opened the saved newscast of The Herald Center, freezing the screen on Angie's face…and stared at all he had lost.

Retrieving the crumbled journal entry, Nathan held the jar of ashes. He dropped the jagged sphere in and flicked the lighter. As always, he secured the lid when the last edge of white paper singed. The smoke clouded and blackened the inside surface. A red ember flickered, trying to hold onto life, but the oxygen had been squeezed out, rendering it helpless, just as he had done to Ramón Garcia. Smoke clouded the jar, hanging heavy over the sooty surface. Nathan held the jar up until the cloud disappeared. The powdery ashes from ten years of consistent journaling were reduced to less than half of the jar. A poor measure of a man's life.

Time to stop this futile exercise. He'd kept it up over the years so he wouldn't forget the cost of his stupidity. He'd convinced himself that Ramón Garcia deserved that. To what end? It helped nobody, changed nothing.

He swiveled his chair back toward the TV and Angie's smiling face. This was his reminder. It humanized the consequences of recklessness in a way that writing hadn't fully accomplished. He could print this as a daily reminder of what he'd lost and what he'd cost this family. But he wouldn't do that. He wanted a painful reminder, but that would be too much.

Nathan opened his laptop to Apartments.com and searched Atlanta. On paper, his budget spreadsheet said it could work. If book sales remained strong, he could meet the payment plan for his father's debts, continue subsidizing his mother's social security, and afford a small apartment in some areas of Atlanta. It wouldn't match his old lifestyle, but it would get him out of Greenville, away from The Herald Center. The longer he delayed, the harder it would be.

27

Disappointment gripped Angie when Nathan made no mention of seeing each other again. She'd had hopes of a dinner invitation. But he'd already told her he was under pressure from his publisher. She would have to be patient.

Their last evening together had been perfect. She relived that kiss over and over, imagining the next one. Longer, deeper, resting her head against his beating heart. Never before had she felt this way. Had God finally provided the one He ordained for her?

Wednesday came and Angie watched the clock, waiting for Nathan to saunter in that door, his eyes roaming, looking for her. He'd wear that easy grin.

She saw Mayzie, always with a clipboard in her hand, standing on spiked heels. Mayzie liked Nathan, and she was bolder than Angie.

Angie had overheard Mayzie's conversation with Nathan at the park.

She'd seen Mayzie tuck a card into his pocket.

But Nathan had set his eyes upon Angie. She could relax in confidence that good things were ahead.

There he was across the gym. Somehow, she'd missed him coming in. He stood chatting in the midst of a few volunteers. She'd have to be content to see him after tutoring.

The clock seemed stuck. Each time she glanced, it turned out to be five minutes after the last time. Would they never come out? She paced up and down the tutoring hallway, checking in each room. Del and Nathan crouched over the table with papers between them. Del occasionally wrote something down. Angie couldn't stand and stare so she made her way to other windows, observing other tutors.

Finally, the tutoring time ended. As always, Nathan and Del headed back toward the basketball hoop. Angie walked closer, leaned her back against the wall, and watched the action. When it ended, she joined them. "Del, congratulations on getting back on the team. I knew you could do it."

"Thanks Miss Angie. Nate's coming to watch me play. Think you'd like to come to a game?"

"Nate? I've not heard you call him that." She looked from one to the other.

Del thrust a ball toward him. "Close friends call him that."

Angie saw the crooked grin that Nathan attempted to suppress. "Well, I might have to begin calling him that. And yes, Del, I'd love to see you play. Perhaps I could tag along when Nate comes."

"It'll be a while. Right now, we're just practicing."

They returned the ball and grabbed their backpacks. Del waved and walked out the door. Nathan headed in that direction. "Hey, I'm in kind of a hurry today. I have a few errands on my way home."

Angie's shoulders slumped and a sigh escaped. "Well, I suppose I'll see you Friday?" She hoped that would remind him of the upcoming weekend.

~*~

The weekend passed without any word from Nathan. He had a deadline, but surely a few hours away from his computer would have been good for him. He had arrived at the last minute today, reaching the basketball court the same time as his kids.

Mayzie had laughed, saying, "Finally! I thought I was going to have to do basketball today wearing these." She lifted her foot in reference to today's platform heels.

The thud of the basketball hitting hardwood kept Angie aware of Nathan's nearness. When all sound ceased, Angie sprung up to see why. Jonas stepped out of the boy's restroom, his arm around Thomas's shoulder and his hand gripping Chaz's forearm. Jonas's stern face motioned toward Nathan.

"Nathan, will you take care of Thomas? He needs some medical attention. I'll stay with the boys. Chaz, we'll deal with you later. Sit out right there." He pointed to the only chair in the gym.

Chaz glared at Thomas before plopping into the chair.

~*~

Nathan brought Thomas to the office, blood coursing from his nose as his face showed the first signs of swelling. Angie ran for an ice pack while Nathan brought Thomas tissues to cover the bloody nose.

Nathan pulled two chairs in front of Thomas. "Can you tell us what happened?"

Thomas took the ice pack and held it on the swollen cheekbone. "He hit me," were his only words.

"That's evident, but why did he hit you?"

"He wanted me to switch sides, to get off of his team. I said I couldn't 'cause you put me with them."

Angie leaned in to comfort him. "Thomas, I'm so sorry he was cruel. Please be assured we will deal with Chaz. This is a place where you should be protected, and I'm saddened that this happened."

"He's always saying stuff like that." A teardrop escaped, and Thomas quickly brushed it away. "I hate him."

Angie tilted her head, dismay on her face. "Oh, Thomas. I know you're hurting right now, but hate is such a strong word."

"I can't help it." Thomas spoke through gritted teeth.

"Actually, you can. God wants us to love our enemies. He can help us to do that."

Thomas covered his face with his hand. "You don't know how hard it is. You probably never hated anyone."

Angie reached and moved his hand, looking him in the eyes. "Oh, but I did. I did hate, but God helped me through that."

Nathan turned startled eyes her way. Hate was too out of character for Angie. He couldn't fathom it.

Thomas must have been taken by surprise as well. "Who'd you hate, Miss Angie?"

She sat back in her chair, ready to tell her story, no doubt an analogy to help Thomas. "Someone I never knew. You see, my uncle, whom I loved very dearly, was killed in a car accident. But we were never convinced it was an accident. Some people said another vehicle was driving recklessly, and the driver may have been intoxicated. But they never found the person."

A rush of air left Nathan's lungs, making it difficult to breathe. He felt the color drain from his face, his pulse rate increasing.

"I had so much grief and watched all of my family grieving. Our lives were changed forever. I kept thinking about the person who caused it, and my heart hardened with hatred. Would my uncle have lived if he had stopped to help? I imagined him driving away, never thinking about it again while I lived with it every day."

The throbbing began in Nathan's chest as he tried to get air. The walls were closing in on him. He strained to breathe deeply as he'd been taught but couldn't remember the counts. He tried to imagine himself somewhere else. Somewhere safe, but his mind couldn't find that place.

"But you see, the hate only hurt me. It didn't hurt that other person. So a dear friend helped me. She suggested that I pray for him every day. I was resistant. It's hard to pray for someone your heart is hating. But in obedience, I prayed."

The room was swimming around Nathan. He wouldn't be able to stand. Would he pass out right here in front of them?

"I prayed that he would remember my sweet uncle. I prayed that he would never hurt another person in the same way. I prayed that God would capture his heart and turn it toward Christ. And do you know what happened? My heart softened. If you pray for someone every day, pray honestly and truthfully, you can't keep hating them."

The spinning eased up, and his heart rate slowed. Nathan sucked in a shallow breath of air. Slowly,

slowly, the breaths deepened.

"So, Thomas, I want to challenge you to pray for Chaz. Pray every day and allow God to take away the hate. It will help you and Chaz. I'll probably never meet the person I prayed for. Never know how God worked in his life. But that's OK. I have faith that God answered that prayer according to His perfect will. And He will answer your prayers."

Angie turned her eyes to Nathan, unaware that a panic attack had subsided. "Nathan, do you have anything to add?"

He shook his head, not trusting himself to speak.

"Thomas, I'll call your mother and let her know what has happened. You are free to go back to the gym, and I'll talk with Chaz."

"Miss Angie, Jonas asked me if I wanted to switch to another activity. I think I'd like to move to art."

"I'll be happy to move you if that's what you really want. But if you want to play basketball, please be assured this won't happen again."

Thomas sat stone faced. He lifted his eyes to Angie. "I'll do art."

Thomas stood, and Nathan joined him. "I better get back to the boys. I'll send Chaz in." Without another word, he exited.

~*~

Nathan left the center after tutoring. No one-on-one time with Del. He'd simply told him he was unable to stay today. He needed distance between himself and The Herald Center. He couldn't allow a return to panic attacks. They had almost crippled him years ago. Two more days, Wednesday and Friday, then it was over.

28

He had been avoiding her. Angie suspected it, but now she knew it. Two weeks had passed since the concert at the Peace Center. Nathan retreated after that. He must have decided that she wasn't the one for him.

A weight lay heavy on her heart. This was more than a passing attraction. Angie had grown to care deeply for him. But since his retreat, she refused to think about that. She would protect her heart.

When rec time ended, Nathan stopped by the office on his way to tutoring. Angie's heart accelerated at the sight of him standing in the doorway. "Carlos is out again. Everything OK with him?"

Her stomach knotted. She worried more about Carlos than any of the others. Too many issues at home. "As far as I know. I haven't heard. I'll let you know if I do."

An hour later, as tutoring ended, Angie hoped to run into Nathan again. She watched him head to the hoops with Del. The office phone rang, but Jonas was closest. She turned toward the doorway when she heard him talking.

"Whoa. Slow down there, son. Angie, you better take this. I can't understand him."

"Hello, this is Angie."

"*Mi mamá está herida. Necesito una ambulancia. Creo*

que está muerta. Apresúrate."

"Carlos? Is this Carlos?"

"Yes, *Mi mamá. Apresúrate.*" He screamed the words.

"Carlos. I'll be right there. Did you call 9-1-1?"

"No, hurry. I think she's dead."

She hung up the phone and went into action. "Jonas, get Carlos's address from the file. Call 9-1-1 and send an ambulance. Hurry. I'm going there now."

"Not alone. I'm coming with you."

"No, Jonas. You can't leave the center to volunteers."

Angie saw Jonas run to the gym and heard him call to Nathan. "Nathan, we need you. Hurry."

~*~

Nathan sprinted over as Jonas pulled out a file.

He scribbled something on a notepad and handed it to Nathan. "Can you go with Angie? Carlos is in trouble."

"What kind of trouble?"

"Somebody's hurt. We called for an ambulance." Jonas's hand circled Nathan's arm, turning him toward the doorway. "Go. Catch up with Angie."

Nathan took the address and ran after Angie who was almost out the door. "My car's right there. Do you want me to drive?"

She turned, a mixture of panic and confusion. "Yes. Yes, please."

He hurriedly punched the address into his GPS and sped off, following the robotic instructions.

"Angie, what do you know? Who's hurt?"

"Carlos was hysterical, saying he needed an ambulance. He thinks his mother is dead. He sounded so scared. Oh, Nathan, do you think his father broke the restraining order?"

"Well if Carlos made the call, we know that he's all right."

Nathan turned onto Carlos's street and left the car haphazardly parked. They ran to the house. Angie was steps before him as he came around the car. She opened the front door, and Nathan heard the scream. Angie's knees buckled, and she knelt with her hands covering her face. He lengthened his stride.

Nathan's muscles tightened as he looked in the doorway. He fought the urge to back away.

Blood was splattered around the living room and pooled near the body of a man. His mutilated face had obviously taken a bullet at close range. A woman lay a few feet from him.

His delayed response lasted only a moment. Nathan dashed into the room. The man was clearly dead, so he ran to the woman. She had multiple stab wounds bleeding freely. He felt her wrist and found a weak pulse. There were shallow breaths, but she'd bleed out if they didn't hurry. He had to slow the bleeding.

Nathan glanced around for anything clean that he could use as a compress. He didn't have time to search, so grabbed a blanket from the sofa. He applied it to the wound with the heaviest bleeding at the front base of her shoulder blade. Holding pressure on the wound, he glanced around to see if any others needed immediate attention. Her abdomen seeped blood, soaking her blouse. Her clothing covered the wound, but he stretched the blanket and his arms to apply pressure to both areas.

Angie still stood at the door, doubled over with her hands shielding her eyes from the bloodbath. "Where's Carlos?"

"He's not here. Angie, wait out there. Watch for the ambulance."

He needed her out of the house. Nathan looked at his hands, blood seeping through the blanket, and remembered all of the blood-borne-pathogens training videos he had seen when he taught school. He had just broken every rule. *God, please keep her alive 'til they get here.*

The peal of sirens had never sounded so good. Three EMTs dashed into the room. One took over, immediately replacing the blanket with sterile gauze pads. Another checked the man for any sign of life. One met him with disinfectant wipes, cleaned his hands, and doused him with Betadine.

Nathan ran outside, the sound of his own heartbeat pounding in his ears. Angie leaned against the house, bent over, her breathing labored. She looked frightened, like a cowering puppy, and protectiveness moved Nathan toward her.

"Angie." He hurried to her then saw the blood that covered his jacket. Nausea rose in his throat as he slid his arms out and tossed it to the ground. Then he closed the distance between them and pulled her into his arms. "Are you OK?"

"Oh, Nathan. It's so awful. I couldn't go in."

He rubbed her back in circular movements. "It's all right. They've got this now. Take some deep breaths."

"But where's Carlos? Oh, Nathan. He must have seen this. How awful for him."

Nathan shushed her and tried to get her to relax. His mind raced through the possibilities of what happened. He came up with only one explanation. There was no gun on the floor. Carlos did more than just see this. He must have been the shooter.

Angie's breathing slowed—her pants turning to raspy intakes of air. She pulled her arms around Nathan, and he held her head against his chest, stroking her hair.

Blue lights appeared as two police cars pulled into the parking lot. Between the police and the ambulance, the street looked like a blinking Christmas display. The officers approached, and Nathan released Angie but kept an arm protectively around her shoulder.

An approaching police officer held up a badge to identify himself. "I'm Officer Ackerman. What happened here?"

Nathan introduced himself as a volunteer at The Herald Center and introduced Angie. "She took a call from Carlos, one of our students, and we rushed here. A man's dead. He's been shot. The boy's mother has multiple stab wounds and a weak pulse. The EMTs are with her now."

"And the boy?" The officer lifted one eyebrow.

"He's not here." Angie's breathing became heavy again, and Nathan pulled her closer.

"Let me go take a look. Stay here. We'll need your statement."

As the officer left them, Nathan turned Angie to face him and took both of her hands in his. "Angie, are you all right? Can I have the EMT look at you?"

"No. I'm OK. I've just never seen anything like that before. Nathan, we have to find Carlos. Where could he be?"

"Don't worry about Carlos right now. He's not here, and that's a good thing. We'll find him."

Angie leaned into him, laying her head against his chest.

Nathan pressed his back against the building holding Angie close. Just like he had with Connor, the baby boy, Nathan found himself filled with protectiveness. He had wanted to flee with the child and save him. The same feelings overwhelmed him now. If he could just take Angie away. Somewhere safe, far from The Herald Center, far from the poverty and hopelessness. Far from the memory that came between them.

Angie took a few steps back and looked up into Nathan's face. "I almost came here alone. Thank you for not letting that happen."

With her upturned face, so close and vulnerable, Nathan moved toward her and softly kissed her lips…exactly what he had determined not to do.

A moment later, the EMTs emerged with a gurney holding Carlos' mother. Nathan followed them to the ambulance.

"Which hospital?"

"Greenville General, the downtown branch." Then they closed the doors, sounded the siren, and sped away.

Nathan took Angie's hand and spoke in a whisper. "I think I know where Carlos is. The police are going to want to talk with him, but it would be good if we could do that first—just to prepare him."

Angie jerked her head back. "How do you know where he is?"

His eyes darted behind the house. "I could be wrong. Do you see the storage shed? The window blind has moved. It was a few inches up at the bottom, and now it's fully closed." His gaze moved toward the house. "They're busy with the crime scene. Let's check it out."

They walked quietly past the door and into the backyard. A dusty pick-up truck sat beside the shed under the shade of a towering oak tree. Angie turned the knob on the rusted metal door. It opened easily, sending out a musty odor from the damp, wood floor.

Carlos sat against the back of the shed, crouched between a lawn mower and wheel barrel. He held a gun in his shaky hands, pointed toward the door.

Angie took a tentative step toward him. "Carlos, it's us. Angie and Nathan. Please put the gun down."

"No. Go away."

"But Carlos… "

Nathan gripped her arm and moved her out of the doorway. He stooped down, off to the side, away from the direct line of the gun's barrel. The pulse in his neck throbbed with tension. "Carlos, they took your mom to the hospital."

Carlos still held the gun, unsteadily, pointed forward. "But my dad's dead."

"Yes, Carlos. He is. But that's not your fault. It was self-defense. He would have killed your mother if you hadn't been there."

Carlos's hand shook, his finger hooked around the trigger. A bad combination. "Will you put the gun down now? We're here to help you."

"No. They'll still take me to jail."

Nathan startled as a breeze sent acorns pelting the shed roof. He steadied himself and tried again. "Carlos, you saved your mother's life. Please trust us."

Angie was beside Nathan now. "No, mi amigo.

They won't take you to jail. They will only talk to you to see what happened. They won't hold you responsible. And I'll stay with you the whole time they talk. I promise."

Carlos continued to hold the gun, his hand wracked with tremors.

Nathan took a deep breath. "Carlos, I want you to look at your hand. You have your finger hooked around the trigger, and your hand is shaking. I know you don't want it to go off. You don't want to hurt Miss Angie or me. What happened in the house was self-defense. If that gun trips out here, it won't be self-defense. Don't make this situation worse. Please lay the gun down."

Carlos quickly pulled his finger away from the trigger but held the gun in a clubbed hand. "Don't let them put me in jail."

Angie held her arms out toward him. "They won't. You saved your mom's life. Come with us."

He looked down at the gun in his hand and then laid it on the floor of the shed. In a slow, deliberate motion, he pushed himself to his feet and ran into Angie's arms. Once firmly in her embrace, he cried like a little boy.

Nathan moved as though slowed by the special effects of a movie camera. His tense joints creaked as he bent down and stretched his fingers toward the gun. He was inches from touching it when he jerked his hand back. No. If he picked up the gun, he would leave his prints on a murder weapon.

Nathan reached for an oil slick towel that had been draped over the handle of the lawn mower. With his finger around the cloth, he slowly picked up the gun and clicked the trigger lock into place. He set the gun on the wooden floor of the shed and stepped outside.

He leaned against the rough wood of the shed and took deep breaths as Angie walked Carlos to his Jeep. For a fleeting moment, Nathan saw himself, eighteen years old and terrified with the possibility of going to jail. He shook off the memory and walked the path back to the house.

Angie and Carlos sat in the car while Nathan went to the door to get an officer. A crime scene photographer snapped pictures of the carnage. Nathan glanced at his jeans which still held blood stains. Had he done all he could for Carlos' mother? Would she make it? Had he been correct when he told Carlos they wouldn't charge him?

"Officer, we have the woman's son, Carlos, sitting in my car. He was behind the house. We'd like to get him to the hospital to check on his mother. I'm guessing you'll want to talk with him first?"

"Yes, we definitely do. We need his statement."

"But not in the house." Nathan stated firmly.

"Of course not. I'll come out to the car."

Nathan opened the car door and the officer stood beside it. He stooped down to see the teen. "Hello, Carlos. My name's Officer Ackerman. I need to hear what happened here today, and then we'll get you on your way to see your mom. Can you step out of the car so we can talk?"

Carlos nodded and got out, followed by Angie. Her arm rested across his shoulder.

"How old are you, son?"

Carlos looked at the ground. "Fifteen."

"What's your last name, Carlos?"

Angie reached and tipped his chin so he'd look up while he spoke.

"Martinez."

"OK, Carlos. Just take your time and tell me everything you can remember."

"I was in my bedroom when I heard loud noises. I ran out and my dad was there yelling at my mom. He's not allowed to be here."

"There's a history of abuse and a restraining order," Angie interjected.

The officer nodded and turned back to Carlos. "What happened when your dad came?"

"He was drunk and started hitting her. I ran over and tried to get her away. I struggled with him for a minute, but he pushed me across the room. When that was happening, my mom ran to the bedroom. She keeps a gun in the nightstand drawer." Carlos stopped talking when his voice cracked.

"That's OK, son. Take your time."

Carlos swiped at his face catching a tear that started to form. "My mom pointed it, but I think she was afraid to shoot. He charged toward her and knocked it out of her hand. I was still on the floor where he pushed me, and the gun came flying right next to me. I don't think he saw me pick it up."

Carlos looked up at Angie, and she nodded for him to keep going.

"He yelled something about her getting a weapon and then he pulled out a knife. He clicked it and it sprung open. Then he slashed her. She screamed and he kept stabbing. When she fell, he pulled his arm back to stab again, and I knew he'd kill her. That's when I shot the gun."

The police officer pushed his glasses up and rubbed the bridge of his nose. He took a deep breath before proceeding. "Did you think your dad was going to hurt you?"

Carlos shrugged his shoulders. "I guess he would've since he saw me with the gun. He hurt me lots of times, but never with a knife."

"That's all I need for now, son. Do you have any relatives close by?"

"My aunt. Rosa Martin."

"Do you know her phone number?"

He wrote the number that Carlos gave him.

"We'll call her for temporary custody. Go see your mother."

They arrived at the hospital to find Carlos's mom in surgery. His aunt came within the next half hour. They all waited until the doctor came out to see them.

Wearing green scrubs, his mask hung loose around his neck. "You're Carmen Martinez's family?"

"Yes, this is her son, and I'm her sister, Rosa Martin," his aunt answered.

"She's out of surgery and doing well for now. She had internal bleeding which we were able to stop, and she has multiple stitches. The big concern now is infection. We have her on some heavy antibiotics and pain medication. We'll keep her here for a few days and watch that closely.

"She's in ICU," the doctor continued. "I'll let you see her for just a moment, but she's sleeping and will be for a few hours. I suggest you see her, and then go home and rest."

The doctor turned toward Nathan. "Were you the one with her before the EMTs arrived?"

"Yes. Why?"

"They told me she wouldn't have made it if you hadn't intervened. I thought you should know that."

Angie hugged Carlos. "We will leave you now

while you and your aunt see her. I'll be praying for you and your mom."

29

As they walked down the hallway, Angie reached for Nathan's hand. "See, there was a reason for you to be with me. I could never have done what you did."

Walking to the car, Nathan's phone rang. "Excuse me one second." He pushed the button to accept the call.

Angie listened to one side of the conversation. "Hi, Mom. Yes, I'm fine. I'm sorry I didn't get your call. My phone was off. I'm actually leaving the hospital. Someone from the center was injured, and I came along." "No, she's fine. Just a cut that needed stitches."

Angie's face held surprise. "Just a cut that needed stitches?"

Nathan showed a weak smile. "No sense worrying her. Are you hungry? It's after nine o'clock."

Angie hadn't realized how hungry she was until that moment. "Yes, I'm famished."

Nathan slid his arm around her shoulders as they walked to the car.

She slipped into the passenger seat and waited while he walked around to his side. Once inside, he didn't start the car. Instead, he turned toward her.

They sat silently for a moment, facing each other. Nathan reached a hand up and brushed a finger down her cheek, then brushed her hair back, resting his hand behind her neck. "Are you OK?"

The horrendous scene in the house would stay with her forever, but it caused a breakthrough in the wall Nathan had erected. He had kissed her. It was ever so soft, and it was a gesture to comfort her, but still, it had been a kiss. She leaned forward and lifted a hand to his face, touching him as he had touched her a moment ago. He closed the distance and met her lips with his.

When he sat back, he held her hand, brushing his thumb over the soft surface. "I've been trying hard not to allow this to happen." He didn't look at her but fixed his eyes on their joined hands.

Angie's head tilted in question. "Why?"

He didn't readily answer. When he did, he lifted his eyes to hers. "I'm not the right man for you."

Angie tried to make sense of that. "Why?" Was it her heritage? Because of where she lived? Because she wouldn't fit into his world of writers?

He met her eyes. "Because you're …" He seemed to search for a word. "Good. You're good. And I'm not. I have some history—some baggage. You don't really know much about me."

Angie smiled. "That's the beauty of history. It's in the past. I know you, Nathan. I see how you care. It doesn't matter what's behind. It matters what's ahead."

He released her hand. "I wish that were true." The roar of the car's engine brought the conversation to an end.

~*~

Nathan picked up their sandwiches at the counter while Angie found a booth. He slid in to join her. They made small talk, avoiding the obvious conversation. The question hung heavy. Did they have a chance at a relationship? Nathan found his heart and his brain at war with each other, knowing his brain would win. It felt like a knife to his heart. How ironic. He had saved a woman from her knife wounds but couldn't stop his own from bleeding.

Angie dabbed at her mouth. "Carlos probably won't be returning to the center. His Aunt Rosa told me she plans to take them to live with her. She has two children and was frightened to do it when his father was a threat. If his mother agrees, they will move in with them."

Nathan finished his sandwich and pushed his plate to the side. "I hope he doesn't have to go back to the house for anything, even after they clean it up. It would be way too traumatic."

When they finished their sandwiches, they stood and walked toward the door. Angie reached for Nathan's hand, turning her eyes toward him. Coffee brown with fringed lashes, flecked with light. The eyes that he froze on his TV screen. Could he really walk away from her?

"Is your car still at the center? Shall I take you there or home?" he asked.

"Yes, it's there, but I'm weary. Would you just take me home? I'll ride in with Elizabeth in the morning."

Nathan turned onto her street and parked in front of her house. "Is Elizabeth home?"

"No." Angie raised her eyebrows with a slight smile. "She's with her friend."

Nathan opened his car door. She stopped him. "I'm fine, Nathan."

He ignored her and walked around to open her car door. Angie walked beside him, fishing her keys out of her pocket. When they reached the door, he took the key from her and unlocked the front door.

They entered in the darkness until Angie reached the light. "I never expected to be this late or I'd have left lights on."

Nathan glanced up toward the porch. "You should have motion-detector lights here. OK if I check your house out? Your dad would want me to."

"Yes, worrywart." But pleasure glowed from her eyes. "Shall I make us some tea?"

He should check the house and leave. There was no good that could come from spending any more time with her. After a prolonged pause, he nodded. "Sure." As Nathan did a quick walk-through, another irony hit him like a boulder. He was walking through Ramón Garcia's home. This is where he'd lived, laughed, loved his wife, raised his daughter. And now, ten years later, the man who killed him walked through his home. Nathan returned to the kitchen.

"No monsters under the beds?" Angie teased as she reached the mugs.

"Nope. All clear." *Only me.*

They carried their mugs to the living room. He should have chosen the chair, but Angie sat on the sofa and looked up at him with those doe eyes. None of this was her fault. They had started something, and he owed her more than a brush off. He sat beside her and placed the steaming mug on a coaster before moving an arm behind her.

"Angie, it was wrong for me to kiss you. Wrong to

care for you as much as I do. There's no possibility of a future for us. I know you don't understand the reasons, but please trust me on this."

"Why don't you just tell me the reasons? How can I trust you when I don't know? You said it's something in your past, but I don't care about your past. I care about the man sitting here with me today."

"You can say that because you don't know everything about me. If you did, you'd probably hate me."

She raised her hand and laid a curved palm against his cheek. "I could never hate you, mi amor."

Mi amor, *my love.* It was Nathan's undoing. He pulled her close and held her as he had done at the crime scene. Only now, she was the strong one, and he needed a place of respite. Her hands went around his neck, buried in his hair as she cradled his head against her. Her lips touched his cheek, and he turned to meet them. The kiss deepened, leaving him breathless.

"Oh, Angie," he whispered against her.

She stepped back and tilted her head so she could see his face. Her eyes twinkled. "Nathan, here's the wonderful thing. You have a mysterious secret in your past, but that is past. You say we cannot have a future together, but the future's not here. Today is not the past or the future. It's the present, so it's our time together."

Her words brought a curve to the sides of his mouth. "Yes, it is. But what does that make tomorrow? Isn't that the future?"

"Yes, but here's the beauty. When it arrives, it will then be the present."

He suppressed a chuckle. "And next week?"

"It's also the future that will soon become the

present."

He allowed the smile to grow. "Angie, Angie. Always the optimist. Are you ever a skeptic?"

"Not if I can help it. What good does it do? We can choose sorrow or joy. I choose joy."

He leaned in and kissed her again.

She held her face inches from his. "Nathan, do I make you happy?"

He rested his forehead against hers. Had he ever really been happy before Angie? He'd had accomplishments that pleased him. He had enjoyment playing basketball. But those were temporary— superficial feelings that didn't touch the heart. Angie awakened something deeper that had been missing. "More than anyone ever has."

"Then choose joy, mi amor. Choose joy."

Could he do that? Could he choose Angie? How could he walk away from her now? He had lived with ten years of guilt, with panic attacks that had paralyzed him. He lived with nightmares of cell doors clanging closed, locking him in. The hidden jar of ashes was never far from his writing desk.

Maybe it was time to let it all go. Sam had done it. He had done exactly what he said. They were never there. They took a different route home, never passing the accident site. It wasn't them. He'd convince himself of an alternate truth. He'd move forward, and he would choose this angel of grace.

With his arms wound around Angie, he mouthed a silent prayer asking God to free him of his guilt.

30

Guilt was a thief that had robbed Aiden of too much already. He wouldn't allow it to steal Maggie from him. She was worth the battle, and he would fight for her. Life without her was unthinkable.

Yet it would be easier to do battle with a visible enemy. This adversary resided inside of him. He knew him well, had been acquainted too long, and recognized him to be a fierce opponent. Aiden retrieved Maggie's picture, keeping it in his sight. He would need the reminder to be fully equipped for the fight. He intended to win, to defeat the adversary named Guilt.

~*~

Nathan walked into The Herald Center Friday for his last session with Del. He'd still see him when he needed help. He'd attend some games and see him playing ball. He told Angie and Jonas that he'd take a reprieve from volunteering to catch up with his writing responsibilities and would probably return to the center in the spring. All thoughts of Atlanta were shelved. He and Angie were moving forward. The future remained uncertain. She was looking for prospects to join an orchestra. It might be good for them if an opportunity took them to another city. They could start fresh and new, building their own memories. He was looking far into the future—a future that she had to be part of. A new city would remove the constant reminders of the past and her connection to it. Warmth radiated through him, and he couldn't suppress a smile.

Del was like a kid on the last day of school. He had mentally checked out. Nathan didn't push it. The last history quiz sported a big, red A. They worked a little, but spent time talking sports. Angie peeked her head in the window of their door. Del saw her and motioned her in. She carried a brown, paper gift bag with tissue spilling over the top and handed it to Del.

He, in turn, handed it to Nathan. "Miss Angie helped me wrap it. It's just to say thanks." A card with Nathan's name scrawled in Del's messy handwriting peeked up from the tissue.

"Thank you, but this wasn't necessary. I've enjoyed the chance to beat you at the hoop."

Del laughed. "Yeah, you beat me like once in the last four months."

Nathan opened the envelope and slid the card out. Again, Del's scribble met him. He had become adept at deciphering it.

"I always thought I was stupid. Thank you for helping me learn the truth. You better come to see me play. Del"

Nathan pulled the tissue from the bag. He peeked in to see a man-sized coffee mug. He lifted it out with a smile. "You know I love my coffee." Turning the mug to face him, Nathan read the scripture printed in bold script. "You will know the truth, and the truth will set you free." John 8:32.

"I was telling Miss Angie how it helped me to learn the truth about how my brain works. She helped me pick it."

"Thank you, Del." Nathan wasn't sure if a hug would be acceptable. He held his arm out and Del met it, going through the steps of their handshake.

Del picked up his backpack and turned his tall form toward the door. "First game's in three weeks."

"I'll be there."

~*~

Nathan set the menu aside, knowing what he planned to order.

Angie sipped the ice water that the waiter had just refilled. "Mother asked me to invite you to brunch tomorrow. We have a special guest coming. It seems that Elizabeth's friendship might be a little more than casual."

"I'm not surprised. You can see the change in her."

"So will you come?"

He lifted his brows. "Of course I'll come. I've tasted your mother's cooking."

She fixed a mock pout on her face. "Oh, so is that the only reason?"

He stroked his chin as if thinking through the question. "Well, I might be enticed by the company. There will be three lovely ladies there."

She tugged her hair forward. "And you'll only have eyes for one. Right?"

He reached across the table and laced his fingers with hers. "Always."

Angie had been anxious to tell him about her search. While they waited for their food to arrive, she shared what she had found. "There are many small orchestras right in this area. Greenville, Spartanburg, Fountain Inn, Newberry, just to name a few. I've prepared inquiries but haven't sent anything yet. I'd like to visit each when they have a performance."

"No Carnegie Hall?"

Angie laughed softly. "I think I'll stick with something attainable."

"Yet, you should reach high. Remember your dream—Carnegie Hall and Musikverein."

A melancholy look crossed Angie's face. "I remember Uncle Ramón telling me, 'You eat an elephant one bite at a time.' I was fumbling through my first Bach minuet, and he said to take it step by step."

Nathan nodded and glanced away.

She touched his hand. "Thank you for the vote of confidence. I think a small venue will be my first step."

~*~

Nathan stepped onto the porch at the Hernandez's home and pressed the doorbell. Angie met him at the door, sneaking a peck on his cheek before opening it fully.

Alex bounded over, his hand extended. "Nathan. Come in. Come in." A blend of inviting aromas wafted into the living room. He detected a hint of garlic and basil. "Come and meet our new guest." Alex led him into the dining room. "This is Adam. Elizabeth's friend."

Adam stood and grasped the hand that Nathan offered.

"Nathan Drummond."

"Nice to meet you. I hear you're an author?" Adam said.

"Nathan, sit. Sit." Alex pulled a chair out for him. Angie moved into the kitchen where her mother and cousin prepared brunch.

He sat. "Yes, I make up stories for a living."

"I'll have to pick one up. I don't get too much recreational reading. I usually have enough real drama in life."

"What do you do that brings real-life drama?"

"Adam's with the Greenville County Police. Keeping our city safe." Alex answered for him, speaking with a voice of pride, like he hadn't just met the man.

"I don't actually get to work the streets. I'm an Internal Affairs Ethics Counselor. That's how I met Elizabeth. I was guest speaker in her ethics class."

Alex shook his head. "Too little integrity in the world today. We need your accountability."

A full debate ensued about rogue officers and the fading respect for law enforcement. Adam scanned back and forth from Nathan to Alex. "Ninety-five percent of our force work hard and honestly. You don't hear nearly enough about them on the news. As soon as one crosses the line, it's splashed on every station and Internet site. We have them vetted as thoroughly as possible before hiring, but not everything shows up."

Adam grinned. "Come see me if you get stuck on a new story idea. I can give you plenty. I imagine you've done some fiction based on real-life scenarios."

"There's nothing new under the sun. Everything writers write has been tried somewhere. Unless, of course, it's a work of fantasy."

The ladies walked into the room, each carrying large plates of food. Adrianna was first to set her plate down. "Antipasti salad. I'm sorry if you were expecting Puerto Rican. Today is Italian."

Angie followed with a tureen of Minestrone soup, and Elizabeth walked behind her with a basket of crusty rolls. She set it down and proceeded to create an olive oil dip for each side of the table, adding sprinkles of garlic, cheese and spices. "We start with soup and salad. Mother has an amazing casserole in the oven—chicken carbonara."

They sat and Alex reached his hands to each side. Adrianna and Angie took the offered hand. Elizabeth and Angie followed suit, reaching their hands to form a circle. Alex asked a blessing on the food. "He exhaled a contented sigh. "A full table. Thanks be to God. It's been a long time since this table has been full."

Nathan focused on the napkin in his lap, his mind seeing a full table with two sets of parents and two teenage girls, talking, laughing, and eating together.

Adam seemed like a nice enough guy, and he clearly made Elizabeth happy. Yet Nathan remained quiet. He still had some hurdles to cross, and today brought too many reminders. He ate, talked, and lingered after brunch for what was an acceptable time before making his departure.

An ethics counselor with the criminal justice system. Nathan reminded himself—*I wasn't there. I came home a different route. I never passed by that intersection.* And Adam wouldn't have been there ten years ago.

31

The air had turned cold, and Nathan reached for a jacket in the back of his closet. It had been a few weeks since he last saw Del. They'd played under the same hoop many days at the center, but today Nathan would see him in a real competition.

Angie waited at the door and ran out when Nathan pulled to the curb. He stepped out and held the car door for her. Then he walked around and climbed in the driver's seat. Before starting the car, he opened his phone to a photo. "I became an uncle last night. Benjamin James Garner. Weighing in at seven pounds two ounces."

Angie lifted the phone to see the newborn. "Oh, that's wonderful. Are they doing well?"

"Yep. No complications. No surprises. Well, one surprise, but it's a good one. We just found out my brother-in-law will finish his residency at Duke. They'll be moving back to the east coast in three or four months."

"Oh, I'll bet your mother is thrilled. Is she cleared to travel?"

"Yes. Actually, a change in plans. She was fretting about Christmas. Didn't want to leave me, but once she goes to Leah's, she wants to stay for a while. So I'm going to travel with her two days before Christmas.

She'll stay, and I'll come home on the twenty-seventh.

"That's wonderful. Your whole family will be together."

"It's the first Christmas without my dad. It will be good to be in a new place."

Angie reached for his hand and gave it an understanding squeeze. "I remember the first Christmas without my uncle. It had been almost a year, but we felt the loss deeply at Christmas. Oh, and that reminds me. My parents would like to invite you to their home for New Year's Eve. We have a family tradition."

He smiled, glad for the abrupt change of topics. "If it's anything like Sunday brunch, I'm in."

Angie shook her head. "Men. It's always about the food. Well, it's not like Sunday brunch, but you won't be disappointed. We fix many appetizers. Some recipes that we brought from Puerto Rico will be new to you."

He started the car and pulled onto the road, heading in the direction of Del's school. After parking, Nathan pulled ten dollars from his wallet and paid for their tickets, and they held out their hands to have them stamped with ink, proof that they'd paid to get inside for the game. They wore the school colors, blue and gold, and sat on the home-side bleachers. It was the same location he had visited to see Del's teacher, but the gymnasium looked to be in better condition than the school.

Nathan's eyes roamed the crowd, glad that he didn't see Marcus. He trusted the promise that he'd come someday. Best not to be the season opener. The team entered the gym and the crowd cheered. Angie said something, but he couldn't hear a word. Nathan had forgotten the cheering enthusiasm of high schoolers.

Angie waved hands over her head. Del, the tallest player on the court, caught sight of them and nodded with a slight grin.

"Do you think his mother's here?"

Angie shrugged her shoulders. "It's doubtful that she can take off work for the games."

The buzzer sounded, and the thud of the basketball started the game. Del dominated the court. No one on either team matched his ability. He shot, rebounded, and passed, but it always came back to him. His teammates knew how to win a game—pass to Del Jefferson.

During intermission, they walked outside to get some fresh air, the inked stamp on their hands showing their paid admission.

"I didn't play a sport because violin took so much of my time, but Elizabeth played volleyball. We would come to every game. Uncle Ramón would holler like a cheerleader. I think it embarrassed Aunt Elena because she would often put her hand on his arm and whisper something. He'd quiet down for a few minutes until he couldn't stand it. Then he'd start cheering again."

A chill went through Nathan, despite the heavy jacket. "It's getting cold. Maybe we should head back inside."

The second half didn't change. The lopsided score could be attributed to Del alone. When the final whistle blew, Nathan and Angie hung around to see him. He came out of the locker room with a cluster of boys but hurried over to where they stood. Nathan slapped his back. "Great game, Del."

Angie shook her head in disbelief. "You were so amazing."

"Do you think Marcus was here?"

"Nope. Not for the opener. Keep playing like that. He'll be here someday. You got a ride home?"

"No, I'm walking."

"Come on. We'll give you a ride."

~*~

Nathan completed the manuscript. He sat at his computer, poised to hit *send*. He stared at the screen of his e-mail, complete with the attached file and addresses for Anya and Brian. His novel ended differently than the real story would end. The real story would end with a welcome release of guilt. An act of will. An alternate truth that he had convinced himself. The novel needed something much more dramatic. Nathan knew this story by heart, but he separated fact and fiction for the sake of a story. His fictional ending would offer the surprise his readers were accustomed to. Authors merged fact and fiction.

He hadn't come up with a title until last night, sometime around 4:00 AM. He had tossed and turned, his mind entertaining dozens of options. He discarded each one until a bolt of inspiration hit him. The fictional ending made this title perfect. This morning, he typed it into the manuscript, whispering a thank you to Del. *Set Free*. He exhaled a long puff of air and hit *send*. It was done.

Nathan lifted his new mug, now filled with tepid coffee that had sat silently with him for the last half hour of indecision. He read the familiar scripture, remembering his prayer. The truth? The truth wouldn't work for him. Instead, he needed his contrived truth, the one he would work to convince himself was real. *I wasn't there. I took a different route home. I was never near the accident site.*

The truth from ten years ago wouldn't set him free. It would lock him up.

~*~

Nathan spent some time with Angie each day, sometimes just lunch, sometimes a movie or dinner. Amazing how different his life was with her in it.

It had been two weeks since sending the manuscript. He headed home after meeting her for lunch when Anya's name appeared on his ringing phone. A wave of anxiety shot through him. What would she have to say about this total stray from the normal? He hit his Bluetooth and looked for a place to pull over. This would need his full attention.

"Hi, Anya."

"Nathan!' She drew his name out in a breathy tone.

"Hello. Hold on for just a second." He turned the car into a convenience store parking lot, slid it into a diagonal space, and cracked the window an inch before cutting the engine. "Sorry, I was in traffic."

"I always suspected there was a latent romantic inside. This is incredible. I never expected a romance."

The last thing he wanted was to be coined as a romance writer. "I wouldn't categorize it in that genre. There's more to the story than romance."

"You can fool yourself, but this is a romance. I talked to Brian this morning. Their ready to go with it. We'll send the contract and he'll get started on a publicity campaign. We need to hype this. It should bring in a whole new audience."

"We need to talk about that. I'd like to keep my two styles separate. I'm thinking of using a pseudonym for this one, and any others that I may write in this style."

He was met with dead silence.

"Anya, did I lose you?"

"I'm here. Why in the world would you want to do that?"

"Lots of writers publish under two different names."

"This book is amazing. Use a penname, and it's marketed like a new, unknown author. You'll start over, building a reader base."

"I'm all right with that."

"Maybe you are. I doubt if McAllen Publishing will be."

Or you. Nathan realized his income affected her income. "Try it, Anya. It's important to me."

"I can take this to McAllen, but don't hold your breath."

They ended the call, and Nathan drove home considering the ramifications of using a pseudonym. It had the obvious drawbacks, but how could he publish this story under his own name?

Nathan went home and began a search for an old college friend that he hadn't seen in ten years. Ryan majored in music and was quite a cellist. Nathan heard that he was first chair for an orchestra but never knew where. He needed to look no further than Facebook. Boston Symphony Orchestra. Nathan hit 'message.'

"Ryan, this is Nathan Drummond from Emory. Hope you're doing well. I see you play with Boston

Symphony. I have recently met a violinist who is quite talented and is looking to use that gift professionally. I wondered if you might have some sway to get her an audition. She truly is an amazing musician."

Now he awaited word back from Ryan and Anya.

~*~

A carry-on was enough for Nathan, but his mother planned an extended stay. Nathan wheeled in her two stacked suitcases and took them to the baggage check in. Once done, they made their way to their gate. The small airport was easy to navigate. Their connecting flight in Atlanta would be a different story.

His mother squeezed his arm as the plane took off. She never liked flying. Once they reached their altitude, she relaxed a little. "So when do I get to meet this young lady you've been seeing?"

Nathan suppressed a grin. "Who said I've been seeing a young lady?"

"You don't have to say it. I can see it written all over you. So are you going to tell me about her?"

"Just a few dates, Mom. I'll bring her around when the time is right."

His mother persisted. "Where'd you meet her? What's her name?"

"Her name's Angie and we met at The Herald Center." Nathan remembered last night, watching her opening the gold bracelet wrapped in Christmas paper, her eyes filled with light. Along with it, he wrapped a mug filled with herbal tea bags. It had a picture of a violin along with the slogan, "When words fail, music speaks."

Angie had given him tickets to Phillips Arena for a Hawks game, and a CD of classical violin music. He'd once told her he wanted to become more familiar with the pieces she played.

He hadn't been truthful with his mom when he said, "Just a few dates." He spent every Sunday with her parents. His mom deserved as much. "When you return from California, I'll bring her over." He opened his book to the page his magnetic bookmark held. He had to keep up with other mystery writers. The time had come to begin writing another.

~*~

His visit with Leah had been brief. With Christmas over and his mother gone, Nathan needed to brainstorm his next project. To any outside observer, it would look like he was doing absolutely nothing for hours. Sitting, pacing, sitting, Internet searching, and more pacing. It's how he always began. He had a new resource in the criminal justice system. If he had legal or crime scene questions, he'd call Adam. But first, he'd start with coffee. He picked up his oversized mug. *You will know the truth, and the truth will set you free.*

~*~

Elizabeth stopped in the office at The Herald Center late in the afternoon, hoping to catch her cousin before she left for the day.

"Hi, Liz. No class today?"

"I'm on my way there now, but wanted to talk

first." She sat across the table from her cousin. "I've been dragging my feet on a decision, but I know you're right. It's time to move on. Mom and Dad wouldn't want me holding on to that old house. I think I'm finally ready to let it go."

Angie didn't jump for joy or allow her enthusiasm to burst. This was hard for Elizabeth, and she had to give solemn respect to the decision. "I'm glad you have come to peace with it. I would never want to hurry you into a decision."

"I have, Ang. It's time. Thank you for being so patient with me."

"So, what are you thinking? Papi reminds me that we could have free rent with them, or we could look for an apartment? Oh, wait! I'm being presumptuous. Maybe you wanted to have your own place. Without me."

Elizabeth laughed. "No, Ang. I have no desire to live alone. I love your parents, but I think it would be hard to live with them. They still think of us as little girls."

"You're so right. Shall we start looking at apartments?"

"Yes. We'll have to move out before listing the house. I have some heavy duty cleaning out to do first. I think Adam will help."

"Maybe we can get Adam and Nathan to do some of the heavier work." Angie pictured a foursome, working together, laughing together, and double-dating. Joy bubbled up inside.

When Elizabeth left, and she had a free minute, she dialed Nathan's phone.

"Hello, Angelina Grace."

He had begun saying her full name when he was

happy or playful. Just like her dad. It was always *Angie* when he was serious. He must be in a good mood. He sometimes became too solemn. She couldn't seem to pinpoint what triggered his mood changes.

"Nathan, I called with good news. Elizabeth has decided to sell the house. She's ready to move on."

"That's really good to hear. I worry about you living there."

"Well, worry no more. We're starting an apartment search right away. We'll need to move out to get the house ready for the realtor."

There was a long pause before Nathan answered. "I thought you'd want to live back with your folks."

"No, we've both become too independent for that. We'd rather get an apartment."

"But that means a lease. What if you get a job with an orchestra?"

"It will be fine. I'm only looking around here."

"Unless something opens up that's a great opportunity. Isn't that what you said?"

"Yes, but since I'm only looking here, it's most unlikely that the conductor from the New York Philharmonic will decide to telephone me." She laughed to keep the conversation light. Nathan had grown serious once again. "And if he does call, I'll just tell him that if he wants me for his violinist, he'll have to pay off my lease."

~*~

Angie joined her mother and Elizabeth on December thirtieth. They would prepare the *pasteles* today. The meat pastries always took the most time.

Adrianna had already prepared the blended mixture of bananas, Malanga, plantains, milk, and oil. It was best to refrigerate this mixture overnight. They began the process of rolling the masa, seasoning the filling, wrapping, and freezing. Tomorrow they would cook them right before serving.

They set out ingredients for the *coquito* and *tembleque*. These would be made fresh tomorrow. Nathan and Adam had eaten everything Adrianna made so far, but Angie wondered what they would think of the unique spices in the pasteles and sweet coconut milk pudding.

The real surprise would be the *parranda*. Her family maintained a smaller version of this musical tradition. They couldn't take it to the streets as the Puerto Ricans do, joined by neighbors and growing a larger crowd as they played. They had satisfied themselves with a family musical evening. Angie lifted the box of instruments from a storage closet, and they began sorting *palitos, maracas, and panderetas*. Elizabeth pulled out the *Guiro*. The hollowed-out gourd had notches cut on one side. The metal stick used to rub it resembled a paint brush but with metal bristles. It created a ratchet-like sound.

Everything had been cleaned and laid out for tomorrow. Angie fidgeted as she paced the room, examining the familiar scene. This was her heritage. What would Nathan think? Would he think their traditions foolish? Would New Year's Eve draw them closer together, or would it show the vast differences in their worlds?

32

Nathan and Adam arrived at the same time. The scent of cinnamon and cloves met them at the front door.

"Come in. Come in." Alex held the door wide.

Nathan peered at the dining room table, heavy laden with food. He glanced around the room, relieved that he saw no party hats or noisemakers. Then he spotted a corner with an array of instruments, including Angie's violin case and a brass trumpet. For the first hour, they mingled and talked while snacking on a wide variety of foods—a blend of traditional American and Puerto Rican.

Alex gathered everyone, ushering them to the living room. "Time for the parranda. Time for music. Elizabeth. Angie. Come. You get to usher this New Year in for us."

Elizabeth moved to the piano and Angie opened her violin. They sat back and listened as the cousins played a beautiful duet of "O Holy Night." Nathan sipped his water while the others drank wine that Alex had poured. "Wine for now. We save the coquito for after music."

When the duet had finished, Alex picked up the trumpet and set up a music stand. The ladies began passing out instruments, starting with Adrianna. She picked up the maracas. That left sticks, tambourines, and something that looked like a gourd. Nathan motioned for Adam to take first pick. It didn't matter to him since he knew nothing about playing any of them. Adam picked up a tambourine. Elizabeth handed him the other two. "Panderetas. It's a set." Nathan reached for the sticks. As he picked them up, turning them to examine, Elizabeth reached and placed them in his hand the way they should be held. "Palitos."

He and Adam exchanged a look before turning toward each other. Adam traded one tambourine for one of Nathan's sticks, and they engaged in a duel. The sticks became swords and the tambourines served as the shield. They had everyone laughing. The sound of the trumpet ended their silliness. They traded back and waited to see what would happen next.

The family began playing cheerful music. Adam and Nathan exchanged a glance, amused and confused. Elizabeth again took charge. "Percussion, come in on the beat. Just play as you like, keeping a strong beat for us."

They continued for the next thirty minutes. When they finished, Alex and Adrianna went to the kitchen. A few minutes later, they came in carrying a tray. The clear glasses were filled with a white, foamy drink. Adrianna carried the tray to each person. "*Coquitos*," she informed Adam and Nathan.

Nathan held his, but Adam took a sip. "Whew. I can't drink this. I'm driving."

Nathan turned toward Angie, whispering his question. "What's in it?"

"She served it *bautisao*—with rum." She turned toward her mother. "I left some without rum, like you used to do when I was younger. It's quite strong, and they are driving."

"Get them a glass of the other." Alex took over.

Angie moved to the kitchen, and he turned back to the men. "But just take a sip or two. It's a traditional Puerto Rican holiday drink."

A glance at the clock showed eleven fifteen. The glasses had been exchanged and they were seated around the living room, paired into three couples. Angie joined Nathan on the sofa, Elizabeth and Adam sat on a loveseat, and Alex pulled a chair up beside where Adrianna sat.

Elizabeth explained what they typically did now. "New Year's Eve is the anniversary of my father's death. It's been eleven years now. That first New Year's Eve, we decided that, instead of grieving, we would use this date to celebrate his life. I've since lost my mom, and I know that you have all had losses as well. Adam lost his sister to Leukemia and Nathan's father had a heart attack very recently. So we'll go around and share memories of the people whose lives we celebrate today."

Angie hooked her arm through Nathan's at the mention of his father. A chill ran through him and he stole a look at the clock. How long would this last?

"Who would like to start?"

Adrianna spoke first. "I would. I remember when Elena and I were young girls. We shared a bedroom in a very tight space. We were getting ready for church. She had gotten a new scarf for her birthday and knew that I was craving one like it. She tied it around her neck, but took one look at me and removed it. She came over and slid the loop around my neck instead. She said it would look so much better with the color of my blouse."

Elizabeth smiled. "That's Mama. Always thinking of others first." She looked around the circle. "Who's next?"

Angie spoke up. "When I was a young girl, Uncle Ramón always called me Angel, instead of Angie. One day I was practicing my violin. He came in the room and just sat, watching me, like it was the best treat he could have. He said, 'Angel, your music is like an artist adding color to an empty canvas.'"

Alex nodded. "He certainly got that one right. I think the most memorable thing I saw Ramón do was with Jonas. Jonas had just gotten paroled from Edgefield. He needed a job, and no one wanted to hire a convict. Ramón hired him, but he also spent time every day, one on one, teaching him the gospel and helping him to recognize his potential. You could see the changes in that man from day to day."

Elizabeth looked from Adam to Nathan. "Would you share a memory about your sister or father?"

"I will," Adam said. "They diagnosed my sister with leukemia when she was fifteen. I watched her go through horrendous treatments. Bone marrow transplants and chemo. We received one bad report after another. While we all cried in discouragement, Chrissy tried to cheer us up. For as long as she was able, she went from room to room in the hospital visiting other patients, trying to lift their spirits. When she died, there wasn't a dry eye at that nurse's station."

Nathan squirmed in his seat, not sure what he should share. He had an irrational sense of competition. Ramón Garcia wasn't the only father with character. "My dad ..." He cleared his throat and started again. "My dad loved his family. He loved people. We'd always be the last ones out of church on

Sundays because he lingered and talked to everyone. And he listened. He'd sit on the side of my bed at night, asking me about school or basketball. I think he just wanted to hear me talk." So maybe he didn't start an inner-city outreach or visit prisons. This is what Nathan remembered—a dad who loved him.

Angie squeezed his hand. "It sounds like your father was a very good man."

Nathan looked up at the clock that said it was eleven fifty five. Five more minutes until the calendar turned to a new year. Alex stood and turned on the TV, then went back to the kitchen. When he returned, he carried a tray with six small bowls. Each one contained grapes.

As he passed them around, Adam reached for one in his bowl. Elizabeth caught his hand. "Not yet."

"We eat one grape with each countdown of the last twelve seconds of the old year. Those who finish before midnight will have a year of prosperity."

Nathan glanced in his bowl, thankful that the grapes were small, and shot a curious look toward Angie.

"A tradition for fun. We don't hold to the superstition."

As the clock ticked down to the last minute, they watched the timer. Nathan stood when he saw everyone else rising to their feet. A small circle formed in the center of the room. When it reached the number twelve, they began popping the grapes, one at a time. All six of them managed to swallow the last grape before the strike of midnight. Then Angie's arms went around Nathan waiting for the kiss. After everyone finished kissing and hugging, Alex shooed them back to their seats.

"As it is common for your culture to read *The Night Before Christmas* on Christmas Eve, it is traditional for Puerto Ricans to read *El Brindis del Bohemio* on New Year's Eve. I've translated to English if you wish to follow along. This year, Angelina Grace will have the honor."

Adam and Nathan took the English script. Nathan glanced at the words to the poem, but stopped as Angie began reading. Poetry lost much in a translation, and the reading held its own beauty, even if he didn't understand the meaning.

Angie and Elizabeth were spending the night there so they could help with the cleanup. Adam and Nathan began carrying dishes to the kitchen, but Adrianna stopped them. "It is late. Most of this can wait until morning."

Angie walked out to the front porch with Nathan. "I hope you enjoyed seeing some of our customs. They may have seemed peculiar, but it's important to my parents that we hold onto a little of their heritage."

"I'm glad I could be here. It helps me to know your parents background. Traditions are good."

As he got into his car and began the short drive home, it struck Nathan that his family had no real traditions that they protected. Traditions were a glue that held families together—something so special that no one wanted to miss it. When he had a family, they would build their own traditions.

33

Nathan made another installment to Ellison Tools and Equipment and Fidelity Tools. The debt was whittling down nicely. He logged on and checked his e-mail. Nothing from his publisher or agent. He moved the curser pad and checked his Facebook. The message icon was lit with a number one. He moved his curser over the icon and saw a message from Ryan. It had been weeks since Nathan contacted him, and he had given up hope of a response.

"Nathan. Good to hear from you. Sorry I took so long to reply. I don't frequent my Facebook account often. Yes, I'm in Boston. It just so happens that auditions for violinists are coming up. Have her send in a resume. Send me her name, and I can at least put in a word for getting an audition. But I can assure you, it's very competitive, and I'll have no influence at that point. She'll have to be good."

Nathan sent a word of thanks and Angie's full name. He'd see her tomorrow. Best to tell her in person. He closed up his computer and bounded down the stairs to fix himself dinner. He enjoyed having the house to himself—eating when he pleased, what he pleased, coming and going without feeling like he had to tell anyone. That's what Angie wanted for herself, but a lease would tie her here. He harbored thoughts that they might move together, somewhere new, just for them. They'd both need their own place for a while. It was far too early to talk marriage, yet he was certain they were on that path. He couldn't imagine being without her.

He pulled a skillet from the cupboard when the phone rang. Anya.

"Hi again."

"It's not going to fly, Nate. They said absolutely not. A few reasons…"

He interrupted abruptly. "I know the reasons, and they're all about money."

"Nathan, this business is about money. You know that. Hear me out. Aside from the fact that Joe Schmoe, who allegedly wrote this, has no following, you know what it took to build your platform. Social media, speaking engagements, book signings. You agreed to all of that when no one knew Nathan Drummond. Are you going to agree to the same thing as Joe Schmoe? Do you think for a skinny minute that people won't recognize you?"

"I think I'd pick a better name." But Nathan realized all that she said was true.

"It's not happening, Nate. I'm sending the contract made out to Nathan Drummond, to be published as Nathan Drummond. You can sign it or not. Your decision."

Nathan hung up, his appetite gone. He opened the cupboard and slid the unused skillet back in. Maybe another publisher? But what would that change? They'd want the same things. And the cost of living in Boston was pretty high.

~*~

This would be the first time Angie had been to his home. Nathan finished setting the table with his mother's best linens, china, and water goblets. A warm vanilla scent flowed from the two candles in the center. He never claimed to be much of a cook, so he ordered a prepared meal of smoked salmon, twice-baked potatoes, and grilled vegetables.

He kept an eye on the front window and saw the car before Angie exited. Nathan opened the door and stood smiling as she got out. "I watched to make sure you went to the right house."

"You gave very good directions. I've been in this neighborhood once before, but it's been years. My parents had a friend who lived a few streets away."

He closed the door and reached to help her remove her coat. Angie breathed deeply, a look of pleasure on her face. "Something smells good."

"Well it should. I've been cooking all day."

One look at his face, and she broke into a grin. "I think you're teasing me again."

"Guilty. But I did order it and pick it up."

Nathan was anxious to tell her about the opportunity in Boston, but would wait and talk over dinner. "Everything's ready. Come and sit down." He held the chair out for her, pushing it forward as she sat down. He placed a kiss on her forehead then stepped into the kitchen for the platter.

She opened her napkin and laid it neatly on her lap. "I'm feeling pampered tonight. I'm not used to anyone waiting on me."

Nathan sat and took her hand before praying, as her family was accustomed to. He rather liked the tradition. They filled their plates and began eating.

"Angie, I've got something important to tell you."

She looked up at him with a guarded expression. "Important? What is it?"

"I contacted a friend from college. He plays cello for an orchestra. He said they'll be auditioning violinists. If you send your resume, and he mentions your name, he's confident they'll grant you an audition."

Angie held her hands against her heart, , knocking her napkin from her lap. "Nathan, that's so wonderful. I can't believe I'll actually get an audition. Which orchestra?" She stood to retrieve her napkin.

"Sit down, my dear. I'll tell you what I know."

She found the errant napkin and sat back down. "Where?"

"Boston." He gave her his most persuading smile but watched hers fade.

"Boston? Are you teasing me?"

"No, Boston Symphony Orchestra. That's a good one, isn't it?"

"Nathan, it's one of the big five. Why would you ever contact them? I can't play for a big five orchestra, and I don't want to move to Boston."

He set his fork down. "Why can't you play for them, and what's a big five?"

"There are five orchestras that have the highest ranking in the US. New York, Philadelphia, Chicago, Cleveland, and Boston. Those are the elitist positions. I'm not prepared for those. And Boston? Nathan, you're here. My family's here. I can't leave."

His eyes never left hers. "Angie, sweetheart, you have to go where the jobs are. I can write from anywhere. If you go to Boston, I go to Boston."

"Nathan." She paused and leaned forward. "You

told me you played basketball in college. Why didn't you play professionally?"

"That's not the same thing."

"Yes, it is. I'm not prepared. I know that. I would embarrass myself at that audition. I'm confident that I can handle the level of a small-town orchestra, but not that. Truly, mi amor. You must trust me on this."

Nathan put his elbow on the table and rubbed his forehead. He picked up his fork and used it to slice a piece of salmon. "Okay." The rest of the meal was cloaked in silence.

Angie helped carry the dishes into the kitchen. They did a quick clean up and put the leftovers away. She walked to him and wrapped her arms around his neck. "Thank you for trying to help me. I'm sorry you're disappointed. But I'm so thankful for you."

"It's a beautiful town. Very historic." He raised one eyebrow.

"I'm sure it is. And buried in snow during the winter."

His arms went loosely around her. "I thought you liked snow."

"I like Greenville snow. Flurries in the morning and gone by noon."

"Greenville has wimpy snowmen."

"You really would have gone with me?"

"How could I not." He kissed her. When the kiss ended, he said what he had been wanting to tell her. "I love you, Angie."

She tilted her head as she gazed into his eyes. "And I love you, sweet Nathan." She rested her head against him. "I'm so happy."

"When aren't you happy?"

"I try to stay happy. I don't always succeed."

He held her close. "I have this idea that it would be wonderful to start fresh somewhere. Just you and me. Build our new life in a new place."

She leaned back to look up at him. "I don't know if I could leave here. And my family loves you. Don't you enjoy being with them?"

"I do, Ang. They're great. That's what airplanes are for."

"So we'd see them once or twice a year? And besides, we're not married. I can't do that."

"I didn't mean it that way. I'd get my own place. Besides, that's a temporary condition. One day we'll be ready to talk about that."

"Nathan, my love, let's enjoy this time. All things will work out in God's timing. My Uncle Ramón always told me, 'Let God carve the path.'"

Nathan released her and took a step back, frowning. "Uncle Ramón. Sounds like he had a quote for every occasion." He turned and walked toward the living room. "Let's go pick a movie."

~*~

Nathan printed the contract and read it over. It was no different from the eight others he had signed, yet he read it and re-read it. He had painted himself into a corner. He couldn't sign this contract. All of Angie's family would read the novel. Yet he couldn't not sign it unless he planned to get another job. For now, he set it on his desk and ignored it. Let God carve the path. Words of wisdom from Uncle Ramón.

He had spent a day pacing and thinking, so now it was time to choose a plot and begin writing. Might as well take Adam up on his offer. A few scenarios were on his mind, but he needed some facts first.

"Adam, this is Nathan Drummond. You said you wouldn't mind a few questions for my next story?"

"Sure. Over the phone or do you want to meet?"

"Can I take a quick run into your office? Twenty minutes of your time is all I'd need."

"I'm good right now if you want to come on into town."

"I'm on my way."

Nathan pulled on his shoes and gathered his notes. He hopped on I-385 and made the short trip downtown. He parked in the large lot on University Drive and found Adam's office.

After a little small talk, Nathan opened his notes. "I have a few possibilities but want a little crime scene clarification before I start to plot. One that I'm considering involves a death-row inmate who maintains his innocence all the way to the death chamber. Once he's gone, well, I'll skip the mystery part. What I need to know is what would happen to a witness who perjured herself to get him convicted? He's now dead because of her wrongful testimony. Can she be charged with murder?"

"Well, I'm not a criminal lawyer, but I think her charge would be manslaughter. Let me check with someone I know and get back to you. It might come down to a perjury charge from the D.A. and a civil suit from the family."

"Next, this is a white-collar crime. If jewelry is stolen that's valued enough to merit grand larceny, and it turns out that the thief got the fake instead of the real, what's the charge? The intent was grand larceny but he got fooled."

"Good questions. They can't charge him with grand larceny, even if they could prove intent." Adam went on to explain the legal consequences.

Nathan had two more questions on his notepad. Adam talked through each one from the legal side.

"Thanks, Adam. Gives me a lot to think about."

"Hey, glad to help. Let me know what plot you choose. Will I see you at brunch on Sunday?"

"I'll be there. I think it's expected." Nathan stood and turned toward the door. A plaque had been displayed on the wall beside it. *Stay strong. Integrity requires courage.*

He turned back toward Adam. "Hey, one more scenario. An underage kid, drinking and driving. His recklessness causes an accident resulting in death, but they never caught him. It would have been vehicular homicide, but what if it was years later before he was caught. Is there a statute of limitations? Does the fact that he was underage at the time still factor in?"

"Homicide is murder so there's no statute of limitations. He'd most likely do some time. I'd say he doesn't skate now just because he was underage, but sentencing might be lighter. Everyone knows teens do stupid things. Probably depends on his lifestyle since then, if there's anything else on his record, that kind of stuff. A sentencing judge holds a lot of power, and he'd look at all of that."

A clammy, cold sweat formed on Nathan's forehead. The old familiar tightness gripped his chest. Breathe deep. Breathe deep. He had to get out of the office and to his car. He said a quick good-bye and left. The cool, autumn air hit him, helping to ward off the attack. Nathan found his car and stood, hands on the hood, inhaling the crisp air. He had no courage. He couldn't sign the contract.

34

Calls from Brian and Anya went unanswered. Both had left voicemails asking him what he'd decided.

He closed his eyes, but sleep wouldn't come. He kept seeing the contract. He should have just shredded it. He wouldn't sign. The risk was too great. In fact, he should get rid of the whole manuscript. It held him back from fully convincing himself. *I took a different route home. I was never near the accident site.* He told himself over and over, but his mind kept seeing the old familiar picture of the red car spinning, and of a jail cell clanging closed.

Every time he heard Angie say Uncle Ramón. Every time he heard the name Garcia, even if it wasn't in reference to the man. He'd look at Adrianna and remember that her sister looked like her. When he sat at the Hernandez's dining room table with five others, he imagined the six that sat in those same chairs ten years earlier with two teenage girls. Twenty years earlier, two sets of young parents with eight-year-olds.

The panic attacks were attempting a return. Nothing like they were in college, but the tightness in his chest and flushed feeling. He couldn't allow them to return fully. They had crippled him during college. The counselor at Emory had helped him through it, providing strategies that would ease the symptoms. It was always assumed that the rigors of college were the culprit.

Yet when he thought of walking away, he saw Angie's face. So sweet and innocent. So full of goodness. He could never leave her.

Exercise was an effective help for stress. He had neglected that since he wasn't playing ball. He'd join a gym. That would be his new discipline. Maybe it would help him hook up with some basketball enthusiasts. The decision felt right. Exercise would make him healthy. This was his new truth, the one that would set him free.

~*~

Angie and Elizabeth signed the lease on their two-bedroom apartment. It had a shiny new kitchen and a patio with a view of the mountains in the distance. Angie gazed at them with pleasure. This was so much nicer than the old home they were moving from. To her father's delight, it had gated security.

They went back to the house to meet Nathan and Adam who would help to move their personal items and beds. Tonight, they'd stay in the new place. The rest could be moved over the course of the week.

Empty cardboard boxes waited in the living room. Nathan brought one to Angie's room where she worked, loading her clothes, shoes, and other personal items. "Nathan, will you do the books on my shelf? Use the smaller boxes because they'll become very heavy."

He retrieved a box and set to the task, grinning when he saw three of his books among them. "Only three? I remember writing eight."

She turned her head to glance over her shoulder. "Public library. Your hardbacks are too expensive for my budget. I bought the last one because the waiting list was too long. The paperback wasn't out yet."

"So what I'm hearing is that you just couldn't wait."

"Don't be boastful, Nathan. It's not becoming." She walked past and gave him a playful swat. A photo album caught her attention. She pulled it from the shelf. "Oh, I haven't looked at this in so long. Take a break and let me show you."

They sat at the foot of the bed, and Angie spread the album cover between them. "My parents had this made for me when I graduated from high school." It started with her baby picture and a very young Alex and Adrianna.

He tipped her chin and examined her face, pointing to the newborn. "Yep, you haven't changed a bit."

"Very funny." The next page showed two sets of parents and two babies. Angie was newborn, and Elizabeth was six months old. It was easy to tell the two mothers were sisters, even though Angie's mom was more slender. Her Aunt Elena rarely had her hair styled or wore clothing as nice as her sister. But she was the kindest person Angie knew. That showed through the photograph. Soft eyes. A gentle smile. Angie touched the picture lovingly.

Nathan made no teasing remarks. His face became impassive as Angie worked her way through the book. All holidays, vacations, and family gatherings showed their closeness. They were one family, not two.

A page turn showed Angie hanging upside down on an outdoor play gym, her legs hooked on the bar above. Long, dark hair hung down pointing toward the ground. The static caused it to flare out like electricity had jolted through her. She laughed when she saw it. "I remember this." A glance at Nathan found him shadowy. Another moody moment. How quickly he could change.

~*~

The phone vibrated on his desk. Brian. Nathan was tempted to let it go to voicemail, but then he'd have to return the call eventually. "Brian. Hello. You're cutting into my writing time."

"Good. At least you're writing. Mystery or romance?"

"I'm not a romance writer. I told Anya."

"Could'a fooled me. Are you signing that contract or not?"

Nathan drew in a deep breath of air. "Not."

Silence met him. "Are you kidding?"

"Not kidding, Brian. I don't want to be pegged as a romance writer."

"Nate, the novel's good. You put all those hours into it for nothing? What's wrong with romance? It works well for some men, a unique angle."

"It's not for me. I want to keep my mystery writer image. Sorry. I'm peddling hard on this one. I'll have it to you as soon as possible."

Nathan heard Brian's sigh and envisioned him shaking his head.

"Don't you think this pseudonym idea would have been worth talking about before you put four months into it?"

"In retrospect, yes. Brian, I've got to go. I'll let you know when this is ready."

~*~

The hair dryer whirred in the bathroom as Angie dried her hair, brushing it smooth and shiny. She wished they had gotten an apartment with two baths. Elizabeth tried to use the same mirror, applying mascara. She leaned close to the mirror while Angie stepped away from it, giving her space.

She turned the hair dryer to low, giving a final puff of air to add fullness to her hair. She wouldn't tie it tonight, but would leave it long and full. Moving to her bedroom, Angie slipped into the sky-blue dress that perfectly fit every curve. The straight skirt complemented her slender form. She reached into the closet and retrieved a pair of shoes that Mayzie would be proud to wear.

She and Elizabeth reached the living room at the same time. Liz was gorgeous in a sparkly silver dress, her hair styled in a short cut with wispy tendrils that framed her face.

Angie stood still and stared. "You look so sophisticated."

Elizabeth eyed her dress. "And you look so sexy."

Her jaw dropped open. "Don't say that. Do you think I should change?"

"Not on your life."

~*~

Nathan sat across from Adam, and between Angie and Elizabeth. He had to force himself to keep his eyes off of Angie. She took his breath away.

Adam began buttering a roll. "So Nate, did you get a new plot going? Any of the ones we talked about?"

"Yeah, I tweaked it a little, but basically the one with the perjured witness."

"That should be a good one. I thought that or the one with the hit and run would make a good storyline."

Elizabeth furrowed her brow. "Are you going to tell us?"

"Nate had some ideas for a storyline and checked with me about legal consequences."

Nathan picked up his glass of water, damp with condensation. His left hand had to rapidly come to the rescue as it almost slipped from his grasp. Adam caught the movement, but Nathan avoided his eyes.

"One scenario closely mirrored what you told me about your dad, only with more details. You can do that when you're inventing the story."

Nathan set his glass down and reached for a roll. "So Angie, anything we should know about—what's his name—Prokov before we hear tonight's music?"

"It's Prokofiev. He's a Russian composer, more contemporary than the classics, somewhere late 1800s to mid-1900. We should hear a variety tonight. Some of his symphony pieces as well as some Romeo and Juliet, and Peter and the Wolf pieces. I'm hoping they perform his *Violin Concerto No. One*."

Adam rested his chin on steeped hands, sending Nathan a perplexed look.

Elizabeth shifted the topic back as if Nathan hadn't

spoken. "So with the hit and run, did they catch the guy?"

Nathan finished swallowing the bite of roll. "I didn't write that one. It was just part of my brainstorming."

"Did Angie tell you we always suspected there was another driver? The police report showed it as a one-car accident. But we all speculated."

Nathan felt Adam's stare but refused to look his way. "Yes, she told me that."

Elizabeth sat back, shaking her head. "I just wish we knew the truth about that night."

Following dinner, they walked to Peace Center. Nathan excused himself to use the restroom. He wanted no more small talk. Hopefully, lights would dim immediately when he joined them.

~*~

It disappointed Angie that Nathan became moody again. It should have been a delightful evening. Thankfully, she and Nathan came separately so they didn't have to ride home with Adam and Liz. He walked with his arms swinging and his head down. She wanted to feel his arm around her shoulder or at least have her hand in his.

When they climbed in the car, she reached a hand to his arm. "Mi amor, is something wrong? You seem distracted."

"No. Just tired."

She stroked his shoulder. "You must be writing too much. My Uncle Ramón used to say, the best thing about fatigue is that it's temporary. A full night's sleep and you'll be good as new." Under her hand, his muscle tensed.

Nathan whipped a glare toward Angie. "Can we ever spend one night alone without your dead uncle in the seat between us?" He turned back and started the car, spinning his wheels as he left the parking lot.

Angie held on to the side of her seat as he drove with rugged starts and stops, her anger mounting with every minute. She tipped her chin up and shifted her weight closer to the passenger door. How could Nathan be cruel about a man who was so kind? He'd never even met her uncle. When he pulled into the parking space in their apartment complex, she exited the door. He stepped out and was met by Angie's extended hand. Her outstretched palm left no mistake. He wasn't welcome to join her.

"Good night, Nathan." She spun on her spiked heel and went inside alone.

~*~

Angie stayed in her bedroom most of Saturday morning. Elizabeth called in a few times, but Angie told her she wanted to catch up on some reading. Shortly before noon, Liz knocked again. "Delivery."

Angie opened her door. Liz held out a beautiful arrangement of yellow roses. She gave her a knowing smile. "Now I know what's been wrong with you this morning. Lover's spat?"

Angie didn't answer but took the vase and closed her door. A card sat angled on a holder in the middle of the roses. She opened the envelope and slid the card out. "I'm sorry. I was out of line. I love you." He had signed his name under the message. Angie held the note to her heart and breathed deeply the scent of roses.

But why, Nathan? Why would you resent my uncle? Angie didn't want to filter her words or refrain from sharing something that came to mind. This was going to require a heart-to-heart conversation.

~*~

Nathan increased the speed of the treadmill. It suited his long legs better than the elliptical. Saturday afternoon wasn't his typical time. He'd been coming every morning at eight thirty, the time when the early morning before-work crowd dispersed. It wasn't time away from work for him. His mind was productive, creating scenes and dialogue while he exercised. Sometimes he set the speed to match the scene. Perhaps he should purchase a treadmill for his writing room. When he could lose himself in fictional scenes, it kept his mind from destructive thoughts.

Today, however, his mind kept returning to last night. His outburst had been uncalled for. Angie had every right to be mad. Sometimes he thought he'd explode if he heard that name once more. And he would hear it. He'd hear it all his life if he and Angie married.

He caught the perplexed look that Adam sent his way. Did he know? Could Nathan have been that transparent? If that weren't enough, he still had the gap in his scheduled releases. He suffered no consequences at the moment since book sales were strong, but eventually they'd fade—usually about the time of a new release. Could he survive the interim if he had reduced income for six months? The answer would have been yes before he'd liquidated everything to bail his father out. Nathan slowed the treadmill and began to walk. After two minutes, he slowed it further for a cool down.

It was the right decision. What good would the income be if he were in prison? He'd lose everything. Angie, his readers, his self-respect. He stepped off the treadmill. Self-respect? No, prison wouldn't alter the actions, just the consequences of his actions. Self-respect had already plummeted. He hadn't been as adept as Sam in convincing himself. He said the words—I wasn't there—but it never became real. He couldn't ignore the truth.

Nathan walked toward the locker room. He glanced around the gym at people coming and going. Carefree people without life-changing decisions festering. He walked past the spinning room, filled with bicycles. Wheels turning and not going anywhere. He should be spinning. That's how his life looked.

He moved on down the hall, hearing soft music, bringing a vision of Angie, her violin tucked beneath her chin. He peeked at the schedule hanging outside the door. Tai Chi Chih. A dozen women gathered, forming a semi-circle, moving with slow grace. The choreographed movements mesmerized him. Soft lights and relaxed music offered a serene backdrop. He leaned with their movements, back and forth, side to side.

Their graceful arms moved down, up over their heads, back to rest in front of them, only to begin again in unison. A peace that he hadn't known in …. how long? Had he ever had this peace?

Arms swayed around in a circle, hands holding an imaginary object, moving it, releasing it, coming back and doing it again. In his mind, so practiced in imagination, he held his secret, released it, found the elusive peace. But he'd tried to release it. It just wouldn't leave him.

Nathan was glued to the spot until the movements ceased, when each of the women became still as statues, standing on one foot, the other resting against it. Their arms came to shoulder height, each forming their own small circle in front of them, eyes closed. The words of the instructor broke through the quiet. "You will find your peace and freedom in the release of all that binds you. Rest in the strength of God."

Nathan stood, not posed as the women were, but statue still. *Rest in the strength of God. Stay strong. Integrity takes courage. You will know the truth, and the truth will set you free. Let God carve the path.*

The music stopped. Normal movement followed as each of the women began to disperse, talking with friends, picking up coats and handbags. He moved away from the door, feeling like a voyeur.

Realization flooded him. He could never release the burden without speaking the truth. That was his only choice. Speak the truth or forever carry the weight of guilt. *Integrity takes courage.* Did he have that kind of courage? *Let God carve the path.* Was he willing to accept wherever the path led? *Rest in the strength of God.* It was the only strength available. He had none of his own. Would it be sufficient?

35

It was the third time Angie had called Nathan and gotten no answer. She hadn't spoken with him since the day she received the roses. He missed Sunday brunch, and she had no explanation to tell her family. Should she be worried? They hadn't been without contact since the terrible day at Carlos's home. Nathan's mother was due back next weekend. Maybe something happened to him and no one was there to know.

She drove to his home and pulled into the driveway. His car wasn't there, but she couldn't see in the two-car garage. It was possible he parked there. It was noon, but all of the window blinds were closed. Angie rang the doorbell and waited. After ringing three times and knocking, she went back to her car. What should she do? Was he in trouble? Did he go away somewhere? Maybe he was needed in Atlanta to meet with his publisher. But why wouldn't he call?

There were too many questions and no answers. She'd leave one more voicemail.

"Nathan, I'm so worried about you. Please call me. I have good news. I wanted to tell you in person, but will tell you here. I have an audition with a small opera house right here in the upstate. I can't wait to tell you about it. Please call me."

~*~

Nathan ignored the doorbell just as he'd ignored his phone and e-mail. Angie, Anya, Brian, his mother. They all tried to reach him. He wasn't ready. Seated on the sofa with a four-day scrub beard, he couldn't imagine talking with anyone. Eleven years of living with guilt. He'd run away from it by moving to Atlanta, but it didn't disappear. It stayed dormant inside of him, never allowing true peace. Never allowing freedom.

He opened the Bible that always sat on the coffee table. He haphazardly leafed through it, not knowing where to go. His mother's highlights stood out, so he randomly flipped pages and read some of the marked passages.

Have I not commanded you? Be strong and courageous. Do not be afraid, do not be discouraged, for the LORD your God will be with you wherever you go. Joshua 1:0

Fear not, for I have redeemed you, I have called you by name. You are mine. Isaiah 43:1

Nathan flipped ahead to the New Testament, still looking for his mother's highlights.

If we confess our sins, he is faithful and just, and will forgive us our sins and purify us from all unrighteousness. 1 John 1:9

"It's too much, Lord. Confessing this is too hard." Every time he thought of it, panic gripped his chest with a familiar tightness. No answer came to him.

~*~

The following morning, Nathan woke and went to his writing room. His work in progress lay dormant.

Nathan turned on the TV and went to the saved newscast, freezing the screen on the picture of Angie.

His eyes roamed, landing on the gift from Del. "You will know the truth, and the truth will set you free." He forwarded the recording and froze the screen on a picture of Ramón Garcia.

They deserved the truth. For the first time ever, that thought didn't bring a sense of panic. Neither did it bring peace. *Be strong and courageous.* "But I'm not strong, God. I'm not courageous."

I have redeemed you. Words were Nathan's livelihood. Yet he struggled with this one. He knew the word redeemed, but what did it mean now, in light of his situation today? Opening his Thesaurus, he scrolled through the synonyms. Saved, rescued, liberated, reclaimed, freed.

Freed? Set free?

I have called you by name, you are Mine. Not a pseudonym. Nathan shook his head in disbelief.

~*~

Thursday. The day he'd see Angie. He showered, shaved, and opened all of the blinds. Timing was paramount. He couldn't risk missing Angie, so he'd be there waiting when she came home from the center.

Elizabeth's class started at six o'clock, so she'd be leaving their home around five thirty. Angie usually left the center around the same time. He had written the code for the gate and parked out of sight in the apartment complex. Elizabeth's car was in his view, but he was far enough away that she wouldn't notice him. At exactly five thirty, she got in her car and drove out through the gates. He moved his car closer, waiting for Angie. Ten minutes later, he saw her entering and stepped out of his car to wait.

Angie parked and nearly flew from her vehicle. "Nathan!" she threw her arms around him. "I've been so worried. Where have you been?"

Nathan provided no answer, just kissed her lightly. "Let's go inside."

They walked in and closed the door behind them. "Nathan, you didn't answer my question. I've been frantic with worry."

"I'm sorry, sweetheart. I had a lot on my mind."

"And you couldn't call? Or answer my calls?"

"I'm sorry." He offered no more. "Tell me about the audition." It took so little to kindle Angie's spirits.

"I sent in my resume and a recording, and they called me. Auditions begin on Wednesday of next week. Mine is scheduled for Thursday at 10:00 AM. They are auditioning twenty people for three chairs."

"That's wonderful. You'll be great. And how far is it?"

"Spartanburg County. Only a thirty-minute drive. It won't require me to move." She rose and sat on the sofa beside him, reaching to stroke his hair. "I know it's not Boston, but I'm happy, Nathan. There's a season for everything."

He stared into her glowing eyes, filled with expectation. He pulled her close. "I've missed you, Angie." He heard his own husky tone. She stroked his back soothingly. Angie always knew when he needed her comfort.

But it was time to do this. It would never be easy. He lacked the courage to do this correctly, to tell her face to face. He wanted to do the right thing, but this was the closest he could come.

"Angie, I have something to tell you. I want you to know it's the hardest thing I've ever done in my life."

"Nathan, you're scaring me."

"I love you, Angie, but I'm leaving. I have to leave. Tonight's the last time I'll see you."

"Why?" It was barely a whisper.

"Long ago I told you that there was no future for us. I tried, sweetheart. I really tried. But the past finds a way into the present. The only thing I can tell you is that I love you. And I've never said that to anyone else. You're all I've ever wanted."

Angie stood and walked around the living room, much as Nathan did when he wrote. She came back and sat on the coffee table, facing him.

"No, Nathan. I deserve more explanation than this. You owe me that much."

"And you'll have it. I have something to leave with you." He'd been carrying his electronic tablet and set it down when he came in. He stretched to reach it and handed it to Angie. "This is for you to keep."

She drew her eyes close together. "Why? Why would you give me this?"

"Because there's something on there I want you to read. I've removed the password. It's the file labeled, *Set Free*." His voice caught in his throat. "I'm sorry I'm too much of a coward to do this myself."

"Should I read it now?"

Nathan offered a sad smile. "No, my love. It's 85,000 words. It's my last manuscript. I think it will explain a lot."

"Please tell me that you'll come back. Tell me that going away is temporary. I love you so much. And I, too, have never said that to anyone before."

He stood and pulled her to her feet. The kiss was

soft, like the kiss in the yard beside Carlos's home. Soft rose petals, brought together by a gentle breeze.

"Good-bye, Angie." He turned to walk out the door as he heard her cry out.

"No. Please, Nathan."

Then the closed door separated them.

~*~

Angie's red-rimmed eyes were too weary to read, but she had to start. Nathan said she'd understand when she read the manuscript. She curled herself in a ball, opened the file to its cover, and then she pressed the arrow that turned pages. Centered on the page was the following dedication:

To Angelina Grace, so aptly named.

May you forever choose joy

Angie moved to the following page. It too only contained one thing.

You will know the truth, and the truth will set you free.
John 8:32

One more page turn brought her to chapter one.

It had been close to five months since Aiden had seen any of his old high school friends. The Christmas holiday break from college brought them all together again.

Angie read through chapter one and chapter two, wondering what she was supposed to learn from this. It was a story about teenagers and a spirited New Year's Eve party. She turned to chapter three. She didn't want to read on. She wanted to cry for her broken heart. But instead, she read, looking for the hidden meaning in Nathan's words.

36

Aiden drove erratically, veering from lane to lane. The lights ahead were concentric circles that blinded him, constantly moving, changing positions. He swerved to change with them.

The truck cab quaked with the pulsations of music. Dan had turned the radio up to deafening decibels until the vibrations were a living, breathing pulse in the truck. He sang with the music while Aiden tried to make sense of the moving lights.

Aiden saw the ramp ahead, but it was on the wrong side of the road. He gripped the steering wheel and spun it hard and fast. It was the only way to reach the ramp. The lights ahead of him turned suddenly, a flash of red spiraling like a child's spinning top. He heard the impact and saw the red metal crushing against the tree.

His truck found the ramp. As he sped away, Dan craned his head to see what was left of the red car.

"Whoa, Dude. Did you see that?" His words slurred. "That guy must be seriously drunk."

They somehow found their way home. Aiden dropped Dan at his place then went the few blocks to his own driveway. It was easier on the quiet streets. No lights were moving and blinding him. He fumbled with his house key and managed to unlock the door. Everyone was sleeping when he crashed onto his bed, fully clothed, and passed out until morning.

37

Angie continued to read, still confused. Did he use their family to develop a plot for a novel? Urban Center. Mendez, a character of Hispanic heritage. Things were so similar. Why would he do that? But Aiden couldn't be anything like the man who caused her uncle's accident, the man she had hated. If Nathan were going to create a story around their situation, at least he could have made the man a villain.

She read for most of the evening despite her weary eyes. Aiden was so tortured that Angie found herself feeling badly for him. But this story only showed one side of the situation. The readers weren't seeing her grieving family.

Angie turned to chapter seventeen. Aiden heard a newscast. He jumped up to listen when he recognized the name of the outreach. He volunteered. He met Maggie. Angie felt the blood drain from her face. No, she chased that unthinkable idea from her mind. But what had he said to her? Things in his past. Something she'd hate him for?

Angie dropped the tablet onto the sofa, a moan escaping from somewhere deep inside her at the same moment Elizabeth's key clicked in the door.

Elizabeth must have seen the stricken look upon her cousin's face, since she quickly moved across the room to her. "Angie, what's wrong."

Angie held her hands up, palms out to stop her cousin. Elizabeth looked at the tablet, the typed words still visible. She reached to read what had caused such distress, but Angie plucked it from her hand and ran to her bedroom, locking the door behind her. Her cousin could never read this. She'd never understand. Papi. She had to talk to Papi. He'd know what to do.

Elizabeth tried to talk to her through the door.

She would not answer. She couldn't.

Finally, the floorboards creaked as Elizabeth moved away from the door. Angie reached for her cell phone and hit a programed contact. "Papi, I need to talk to you. Just you, alone."

38

This would be the last night in his childhood home. Any peace and courage he'd gained, trickled away following the painful good-bye at Angie's apartment. Up to what part had she read? When had she realized what she was reading? Had the truth revealed itself yet? Now there were two reasons for her to hate him—the events from eleven years ago and his deception.

Nathan reached for the Bible and read through more highlighted passages, but panic, his unwelcome companion, continued to grip him. The peace he'd experienced was now elusive. He fell into his bed and spent a restless night tossing and turning. Sweat soaked his pillow until sleep finally came.

Nathan woke to the sound of birds outside his window. Somehow God's peace filled him while he slept. He had no explanation but moved through routine tasks with ease. He cooked a hearty breakfast of bacon, eggs, and grits. How long would it be before he could cook himself another meal? After showering, he pulled on a white polo shirt and khaki pants. Nathan stood before a full-length mirror. What would he be wearing tomorrow? How long before he could choose his own clothing again?

Yet his questions didn't bring a sense of panic. Why had calm replaced the turmoil? Nathan had no idea. Perhaps the agony of indecision was worse than facing whatever consequences awaited him. Maybe the worst was behind him—losing Angie. Everything else paled in comparison.

At twelve twenty, Nathan left for the airport. He and Leah had talked two nights ago for over an hour. It was the first time his secret had been spoken. Leah convinced their mother that she needed to come east to look at the Raleigh area before their move. As promised, he had picked up an infant car seat that Leah borrowed from an old high school friend.

An airport escort assisted his mother and sister with their luggage, having loaded it on a wheeled cart. Nathan waved so they would see his car. His mother hugged him. "Nate, I've missed you. I never expected to stay away so long."

One look at his sister tore at Nathan's heart. Her eyes welled up with tears when she saw him. She quickly swiped them. His mother gave no indication that she noticed the heaviness in Leah's eyes.

Leah put on a smile and turned the baby to face him. "Benjamin, remember your Uncle Nate?"

The infant slept soundly with no knowledge of having seen his uncle previously or even now. Nathan lifted him carefully from Leah's arms. "Well, aren't you just a handsome little guy. You've grown since I last saw you. Let's get you to Grandma's house."

Coming home exhausted his mother, but Nathan couldn't allow that to deter him. With Benjamin tucked into his make-shift basinet, he gathered his mother and Leah in the living room. He glanced at his younger sister. It had been easy to remember her as the lanky teenager, gangly and awkward, the one he always needed to look out for. Today he saw a lovely and mature adult. Why had he assumed that he alone could take care of their mother?

"Mom, I have some things to talk about, and I wanted Leah to be here. First, I need to talk to you about your finances."

"OK. Is everything liquidated from Dad's business?"

"Yes, and that means that there won't be a business account to draw from. I have no idea how much you receive from Social Security or any pensions that Dad may have had. From going through Dad's accounts, I know you have a small savings in your name. I just want to know you're going to be OK financially."

"Oh, don't worry about me. Dad took good care of us for our retirement years." A dark shadow crossed her eyes. "Of course, we expected he'd be here to share it."

Nathan rubbed his temples. "Mom, I saw nothing of significance. No 401K or IRAs."

"That's because Dad separated them from his business to keep them protected. They're in my name with him as beneficiary. I have more than I need."

Leah and Nathan exchanged looks. "Do you have the paper work?"

"Yes, do you need to see it?"

"We just want to make sure you're taken care of."

Mom stood and walked to her bedroom. A minute or two later, she returned with a file.

Nathan scanned the pages, working to maintain a neutral look on his face. Eight hundred and fifty thousand in a 401k. Everything he'd done had been unnecessary? His townhouse, his own 401K, moving to Greenville?

Nathan stood and walked toward the kitchen. "I'll be right back."

He stood looking out the door. Why hadn't his mother told him? But he'd never given her the chance. She didn't know about the debt. All of the pent-up anger with his father had been unfounded.

If he had been honest with his mother, he'd be back in his Atlanta townhouse, writing mystery novels, and playing basketball. It had been a good life. His secret had been well hidden. If he had known, he wouldn't be standing at this crossroad today. But then, he would never have met Angie.

Nathan returned and sat down across from his mother.

"Nate, you look troubled. Do you think I should start drawing on this? I want it to last, and I hope there's some left to leave to both of you."

Leah jumped into the conversation. "Mom, how about if later this week, you and I sit and make a budget. We'll factor in your Social Security and see if we need to start a withdrawal plan on this account."

"OK. That sounds good. You two both sound worried. Is there something else wrong with the finances?"

"No, Mom. I need to tell you something that's very hard for me and will be hard for you. It's something that happened when I was a freshman in college, and I've never shared it with anyone. That is, until I called Leah earlier this week."

For the next half hour, they talked about the tragedy, the journaling, the panic attacks. She cried when Nathan told her his plan.

"There has to be another way. It's been over ten years. Why now?"

"Do you remember when I tried to convince you to have the hip surgery? What did you tell me?"

"When I fell, I told you it was time."

"Before that."

"Before that I told you I'd know it was time when the pain from the hip was worse than the fear of surgery."

"That's where I am now, I have no peace, just pain inside that's become worse than my fear of the consequence. I'm doing what I should have done eleven years ago. I'm sorry, but this has to happen."

Leah took her mother's hand. "I'm going to be here with you for the next week or two. However long you need me."

Mom crumbled against her daughter and cried.

Nathan left them and went up the stairs. He turned on the DVR, found The Herald Center newscast, and allowed himself one final look. He paused it on a picture of Angie and stared at the radiant smile and the gentle eyes. He reached and touched the image of her cheek, but the softness wasn't there. It was just a cold, hard monitor. He stared until he could delay no longer, then he clicked the remote and she disappeared.

When he went back downstairs, he wrapped his arms around his mother. "Stay strong, Mom. I love you."

"Shouldn't we come with you?"

"No. I have to do this myself. Besides, I hear a little boy starting to stir in there. He needs his grandma."

Nathan drove to the downtown police station, not far from Adam's office, and turned himself in.

~*~

Alex gathered the family together. Angie, still numb with the shock, lowered herself to the sofa. She couldn't look at Elizabeth. Would this bring her closure or rip open the scars? Angie stole a glance at her mother. Adrianna lowered her head. Her father probably shared this news with her last night after he left Angie's side. That made Elizabeth the only one who didn't know.

Angie had stayed up half the night reading after her father left her. She had to skim portions to get to the ending, which brought a new rush of tears. Those were the tears that rocked her into a restless sleep.

Angie gasped when she looked into the morning mirror. Three hours of sleep and endless tears left a haggard look. Splashing water on her face did nothing to mask the exhaustion. She reached for her brush and stroked it through her long hair, brushing out the tangles, restoring its smooth onyx shine. Angie slid the bulk of hair through a stretchy band. Another glance told her she would fool no one.

Elizabeth had been quiet as they got ready to leave for her parents' home. It was obvious that something drastic had sent Angie over the edge last evening, enough that she wouldn't share it with anyone but her father. She couldn't tell if Elizabeth felt slighted, offended, or just worried.

Now, seated in the living room of her parents' home, Alex stood to speak. "I..." He cleared his throat and started over. "Something has come to my attention that is best shared if we're all together. Elizabeth, we know who was driving the car that caused the accident."

Angie bit her bottom lip and stared at her lap. She couldn't bear to see the expression.

"Who?" Elizabeth's whisper mirrored the fear that filled Angie's heart. Would Elizabeth hate him?

The prolonged stillness brought Angie's gaze up to her father, his shoulders slouched in defeat. "Nathan."

Elizabeth sprang to her feet. "Nathan? Nathan Drummond? How do you know?" Elizabeth towered over her seated position and looked directly at Angie. "Did he tell you?" Her voice rose with each word.

Angie shot to her feet. "Liz, he's been so tortured by this. He's not the evil monster that I had always envisioned."

"He's been tortured? Was he drunk?" She spat.

Angie could only give a small nod of her head.

"He got drunk, got behind the wheel of a car, and ripped everything that mattered from me. Don't you dare tell me he's been tortured." Every word was spoken with raw fury.

"Liz." Angie put her hand on Elizabeth's arm. "You have to read the book. Then you'll understand."

Elizabeth pulled her hand away as though she'd been slapped. "Book? Please tell me you're kidding."

Alex stepped between them while Adrianna watched. "Girls, let's calm down. Elizabeth, sit and let me tell you what I know."

Alex explained the manuscript Nathan had left. "I believe it's important we read it. All of us. It's the best way to understand what happened on that day so long ago. Angie brought the electronic tablet, and I'll copy it for each of us."

Elizabeth shook her head. "From his point of view. Written and designed to show him in good light." She straightened her shoulders and stood. "Uncle Alex, with all due respect, I have no desire to read an account describing the attributes of the man who did this to me. To us." Her hand motioned to each of them, looking at her aunt. Swinging back to Angie, she narrowed her eyes. "I hope he's going to prison. That's where he belongs. I'm leaving. I need to see Adam."

~*~

The bed in the holding cell turned out to be a three-inch mat on an anchored wooden base, inadequate for Nathan's tall frame. The bathroom, a steel toilet/sink combination offered only the privacy of a concrete block half wall. A barred window, too high to allow a look outside, sent a spray of natural light onto the concrete floor.

Three charges were levied against him, for which he would plead guilty at the preliminary hearing Monday morning. Leaving the Scene of an Accident Involving Death, driving under the influence, and vehicular manslaughter. He had clearly puzzled the officer who took his statement.

"Turning yourself in after all these years?" an officer asked.

Nathan offered very little except the truth. "At some point, living with the secret became worse than admitting to it."

The officer immediately read him his Miranda rights. Anything he said from this point became official. He never mentioned Sam. No one asked if he was alone. Besides, Sam wasn't driving, his silence being his only culpability.

"We'll place you in holding tonight. There will be a preliminary hearing Monday morning. If you plead guilty, they'll schedule a court date for sentencing. You can have an attorney present. If you don't have one, we can assign one from the DA's office."

"That won't be necessary."

Nathan had been in this eight by ten enclosure since then. The silence was deafening. He stretched out on the mattress, allowing his feet to hang over the edge. He did what had become second nature to him in the quiet moments, inventing stories, creating scenes. Would he be able to write in prison? Would they allow him a computer?

He declined the sandwich they brought him at dinnertime, eating just the small salad. Then he slept on and off through the evening and nighttime.

The preliminary hearing was uneventful, lasting about three minutes. They read the charges, he pled guilty, and they scheduled a sentencing hearing for a week from Tuesday. He would remain in holding until that time. He'd go crazy staring at the ceiling for eight more days. He inquired about getting a computer or some reading material. The computer was immediately denied, but he made a call to Leah to bring him some reading.

"How's Mom doing?"

"She's taking this pretty hard, Nate. I'm trying to convince her to come home with me. Brad's at the hospital most of the time anyway. It would be good for both of us."

"The sentencing hearing is next week. Make sure she knows that they'll be sending me someplace different. She probably won't be able to visit anyway. She should go home with you."

Leah promised to be there as soon as she could gather some things for him.

Twenty minutes later, a guard appeared with keys jingling from a circular ring.

"There's a lady here to see you. I'll take you to the visitor's room."

Nathan stood while the guard unlocked his door. He was surprised how quickly Leah came. They walked down a long hallway and through a door. But it wasn't Leah.

Elizabeth sat at the table waiting for him. Nathan walked in slowly, glad they hadn't handcuffed him. There appeared to be some relaxing of procedures for someone who turned himself in. He sat across from Elizabeth. The guard withdrew as far as the door, but remained and watched them.

Silence sat like a weight, crushing him. Her stony eyes never moved from his. "Wasn't it enough that you tore our family apart? You had to come and rip out my cousin's heart? Why, Nathan?"

Nathan lowered his eyes, gathering his words. "I never intended that. I'd do anything if I could go back and change what happened. I'm so sorry, Elizabeth."

"Sorry?" Fresh rage filled her eyes. "You're sorry? Like that erases eleven years of grief. My mother spent eight months in rehab and still couldn't walk without pain."

Nathan had no response. There was no justification. He deserved her wrath.

"You ate with us, spent holidays with us. And you didn't even have the courage to tell us face to face. Now you have the audacity to capitalize on it. Is this," she motioned her hand around the jail setting, "part of the plan? Publicity to increase book sales?"

"There is no book, Elizabeth. I didn't sign the contract."

"How noble of you."

"There's nothing noble in me. I have no defense." He answered, despite the palpable sarcasm.

Silence returned. Finally, Elizabeth stood. "I needed to look at the face that cost me everything that mattered. When you get out of here, stay far away from my cousin."

39

Angie stood with the violin tucked under her chin, not sure she could get through the audition without tears. She had wept for days, and now she needed to put that all out of her mind for this audition. The committee had chosen three selections.

Angie played the first two pieces using every technique she had been taught. For the third and final selection, the committee had chosen a Puccini aria from *La Boheme*, the tragic love story of Mimi and Rodolfo. The mournful tones spoke of his great loss as Mimi died in his arms. Violins were crucial to building the emotional trauma.

As Angie's bow began its slow glide over the strings, she became lost in the music. She had seen *La Boheme*, watched the agony of lost love. Her violin cried out Rodolfo's pain. She played until she was no longer part of the opera but deep in a requiem to her own grieving family, to each day of torment that Nathan suffered, and to her own loss. She moved beyond technique and became one with the music, unaware of her own tears. The tension built, rising to a crescendo, pausing, and slowing to the mournful conclusion. The music, Mimi's final breath, and her own lost love. Together, they ended.

As she lifted the bow from the strings, Angie realized her cheeks were streaked with moisture. There was a delayed pause before all five members of the audition team sprang to their feet applauding. She watched as they turned to each other, comments flying.

"Amazing."

"Incredible."

"Powerful."

Angie took a slight bow. The committee chair thanked her. "We'll be in touch."

~*~

Five more days until sentencing. Nathan paced like a caged tiger, attempting to shed some nervous energy.

Repetitive sounds of footsteps clip-clipped in the hallway. A guard came into view followed by another man. Tony Willis.

What was he doing here?

Unlocking the cell door with the large ring of keys, the lawyer entered and the guard locked the cell behind him.

"Mr. Willis, I'm surprised to see you here."

"I might say the same. Your mother called me. She'd like you to have representation at the sentencing."

"Please. Have a seat." Nathan pointed to the one wooden chair in the tiny space and then he sat on the edge of his mattress. "Mr. Willis, that isn't necessary. I came to the police of my own accord. I've already pled guilty."

"Understood. But sentencing can go in many directions. I'm not a criminal lawyer, and can get you someone else if you like, but I'd strongly advise against going to that hearing without representation."

"Can that really make a difference?"

"Huge difference. This judge has a range of options within his power. The length of the sentence, time until you come up for parole, the facility where they send you. It could be anywhere from minimum to maximum security."

Nathan rubbed his eyes. "OK. I guess I better take your advice."

"Good." He pulled open a notepad. "Let's start with a few questions. We're going to focus on the accomplishments in your adult life."

After thirty minutes of noting every aspect of responsibility and citizenship, the lawyer closed his notebook. "I'll stop in Monday morning to touch base before Tuesday's hearing. If you think of anything else that could be helpful, write it down."

~*~

Nathan closed his book and set it on the floor beside his cot. Angie should have had her audition this morning. He hoped and prayed that she had gone and none of this had stopped her from auditioning. He had no word from her or about her, not that he expected to. It was over. He had ripped their family apart. It was only right that his own heart suffered the same fate.

Where would he be sent? In this holding cell, he suffered from isolation. Would he be wishing for that isolation when he was placed in the general prison population? Could Tony Willis get him a minimum-security placement? His wasn't a white-collar crime, but perhaps when all other factors were considered…That became his constant prayer, not to be placed with murderers and rapists.

The week passed slowly, filled with reading, pacing, and praying. No other visitors came until Monday. Then he had two. The first was Tony Willis. He reviewed the specifics of his argument for the next morning.

He stroked his beard, eyeing Nathan. "You made a big sacrifice to help your mother following your father's death. I believe that would go a long way to establish character. I'd like to share that with the sentencing judge."

It took Nathan a moment to process that information. "Do you mean the debts? But I expect my mother may be there. She's not aware of that situation. She doesn't even know there were debts to settle."

"I understand that, but maybe it's time to make her aware. Those debts aren't paid off. That may be information to convince the judge of her continued need for you."

Nathan ran his hand through unkempt hair. He needed all the help he could get. Yet he had just handed his mother a huge heartache. He couldn't taint his father's character as well. She didn't deserve that.

"I'm sorry. I can't do it. Surely I have enough to establish character without it."

"You do, but it would help. Are you sure?"

"Yes. I think I've done enough damage. I'll take whatever I get."

When Tony Willis left, the guard told him a lady was waiting in the visitor's room and led him down the hallway. Could it be Angie? He longed to see her, but not like this, filled with shame in an orange jumpsuit escorted by a prison guard.

He need not worry about that. It wasn't Angie. Instead, Anya, in all of her colorful regalia, sat waiting for him. Orange slacks tapered to fit neatly in her fashion boots, with a bright orange top under her fleeced jacket. Her cheeks were heavily rouged under eyes blackened with liner. She tugged at the jacket, revealing the color beneath. "Solidarity. I was hoping they hadn't changed their color scheme in here."

"Anya, I hope you didn't go shopping to buy orange for the occasion."

She gave a dismissive wave of her hand. "No worries. My closet is quite extensive. You'd be surprised what I can find in there."

She had managed to tease a grin out of Nathan. "And what are you doing here?"

"The real question is, what are you doing here? Nathan, you didn't tell me the book was autobiographical. Do you have any idea what that will do to sales? They'll skyrocket."

"Always looking at dollar signs, aren't you? You shouldn't have come. I don't look good in orange."

"Well I'm still your agent, and you don't exactly have e-mail. I didn't know what else to do."

He leaned forward, arms on the table. "I'm not publishing it."

She rested her chin on her palm. "You might have to change your mind on that, Nate. I have some bad news to bring you."

"I'm getting used to it. That's all my news is these days."

Her face softened. "They rescinded the movie offer."

He stiffened, sitting upright. "They can't do that. We have a contract."

"And that contract has a little clause. Apparently…"

Nathan finished her sentence for her. "Apparently, they don't do business with felons."

"Sorry, Nate. The advance is yours, but you won't see the rest of the money."

"No problem. I hear they don't have a gift shop where I'm headed."

Anya squirmed in her seat, highly out of character for her bold, in-your-face business dealings. "McAllen is cutting you loose."

His mouth dropped open. "What! You've got to be kidding."

"I wish I were. They aren't going to pull what they've published. It brings in too much. But they also have a policy." She let the last words drop. "Sorry, my friend."

Brian. Drake. All the editors who knew him well. Did they read the manuscript? Didn't they know that isn't who he is today? "Well, so much for friendships. I guess my value was defined by the numbers on a balance sheet."

"Look. We'll find another publisher. Not all of them worry about …" Again she trailed off.

"Integrity? Ethics?"

"I didn't mean it like that."

"It's all right. Even when I'm out, this will be my new normal. Will you look for a publisher that will work with me? I won't exactly be able to jump back into teaching either."

"I'll get right on it, and you get writing. Remember we can always go indie. You've built a name. And Nate, we've got to get that manuscript published. Think about it."

They both stood. "It's off the table, Anya. No matter what happens. Don't ask me again."

40

Nathan fastened the tie that Leah had brought and then slipped the jacket over his dress shirt. Tony arrived, his goatee neatly trimmed, diverting attention from the bald head. "You ready?"

"I don't think I have a choice."

They walked into the courtroom and stood until the judge was seated, his mother and Leah directly behind him. Nathan looked at the judge, donning a black robe, perched in his elevated position. A middle-aged man with power in his hands.

Judge Kevin Murray got right to business. "Mr. Drummond, you've pled guilty to the charge of leaving the scene of an accident, driving under the influence, and vehicular manslaughter resulting in the death of Ramón Garcia. I'm dropping the charge of underage drinking and driving under the influence due to the statute of limitations. Today will be the sentencing trial for vehicular manslaughter. I've read the details of your case. I'll now hear any evidence that might be a factor in rendering a fair and just sentence."

Tony Willis stood. "Anthony Willis, Your Honor. I'm counsel for Mr. Drummond. We'd like to make the court aware of a few issues pursuant to the sentencing. At the time of the accident, my client was eighteen years old, a freshman in college. That doesn't excuse anything, but it does help to explain. The antics of college students are well documented. Since that time, Mr. Drummond has been a model citizen. Graduating from Emory University with high honors, he went on to have a successful teaching career before moving into the world of publishing. I've thoroughly investigated his driving record and financials. He's never had a driving violation, not even a parking ticket. From the time of his college graduation, Mr. Drummond has not incurred any late charges on any bills, and maintains the highest level of excellence in his credit rating. He has been a guest speaker on numerous radio talk shows, and has lectured writers on various topics related to publishing.

"My client came to the police of his own accord and turned himself in, an act of conscience that is rare in today's society. Because of his excellent display of character in his adult life, we would like to request that time served and community service replace any additional imprisonment. In the event that Your Honor does sentence him to additional time, we would argue that a man of his character who admittedly made a foolish teenage mistake, not be placed in a facility with violent criminals, but be permitted to serve his time in a minimum-security setting.

"Additionally, Your Honor, if the court will allow, we have a few people present who would like to speak on his behalf."

"I'll hear them. Have them walk up to the microphone please." He indicated one at the end of a row of seats, one that would still face the judge when they spoke.

Movement came from behind him, followed by Leah's hand brushing across his shoulders. She stepped toward the microphone. "My name is Leah

Garner, and Nathan Drummond is my brother. I live on the west coast and cannot easily travel to Greenville. Nathan has lovingly taken care of our mother since our father died. My father had been a businessman with some untidy accounting. I call it honest negligence. He just didn't do well at bookkeeping."

Nathan groaned inwardly. Tony Willis had the restraint of client confidentiality. Leah had no such restriction.

"Nathan went above and beyond the responsibility of an adult son, selling his home in Atlanta, liquidating assets, and paying my father's debts. He made a complete life change, moving back to Greenville so our mother would avoid the hardships that faced her. My mother is still grieving the loss of her husband of thirty-seven years. Please don't make her grieve the loss of this faithful son by sending him away." She thanked the judge and returned to her seat.

Nathan turned his head to see where Tony pointed next. His heart swelled when he saw Del, all six-foot seven before his spiraled cornrows, awkwardly walk forward.

"I just want to say …"

The judge interrupted him. "Please state your name first, and how you know the defendant."

"I'm Del Jefferson. Nate was my tutor at The Herald Center." He turned and stole a quick glance at Nathan. "He's, like, the best person I know. He's the only one that ever told me I could do things, like you know, school things. He helped me understand why my brain didn't work the same as other people's brains, and what I had to do to learn stuff that was hard. I was ready to quit school 'til I met Nate. He brought me books I could read and took me to a basketball game. Stuff nobody ever did for me. I don't know much about when he was my age, but I know that he's a good man today."

Del lumbered back to his seat. Nathan locked eyes with him, moving his head with the slightest nod. Tony made another gesture and a man and woman walked forward. Nathan didn't know either. The woman walked to the microphone and tapped it. The sound sizzled and startled her.

"Me English not so good." She leaned in and whispered to the man.

He changed places with her and spoke, "My sister-in-law asked me to come up with her. She's afraid that her language deficiencies will hinder what she wants to say. May I translate?"

"Yes, I'll allow it. Please start with her name."

"This is Carmen Martinez. Mr. Drummond coached her son."

She rattled off some rapid Spanish, and he translated.

"My son, Carlos, attended the afterschool program at The Herald Center. That's where he met Mr. Drummond. My husband was abusive and attacked me in our home. I was stabbed in many places. Carlos called the center and Mr. Drummond came with Miss Angie. They arrived before the ambulance. I had lost consciousness, but my doctor told me the details later. Mr. Drummond saved my life. He stopped the bleeding and held the cuts until the ambulance arrived. They told me I was near death and would not have lived otherwise."

She continued her rapid-fire Spanish, pausing occasionally as her brother-in-law translated.

"When I was healed, my son and I moved, and I never had a chance to say thank you. When I heard about his trouble today, I had to come and speak. I am hearing that a man died long ago because of a mistake that Mr. Drummond made. A man might have lost his life, but I had mine given back to me."

She turned directly toward Nathan. "*Gracias y que Dios te bendiga.*"

The man also looked at Nathan. "Thank you, and God bless you." Then they returned to their seats.

Tony stood up. "Your Honor, the family of the deceased has also asked to speak."

Nathan hadn't seen them when he entered. He turned and found them in the far back of the room. Elizabeth, Alex, Adrianna, and Angie. The others were quietly conferring, but Angie's eyes were looking down. He quickly turned away. He wouldn't be able to bear it if he saw her contempt.

Only Elizabeth walked to the microphone. Nathan's eyes were downcast when Tony jabbed him. He gave a sideways whisper. "Don't look down. It shows disrespect."

He forced his head upright. Whatever she had to say would be what he deserved.

"My name is Elizabeth Garcia, daughter of Ramón and Elena Garcia. I am speaking today on behalf of my family." She motioned behind her. "My Aunt Adrianna Hernandez was my mother's sister, her husband is my uncle, Alejandro Hernandez, and their daughter, Angelina Grace Hernandez. We have spoken as a family and come to a place of unity that we'd like to share.

"My father was a man of great compassion. His legacy in this community is infamous. He spent his entire life reaching out to people in need, primarily those at risk in underprivileged areas, those battling poverty and crime and drugs. The testimonies at his funeral were phenomenal. In my father's eyes, there was no person beyond the reach of Christ, no one who couldn't be redeemed and forgiven."

Emotion hung heavy in each word. Elizabeth paused, clearing her throat.

"This has been a very difficult week for my family, for me in particular. I've held on to anger that would greatly disappoint my father. If he were here, he would say, 'Elizabeth, look deeper. Look at the heart of this man.' My father would remind me of the parable of the two debtors. He who has been forgiven much is called to forgive." Her voice began to crack, and she stopped to catch her breath. "Therefore, on behalf of my father, I, along with my family, would like to grant our forgiveness to Mr. Drummond and appeal to you, Your Honor, to have leniency. Thank you."

Elizabeth pivoted and returned to her seat. Nathan's gaze followed her, wanting to communicate his thanks. She never looked up, but Angie did. Her eyes met Nathan's, her hand springing to her heart. The small gesture could say so many different things. It could speak love or hurt.

Judge Murray's voice shifted his attention back to the decision about to be rendered. "If there are no others, we'll proceed with sentencing." He waited through a pause, then resumed.

"Will the defendant please rise." Nathan and Tony stood and faced the bench.

"Mr. Drummond, I've read the file and heard arguments convincing me of your character and responsibility. I know that you willingly came forward, albeit eleven years too late. I have teenage sons, and I was once a teenage boy myself. No one wants to be remembered by their actions from that stage of life.

"However, a man has died, and I can't overlook that. I cannot, in good conscience, reduce this to community service in exchange for a man's life. Therefore, I sentence you to one-year imprisonment to include time served. Due to your cooperation, a minimal flight risk, and prison overcrowding, the sentence may be served as house arrest, provided a suitable site is available. You'll be returned to the county holding until equipment can be installed, which will be no longer than two weeks from today. Court is adjourned.

Relief surged through Nathan. House arrest instead of a prison cell. He turned and hugged his mother and sister. The guard reached for his arm to return him to holding.

"May we have a word?" Nathan turned at the sound of Alex's voice.

The guard looked at the judge.

"Give them five minutes."

Tony and the guard stepped back. Leah tugged at her mother's arm. "Nathan, we'll stop to see you tomorrow." They walked out of the courtroom.

Alex and Adrianna stood facing Nathan. "Why didn't you tell us?" The question held no accusation, just compassion.

"I couldn't, Alex. I was so ashamed. I am so ashamed. I came to the center hoping I could give something back. I never counted on falling in love with your daughter."

Alex glanced at his wife. "I can see how easy it would be to fall in love with her."

"I can't adequately express my sorrow for what I did, or my thankfulness for your family's words today. I know how difficult that must have been for Elizabeth."

"Elizabeth is hurting. Her heart will catch up with her words. Give her some time. She'll come around."

"I've hurt you and hurt Angie deeply. I have no expectation that you'll want to see me again after today."

Adrianna lifted her chin. "I think Angie has some other thoughts." She tugged on Alex's arm. "Three minutes left. We better give her some time." Alex shook hands with Nathan, and they stepped back.

Angie had been waiting off to one side. She came to him and opened her arms, wrapping them around his neck. He embraced her, holding her close. "Angie. Angie." His voice cracked with emotion.

She leaned back and looked up at him. "Nathan, house arrest. That's so wonderful."

Nathan shook his head. "Always the optimist."

"Yes, I am. But it is wonderful. I can come to you. Maybe I'll convince my mother to take Sunday brunch there one day."

He fought to control the trembling of his hands. "I didn't think you'd ever want to see me again."

She brushed her hand across his forehead. "How could I not, mi amor?"

"Even knowing what you know?"

Her eyes turned somber. "Nathan, it was a terrible, terrible accident. Yes, you were foolish, but you never intended to harm anyone. We've suffered. You've suffered. It's time for healing. I choose joy. That means that I choose you."

A tap on his shoulder told him it was time. He

kissed her softly. "I love you, Angie. One more thing, don't visit me here. I'll see you in two weeks or less."

She put on a pout.

"Please. There are enough bad memories."

She nodded. "Two weeks."

As he was ready to pass through the door, he remembered. Looking over his shoulder, he called back to her. "The audition? Did you go?"

A bright smile filled her face, and she nodded. "I got the job."

~*~

Three days later, Nathan was released. An escort returned Nathan to his mother's home. He had no new novel, so no finances for getting another place. She'd be stuck with him for a year. Somehow, he didn't think she minded. And the comfort of home would go a long way to help this journey.

He couldn't attend Del's games or Angie's concerts. Sunday brunches would find his chair empty. But gratitude filled him. It wasn't a barred cell, no clanging locks behind him. And Angie would be here soon. Bright-eyed, joyful, optimistic. She'd fill the room with chatter and light.

His mother's dog-eared Bible sat on the table. Nathan reached for it and opened to the gospel of John, chapter eight. He read the familiar words in verse thirty-two. *"You will know the truth, and the truth will set you free."* Nathan read on beyond that verse. The people reminded Jesus they had not been enslaved. How could they then be set free? Jesus' words resonated deep within Nathan.

"Truly, truly I say to you, everyone who practices sin is a slave to sin. The slave does not remain in the house forever; the son remains forever. So if the Son sets you free, you will be free indeed."

The irony didn't elude him. He, the son, remained in his mother's house. The same house that enslaved him before he spoke the truth. The same house he had avoided for years, afraid of the panic within him. He glanced at his ankle, the device securely in place, restricting movements beyond the perimeter of the yard. He inhaled a deep, peaceful breath.

At last, he had been set free.

Epilogue

Five Years Later

Nathan watched as Leah and Brad turned into the driveway. They had driven in from Raleigh for the occasion. He stepped out the front door as Leah freed Benjamin from his car seat. He darted to the house where Nathan picked him up to swing him around. Brad and Leah gathered two-year old Tessa along with the diaper bag and toys.

Angie had been helping his mother in the kitchen but came out when she heard the voices. She ran to greet her sister-in-law. "I'm glad you could come for the weekend. We're so excited about tonight."

Leah looked around. "Where's Micah?"

Angie glanced toward the baby monitor. "He's upstairs sleeping. He should be up soon."

Nathan's mom emerged from the kitchen. Benjamin ran to her while Tessa buried her head behind her mom.

Brad set the supplies down and pried Tessa from her grip on Leah's leg. Benjamin had never been as bashful. "We need her to get comfortable with this small group before the big gathering tonight. Who all will be there?"

"My parents are coming, and Elizabeth and Adam with their two little ones." She turned toward Nathan.

"Did you ever hear back from Del?"

"He called, but he couldn't make it to Greenville and back in time. They have an away game against the Celtics, so he has to be in Boston tomorrow."

Benjamin had already opened the toy bag and scattered some around the living room. It had been his playroom at Grandma's house since they moved back east. The room had been childproofed a few years ago for Benjamin and Elizabeth's children. The two families had been alternating the location of Sunday brunch since Nathan's homebound year.

The baby monitor sounded as Micah woke. Angie started toward the stairs, but Nathan interceded. "I've got this. You're better at warming up to Tessa."

He bounded up the steps to his old writing room where the six-month old infant waited. Reaching into the crib, Nathan lifted Micah into his arms. "Hey, little man. Daddy's here." Every time he held his son, Nathan's heart swelled with an inexplicable love. Is this how God loved him, so completely and unconditionally?

Nathan moved to the changing table and reached for a clean diaper. For Micah's first month of life, Nathan couldn't change a diaper without thinking of baby Connor, wondering how he looked today. He'd be close to six years old now.

A glance on the wall behind the changing table reminded him of why he and Angie chose the name. He read aloud while changing the diaper. "He has told you, O man, what is good; and what does the Lord require of you but to do justice, and to love kindness, and to walk humbly with your God?" He spoke the words from Micah 6:8 to his infant son. "Just like your Great Uncle Ramón."

Carrying him proudly down the stairs, Nathan handed him to Leah's waiting arms. "Hold him while I warm his bottle. After he's fed, we're going to take off and let you have some Grandma time. We'll see you at our house tonight around seven."

~*~

Angie stood in her living room holding Micah. Their families would be here any moment. She turned him toward the framed pictures on the shelf. Their wedding picture, a picture of them holding Micah, Elizabeth and Adam with their two children, Leah and Brad with their family, her parents, Nathan's parents, and her Uncle Ramón and Aunt Elena. She hadn't put that one on the shelf. When Nathan found it with her old photos, he'd framed it himself and included it with the family pictures.

She had been hesitant. "Mi Amor, I don't want this to be a painful reminder for you."

His response was to cup her face in his hands. "I spent years determined not to forget what I'd done. I'm able to rest in forgiveness, but not forgetfulness. They're part of our family. They belong on this shelf."

The doorbell rang. She and Nathan both moved to answer it.

Everyone seemed to pour in at once. Elizabeth hugged Nathan, then lifted her little Lolita to see Micah. "Use gentle hands on the baby," she cautioned the toddler.

After the greetings they settled the children in the playroom with the sitter Nathan had hired. The adults gathered around the television. Nathan inserted the

DVD into the player, but turned to speak to everyone first. "This is my preview copy. The show will air next Sunday evening on television. You all know the story, both the fictional version and the real-life one. I said no to my agent for three years, but Elizabeth encouraged me to submit it. All proceeds from the book and the movie have been designated for The Herald Center in honor of Ramón and Elena Garcia."

Nathan had previewed the movie alone for the first time. The accident was shown in a slow motion surreal scene. It lacked the graphic violence that could have been depicted. Even so, nausea burned his stomach with vivid memories. The strength of the movie was the portrayal of Ramón Garcia. Every viewer would see the kind, gentle servant who gave his life for others.

He hit play and the screen filled with the words *Set Free, based on a novel by Nathan Drummond.* Nathan sat back to watch, surrounded by the family of Ramón Garcia, and thankful that God had carved the path.

A Devotional Moment

Then you will know the truth, and the truth
will set you free. ~ John 8:32

There are times when we are trapped by our
past mistakes, afraid or unable to break free from
evil or wrongdoing because guilt threatens our
current status. But our faithful God whispers in
our hearts, and the driving need to be free of sin
and guilt becomes overwhelming. We may
wallow in shame, but we work to build the
courage to face our fears. Whatever justice is in
store for the sin we've committed is also fraught
with repercussions, but with prayer we can
weather the storms. God renews hearts when we
face the consequences for past sins.

In **Beauty for Ashes** a past sin impedes the
protagonist's walk with God. When he is ready to
confess and face the consequences, a new person
enters his life who will be directly affected by his
former mistake. Finding the courage to address
the issue becomes difficult. The repercussions are
devastating, but God's comfort is at hand.

Have you ever been so racked with guilt for your past mistakes that you can't be happy in your present circumstances? Remember that you are a child of the Most High God. He loves you no matter what you've done, and He is ready to relieve you of your guilt, even if there are unavoidable consequences to your actions. The truth is what sets us free. Christ died to relieve you of your burden. That is the truth!

LORD, TEACH ME THE WAY TO RIGHT ANY PAST WRONGS. GRANT ME THE COURAGE TO FACE THE TRUTH AND THE GRACE TO ACCEPT YOUR MERCY, SO THAT I MAY BE FREED FROM ANY GUILT MY FORGIVEN SINS MAY CAUSE ME. HELP ME ALWAYS TO WALK IN YOUR TRUTH AND LIGHT. IN JESUS' NAME I PRAY. AMEN.

Acknowledgements

First and foremost, I would like to thank my family for encouraging me, supporting me, and filling in the gaps at home while I write. Thank you to my sisters who are my biggest fans.

I rely on people who have expertise where mine is limited. I'm thankful to Jackie Waingart for all things Puerto Rican. Our friendship inspired me to include a Puerto Rican family. Thank you, Jackie, for reviewing my draft, correcting when something was amiss, and affirming when I managed to get some things right. The best part was topping it all off with our Puerto Rican lunch.

Thank you to Christopher Wu, whose talent I so greatly admire. Chris holds first violin chair for the Pittsburgh Symphony Orchestra, as well as teaching for Duquesne University, Carnegie Mellon University, and Geneva College. The *Tribune-Review* describes Christopher Wu as a musician of "virtuoso command with depth of musical understanding." I'm honored to describe him as friend. Chris, you added authenticity to the musical parts of my story. Thank you for sharing your gifts with so many people.

Thank you to Harold Hess for providing feedback on business structures and liability, and for correcting my misconceptions.

Thank you to my oldest son, Brian Neely, the ultimate sports fan. I know basketball a little better than I know Puerto Rican culture and classical violin, but my knowledge pales compared to yours.

Everything I write passes through my critique partners, Cynthia Owens and Tim Suddeth. It's a joy to work with you and watch how iron sharpens iron. While critique partners see a work in progress bit by bit, week by week, a beta reader is the first to review the manuscript in its entirety. Thank you, Erin Greene, for visiting *Beauty for Ashes* before anyone else. Your suggestions and words of encouragement helped to shape this story.

I'm so grateful to be part of Pelican Book Group. Thank you to the Pelican family and especially to my editor, Megan Lee. You see things that I miss. Thank you for your care and vision.

With gratitude,
Kathleen Neely

Thank you…

for purchasing this Harbourlight title. For other inspirational stories, please visit our on-line bookstore at www.pelicanbookgroup.com.

For questions or more information, contact us at customer@pelicanbookgroup.com.

Harbourlight Books
The Beacon in Christian Fiction™
an imprint of Pelican Book Group
www.pelicanbookgroup.com

Connect with Us
www.facebook.com/Pelicanbookgroup
www.twitter.com/pelicanbookgrp

To receive news and specials, subscribe to our bulletin
http://pelink.us/bulletin

May God's glory shine through
this inspirational work of fiction.

AMDG

You Can Help!

At Pelican Book Group it is our mission to entertain readers with fiction that uplifts the Gospel. It is our privilege to spend time with you awhile as you read our stories.

We believe you can help us to bring Christ into the lives of people across the globe. And you don't have to open your wallet or even leave your house!

Here are 3 simple things you can do to help us bring illuminating fiction™ to people everywhere.

1) If you enjoyed this book, write a positive review. Post it at online retailers and websites where readers gather. And share your review with us at reviews@pelicanbookgroup.com (this does give us permission to reprint your review in whole or in part.)

2) If you enjoyed this book, recommend it to a friend in person, at a book club or on social media.

3) If you have suggestions on how we can improve or expand our selection, let us know. We value your opinion. Use the contact form on our web site or e-mail us at customer@pelicanbookgroup.com

God Can Help!

Are you in need? The Almighty can do great things for you. Holy is His Name! He has mercy in every generation. He can lift up the lowly and accomplish all things. Reach out today.

Do not fear: I am with you; do not be anxious: I am your God. I will strengthen you, I will help you, I will uphold you with my victorious right hand.

~Isaiah 41:10 (NAB)

We pray daily, and we especially pray for everyone connected to Pelican Book Group—that includes you! If you have a specific need, we welcome the opportunity to pray for you. Share your needs or praise reports at http://pelink.us/pray4us

Free Book Offer

We're looking for booklovers like you to partner with us! Join our team of influencers today and periodically receive free eBooks and exclusive offers.

For more information
Visit http://pelicanbookgroup.com/booklovers

CPSIA information can be obtained
at www.ICGtesting.com
Printed in the USA
FSHW021122010519
57725FS